With gratitude to our parents, grandparents, and generations of pioneers whose spirit provides foundation for character that refuses surrender in the face of difficulty.

Tyler Woods

# These next pages give birth to a journey.

What would your world be like if suddenly you were unplugged from all conveniences?

RAGNAROK is a Norse legend describing a terrible battle of the gods. In the end, the gods are dead leaving mortals to rebuild without their help.

In this story, the gods of money, technology, and government are suddenly crushed, leaving the survivors to rebuild a life without them.

Jason and Anna Connors embark on a reverse Pacific sail from Hawaii to Seattle. Two days out, the US economy defaults. Unknowing, they sail for a month while calamity rips the fabric of society back home. Almost too late, they are warned off and divert to Mexico where they sneak back into their own country to find temporary safety in the pocket canyons of Big Bend, Texas.

Follow them as they face the harsh reality of civilization gone mad. Discover with them what's necessary for life without electricity, technology, and government.

The events are imaginary as are the characters, but every detail is within likely scenarios today.

Read on and journey with survivors who sift the rubble of a disheveled world to discover a new existence. Witness the effect it has on those who endure hardship and must become more than they imagined.

# Note to Readers

This is a work of fiction only because imaginary characters and modified settings of real places, tell a story that is possible and even likely.

EMP (Electro-Magnetic-Pulse) is but one of the means by which we can lose our supply of electricity for an extended time. This communication destroying pulse can come naturally by a solar flare, called Coronal Mass Ejection (CME), or intentionally, by a nuclear device detonated high in our atmosphere. The grid can also collapse from the weight of its own mismanagement. Our grid routinely operates near its limits during heat waves and cold snaps. There will come a day when those limits are exceeded and the power fails.

When lost, there will be no computing to maintain store inventories. Grocery shelves will not be re-filled, gas stations will run dry, banks will close, credit cards won't process, and emergency services won't dispatch. The result will be complete social collapse. Riot will engulf every metropolitan area as dependents of federal entitlement become desperate and uncontrolled.

Descriptions and responses portrayed in this book are derived from actual events and sound training.

This book is safe for young readers. There is drama that is not deranged; love without lust, and suspense that's not sadistic.

Characters have an unapologetic and strong Christian

faith but it is not the central focus for the storyline.

Names and descriptions of characters are purely random and are in no way connected with real people, except for one singular character who indeed carries the first name of a friend and contributor who has also given permission for its use. My special thanks to Mandy Ecenbarger of YamerPro.com.

I trust you will enjoy following the characters of this book and will want to continue following them in the second book of this series,

**Realm of Ragnarök – Two Worlds Meet**

# About Tyler Woods:

Tyler Woods is an accomplished author, teacher, and disaster preparedness conference speaker with over forty years' experience. He knows firsthand the effects and needs arising from a sudden loss of infrastructure. From personal experience during major earthquakes, floods, blizzards, and one super-class typhoon, he offers first hand insight. His teaching and writing style presents a refreshing positive approach to challenges with emphasis on keeping aware of your surroundings and avoiding conflict.

"The best place to be when trouble breaks out;
is somewhere else."

While maintaining suspense and drama, you will find his writing free of gratuitous violence, gore, and sexual misconduct. The sense of realism will compel you to read on and evaluate your own level of readiness.

# The Cover Design:

Yamerpro has done fantastic cover design for my last two books and is currently designing a third. I recommend them highly.

**www.yamerpro.com**

# Days of
# RAGNARÖK
## End of the gods

By Tyler Woods

# Strange Crossing

Frank Iverson was my father-in-law. I didn't have much time to know him apart from his struggle with cancer but he was a good man, raised his children well, and I feel like I've missed out by not knowing him longer. His extended fight with cancer ended last January, just three years after walking his daughter, Anna, down the aisle at our wedding in Northern Alberta. Frank, his wife Edna, and Anna, had moved to Seattle for Frank's dental business but home was always in the north country of Canada. Edna is a commercial realtor and though she could work most anywhere, Seattle has been very good to her.

Anna's heart is full of stories growing up with the moose and bears. Had she not followed her family to the Pacific Northwest we may not have met but I think she still hungers for the wilderness. A redheaded Dane of thirty-two, Anna is quite a looker and turns heads whether she's in blue jeans or a formal dress. Anna is one of those girls that need no makeup to look her best. I was stunned when we met through her brother Scott. I remember thinking *"Are you the one I've been waiting for?"* It was funny that after our engagement I shared that first thought with Anna and she told me she had the same impression when she saw me. She said when a six foot four, blue eyed Texan with dark wavy hair steps into the life of a girl from Alberta, she better not wait for a second one to come by. We must have been made for each other. Were so many men that stupid to pass her up, or was she so selective that others failed the cut? I didn't wait to find out. Courtship lasted a whole six months and we've been a strong team since. She's no city girl. Most of her extended family still lives at Trout Lake, Alberta, and the door is open to us. Maybe we could retire to a log cabin someday but that's a long way off.

My family has been drilling, refining, and selling Texas oil for three generations. Pop says I was weaned on oil which explains how I easily come by solutions to oilfield problems. I'm not sure of the accuracy of my weaning but I've done OK as an oilfield engineer. My family was growing nervous that the bloodline was ending with me; I'm an only son. Business keeps me occupied and I never found time to pursue a relationship, until I met Anna. Now, at forty-one, I'm starting to take more personal time and let the business grow with good people. I'm Jason Connors and Oilfield Solutions Inc. (OSI) is my company, headquartered out of Houston, but since we occasionally do work in Arab countries, we sub-contract Canadian specialists where a U.S. passport might cause trouble. I keep a forged Canadian passport to get me out of country if I get caught in the midst of one of their frequent uprisings. I nearly had to use it once.

Anna and I have a ranch north of Houston but life has been so busy with the current oil boom that "J&A Ranch" is more of a place than a home. It has about anything you could ask for but we hardly have time to even sleep there. With Anna a Registered Nurse and me working all over the world, our schedules scarcely cross paths. Thank God for cell phones. We even have a private air strip but it serves more for flying out to work locations than for recreation. I guess we've needed this working vacation and it's been a blessing for both of us.

Anna's dad owned a 1982, Pearson 36, blue water sailboat called "Intrepid." Frank kept her moored here at Ko Olina Resort & Marina near their condo in Hawaii. His excuse for not keeping her in the Puget Sound was "If I'm going sailing, I'm going for a good spell and in warm water with sunshine." I guess that ruled out Seattle. We stayed here for our honeymoon and two vacations since. The Pearson may not be the fastest boat on the water but sturdy design and cutter layout makes it very comfortable in open water. It comes into its own when other boats head for the harbor.

I left Oilfield Solutions in good hands and Anna took a leave of absence so we could fly out and close the sale of the condo. We've taken two weeks to enjoy Hawaii and provision Intrepid for our sail back to Seattle.

Blue-water sailing is boating on the open ocean. It's not for a poorly equipped boat or inexperienced sailor. The crossing from Seattle to Hawaii is not complicated. The hardest part is getting to San Francisco. After that you catch the trade winds and follow your GPS to Hawaii. The return trip from Hawaii to the West Coast is a bit more complicated. Timing is critical for good weather with best crossings in late summer. Our first leg will be north to catch the easterly winds off Japan by the first of August. That should carry us to Sitka, Alaska, where we can take the Inside Passage down to the Strait of Juan de Fuca, into the Puget Sound, and then to Seattle. It sounds easy but any crossing can be a challenge.

Anna has been sailing with her dad for over ten years and during my twenties, my diversion from oilfield work was serving as summer crew to retirees who needed an extra hand sailing open water to their winter harbor in South America. Anna and I make a good crew.

I love sailing. Perhaps it's the sound of water on the hull, or the look of energy filled sails with but the isolation and independence have to claim part of the allurement. Out here, for a time, we are cut off from the world and all its problems. It's just Anna and me; our time alone is sacred.

Sailing open water offers a lot of free time and Anna loves her perch on the bow where she soaks up sun while reading a good e-book. What she accepts as a necessary evil is the harness and tether line. Falling overboard can happen and it's always unexpected. If it happens in the middle of the ocean and you are without a tether to your boat; you probably won't live to tell about it.

Anna cheats a little when she tans in calm weather. She fastens the waist belt and lets the shoulder straps down to avoid massive tan lines.

"Don't burn up there! You're only good for about ten minutes a side or your freckles fall off." Teasing Anna about her fair skin and freckles always falls on deaf ears but she knows I love her skin. It's funny that girls tend to be ashamed of the freckles that guys are nuts over.

Anna loves the sun but knows I'm right about her skin. As a nurse she knows all too well the sun's effect. However, a little sun is healthy and even for the short time she has, she enjoys being in warm air and a swim suit. It doesn't do any harm to show off her curves and a little skin for me either. Anna knows how to keep my attention. I never give her reason for jealousy but at the same time, she is skilled at keeping my heart at home and it adds to the strength of our marriage. When I have to be away on a work project, Anna plans a fabulous dinner date and a romantic evening alone for the two of us the night before. It makes it difficult to keep my mind on work while I'm away but she knows how to make me want to get back home.

Things are going well. The seas are behaving, which is more than I can say for Intrepid's electronics. Twenty days sailing out of Hawaii, the GPS dies.

Anna sees me fussing with the Electronic Charting

System (ECS).  "What's wrong?"

"I think it's dead." I say, "The system checks out but it can't establish a link.  The portable at the helm is offline too."

"What about the one in the ditch bag?" she says.

A 'ditch bag' is a waterproof sea bag with emergency equipment you need if you ever have to quickly abandon your vessel.  There is a hand-held GPS in it and I get it out.

"It's dead too.  This is weird.  Anna, I think we should head back for repairs."

Anna sees it differently, "We don't need GPS to find Alaska or Canada but finding Hawaii without GPS might be challenging.  We have good charts and Dad always keeps a sextant on-board.  Let's do it!  We're two thirds the way there anyway."

Well, she makes a good point.  Compared to Alaska, Hawaii is just a dot in the ocean.  We decide to make like Magellan and chart our course by the stars.  There is room for error and we have plenty of time.  This will be fun in the sun, and the sight of Anna taking a sextant reading in her bikini top and short-shorts will forever be etched in my mind.  North to the easterly trade winds and then on 'til we hit Alaska... or Canada.  They're both rather difficult to miss.  We can find Sitka from there.

We post text message updates over the SPOT.  It's a tracking tool that allows Edna and the rest of the family to see our progress online and saves calls on the satellite phone. I don't want to talk to anyone besides Anna anyway. She deserves my undivided attention. The SPOT is great for updates but it uses proprietary satellites and is a bit slow. It seems to always be looking for a link.

With the GPS out, it's a good thing Frank thought to install a manual AutoHelm for backup. GPS driven AutoHelm is an electric power hog but accuracy is good. Intrepid has both solar and wind turbine generators but I never like being dependent on power. Besides; the GPS isn't working. Reading the guide for the backup AutoHelm gives me a smile when I see it is made in Denmark, just like Frank. His hand is still in this boat. The Aries AutoHelm is easy to use. Just run the snaffle lines to the hub on the wheel and lock in the course according to compass. No hydraulics and no electric needed. I love simplicity.

At least our Radar and AIS transponder are working but we haven't seen a single commercial ship since leaving Hawaii. I do a couple radar sweeps every now and then just to be cautious but the AIS should alert me if anything is coming. It's strange that we aren't getting alerts because we are spending a lot of time crossing busy shipping lanes. Anna calls these eastbound lanes the "Wally-Mart Express" for all the Chinese container traffic. The Japanese current is much cooler so it's probably good that Anna puts on warmer clothes. We don't want to be the cause of any crew distraction should we find another ship out here.

Aside from electronic problems, this trip has been

fantastic for both Anna and me. For thirty-two days we have been to ourselves and it has been a second honeymoon for us. The only other human voice we hear is the recorded shortwave weather forecast from Australia. Our combined "old school" navigation is pretty good.

Meals for two are special. Spending so much time with Anna is causing me to realize how little I still know of her. Our small-talk opens doors to whole new areas of our lives that we never found time to explore in the past.

Cuddled in my arms as we share some stew for dinner, Anna begins, "Did I ever tell you about the bear I met in the woods near Uncle Ed's?"

"Sounds interesting, do tell." I love hearing stories of her growing up.

Anna continues, "I was fourteen and picking blackberries at Uncle Ed's cabin. Not the big ones but the smaller mountain berries. They're sweeter but the thorns are hooked and go all the way out to the end of the leaves. You have to be really careful picking because the thorns will cling and tear you up pretty bad. As I was working one side of a really good bush, the other side was moving and I thought someone else was picking too. Not too many people live up near Trout Lake so I stood up to say hello. As I stood up, so did a big black bear on the other side of the bush. My Dad taught me that when you meet a bear, stand real tall with your arms up over your head to make yourself look bigger. He also said to make a lot of noise and walk away but not to run. I set down my berries, put my arms up and sang every Sunday school song I could remember until I reached Uncle Ed's cabin. I've never been so scared in my life."

I can tell some of the realism Anna feels because her heart is pounding through to my chest. "Wow! That was close. Did you ever go back for your berries?"

"Uncle Ed went back with me but that bear cleaned out my basket good. I was really mad because I worked hard for those berries and still had scratch marks from the thorns. Uncle Ed leaned his rifle against a tree and helped me pick more berries but the bear got most of the good ones. I think Uncle Ed is my favorite of Dad's brothers, but don't tell anyone."

"Your secret is safe. I won't tell." As I hold Anna tight in my arms, "Have I told you in the last five minutes how much I love you?"

"Not in the past five minutes, " she says. "I was beginning to wonder what I'd done."

Provoked, I begin tickling Anna and end up in a lip latch. I really love this girl.

We take another sighting and update our course as I comment, "I bet your Dad never thought his old school tools would become our primary navigation gear. We should be sighting land soon. The Alaskan coastline is coming up and Sitka is to the south."

Anna takes the binoculars and scans to port. "Land HO! We've made Alaska. I can see the coast. How's

THAT Mr. Connors?"

"Well, with a first mate like you, how could I ever doubt?"

Anna grins back, "I'm also your ONLY mate, Mr. Connors, and I'll never let you forget it."

I take Anna in my arms again and plant a big smooch on her kisser. "No one else could compare, I quit looking when I met you."

# Not So Fast

"Intrepid, this is Scott, do you copy? Intrepid, this is Scott, do you copy?"

Our first voice communication since leaving Hawaii comes over the hailing channel of the Single Sideband Marine Radio (SSB) but what's Scott doing out here and why is he using the radio and not the satellite phone or even one of our cell phones?

Scott is Anna's brother, a geologist and computer programmer. It's an odd mix of skills but it's working well for him. While analyzing seismic data collected by 'thumper trucks' that pound the ground with compressed gas pistons, Scott saw some patterns and correlation with other data that allowed him to write a program to process it into some remarkably accurate location data for finding tar sand. He started 'Can-Geo' and that's how we met. I've contract him to do a lot of spotting for us, especially overseas where his Canadian passport helps. We became good friends through working together and he's the reason I met Anna, so I owe him.

"Scott, this is Intrepid. Jason here, good to hear your voice but what brings you out here?"

"Jason, I need you to by-pass Sitka, take the Eastern Channel to Camp Coogan Bay. I'll meet you there and explain."

Anna has a confused look. "That's my brother but he sounds so serious. Jason what do you think is up?"

"I don't know yet but I trust Scott and if that's what he says, I guess we head to Coogan Bay." We don't talk much about the strange message but as we chat about everything else, meeting up with Scott is on the top of our thoughts.

Scott is waiting for us in a thirty-foot open hull fishing skiff with a single inboard drive. It's loaded with cargo and not much freeboard remains but in the protection of a small bay, it is stable. Our two boats tie up and Scott comes aboard with a good round of hugs.

"Marriage is treating you well, Mrs. Connors."

"Oooh, so formal. Good to see you Scotty." Anna is the only one who still calls him Scotty; to her, it's a term of endearment. After a longer than usual hug, Scott turns to me and converts a quick handshake into a hug.

"I'm so glad you made it. Did you have any trouble?" Scott releases his atypical hug and I notice a welling up in Scott's eyes. Perhaps it's the cold air but something isn't adding up.

"Trouble? Haven't you been getting our progress reports and tracking data?" My confusion is obvious.

"Jason, you don't know do you? You've been at sea the whole time."

"Know what, Scotty?" Anna's curiosity is almost in overload.

"You left Hawaii just in time. The day after you left came the announcement that the United States Government was in default on its national debt. That turned the greenback into toilet paper and the whole world tailspinned. There were runs on nearly every grocery store and gas station but nobody would take payment. I guess they figured their stuff was worth more than money. Then real trouble started. Default happened just before federal subsidies were released and rioting broke out in nearly every major city. You could read by the nightlight of burning buildings. Every city of size has turned into a war zone. Riots are still going in some places."

Scott has my full attention. "Yeah, but how did that screw up the GPS?"

"I'm getting to that, but it isn't good. Just when the country was down at its worst, someone, we think Iran but it may have been North Korea, or both... someone anyway..."

Anna interrupts "Scotty, you're all over the place. Slow down and just tell us what happened."

"I'm sorry; it was a nuke, maybe two." Scott is almost overwhelmed just to say the words. "Best bet is that they launched out of modified shipping containers from cargo vessels some two hundred miles off shore. That much came out in early news breaks but a few minutes later, everything went black. No Internet, no television, no phones, and within an hour there was no power. Everything went together. Nobody knows anything more from the government. We think they went dark to wait out whatever happens next."

I'm speechless as I realize the significance of that date. "August sixth," is all I can say.

"What's special about August sixth?" asks Scott

"The first Atom bomb was dropped on Hiroshima Japan on August sixth, 1945. How ironic."

Anna is really quiet, obviously thinking about others. She has friends all over the states and many in major cities. Thoughts flood her mind that they may have instantly been killed or worse, that they may be suffering a slow and agonizing death from radiation. All she can muster to say is, "Ragnarök."

"What?" I ask. "What's Ragnarök?"

Anna explains. "Ragnarök is the Viking equivalent of Armageddon. The Norse believed that a great end time battle of the world would eventually come and they called it Ragnarök, the end of the gods. Maybe they were right. It looks like the end of America's gods has come."

Scott adds, "Well the gods of money and political power have been slain. Things are melting down pretty fast."

"Where did the missiles hit?" asks Anna.

"Well, they didn't really. The missiles were intermediate range and targeted somewhere over the Midwest; probably over Kansas about a hundred miles up. News updates have been pretty scarce and rumor is all we have."

"What about missile defense?" asks Anna, "Why didn't they shoot them down?"

I join in, "Anna, our continental missile defense is designed for long range missiles. We detect an ICBM at launch phase and can be waiting to destroy them as they re-enter the atmosphere on their way to a target. We don't have as much time to respond to intermediate range missiles and if they are targeted to detonate outside of our atmosphere, they don't re-enter and our missile defense is useless."

Anna looks confused, "But how could they hit all our satellites with just one bomb? If the bomb detonates a hundred miles up, that's over 500 miles short of where communication satellites are."

"The blast doesn't have to get them." I pull out a note pad and pencil. "Nukes create an initial blast but also an electromagnetic pulse, called EMP." Anna understands better when I diagram while explaining. "That huge pulse can toast electronics for twenty to thirty miles within the atmosphere but in space, there's nothing to attenuate the pulse. It will go for many hundreds of miles, even thousands."

"So how does that knock out electricity down here? If the atmosphere is twenty miles thick, shouldn't that have protected us from EMP?"

"It did, and except for older transformers and probably every electric fence charger in the U.S., I'm sure little was damaged. It wasn't the EMP's direct effect that stopped power; it was the result of lost communication." I stop diagramming for a moment. "Remember that movie you like about a hacker who blocked a government attempt to fire an energy weapon into the earth's core?"

Anna loves corny movies. "Yeah, the one where they diverted the grid on the east coast to rob power from Alaska?"

"That's the one; remember the control center where they could see the power production and routing over the entire grid?"

Anna is nodding that she understands.

"Well, those places are real. EMC's are Energy Management Centers and they are all over the country, remotely controlling power production and distribution to meet grid requirements. They use a process called SCADA. It stands for Supervisory Control And Data Acquisition but it depends on sensors and data communication over the Internet, and most of that is over satellite."

Anna is following my explanation. "So with satellites down, those centers are blind, but can't the power stations just run on autopilot?"

"When a station loses communication it has a fall back plan to systematically shut down. A single station shutting down isn't normally a problem because power can be routed from other sources but if everything shuts down...."

"Boom!" says Scott. "And it was like a wave across the US and Canada. We expect parts of Mexico too. Between riots over the money failure and now a complete loss of communication, everything got even worse. There aren't enough law enforcement and military combined to control that many cities in meltdown at one time."

"So what did Mom do and how did you get out here to Alaska?" Anna's concern for her mom has come front and center.

"Mom's OK. You know Dad always kept his truck fueled and with his auxiliary tanks, he could drive 1400 miles without a stop. I was at Mom & Dad's when you left Hawaii. She needed me there to help her worry about your cruise. We received your text when you left the marina and the next one where you said Anna would be fine with the cache of chocolate you stowed on-board. Mom got a kick out of that."

"A girl has needs." Anna is able to give a half smile but

her heart is aching for the millions of people, unprepared for what happened to them in an instant.

"Then news broke about the default, I knew it meant big trouble. Mom decided she would rather be with family up at Trout Lake so we packed the truck and left that evening. Good thing too, because they closed the boarder right behind us and before that, they were only letting Canadian's go north and Americans go south. The drive between Seattle and Bellingham was the worst I've seen. Mom ended up lying down on the back seats just so she wouldn't have to see what was going on outside. Filling stations were choked with angry people who couldn't get gas to get home. Credit cards didn't work and some stations shut down and wouldn't even accept cash. Things got ugly real fast and I'm sure I heard several gun shots. Almost every grocery store had police responding with crowd control. It didn't last long because those with cash cleaned the shelves bare within hours and the stores closed. After that, riots started. News radio told us the border was closing but we were already in Blaine and could see the Peace Arch by then. We got to Uncle Ed's that next day but it took us six hours just to cross into Canada. Things aren't much better up there. Stores are empty with a lot of people upset; at least Canadian's didn't burn down their own cities."

I can't let that slide by. "It's the 'free cheesers' created by liberals, that did that. You let a man live without responsibility and they'll sit and wait for someone to spoon feed them and then wait for someone to chew the food too. In an effort to build liberal vote, they created an army that destroys anything worth having."

Scott agrees but adds, "Well, things are tough everywhere, even here in Sitka. Folks are desperate. I loaded supplies from Trout Lake and drove back here after getting Mom settled. They knew you would be cruising in about now and Seattle is in meltdown, you don't want to go there. Getting back to Trout Lake isn't going to happen anytime soon, I barely had enough fuel to get here and there's none to get back. They send their love and said they will be praying for us until all this blows over. All the family pitched in from what they had in store. With winters up there, they all had plenty but getting out here with a truck full of supplies was crazy scary. I blacked out the windows in the truck cap and traveled by night along the back roads. Good thing most Canadians live within fifty miles of the lower US border and I was going the other way. I drove the truck as far as Prince Rupert and traded it for safe passage to Sitka aboard a commercial fishing boat heading this way. I didn't trust the ferry as it would have given too many people, too much time to find out what I was hauling. The boat ride was the safest I've felt during this whole trip. The captain and crew figured their trip would be a big haul with demand for food going sky high and they have a base of operations north of here with fuel and food to last the season. By the time they get back, they ought to see a huge profit. I think I slept a good part of the way. I did confide in the captain about why I was going to Sitka and he was able to help. By late afternoon the next day, we were getting close to Sitka and the captain told me of a friend of his that might have a boat for me. He made contact with him by radio and we met at his dock south of Sitka. I bought this boat with Canadian currency and was that ever a switch. With the US dollar gone bad, Canadian is in demand. I actually got a good deal. It isn't much of a boat but it floats. The captain towed it to Sitka for me and we transferred the supplies in the East Channel. The guy I bought the boat from said Sitka wasn't a safe place to stay and that I'd be better off waiting for you out here. I've been camped here with the HT radio ever since and have kept a cold camp the whole time. Hailing you every eight hours has been the highlight of my day and I can tell you, sleeping out here with the bears with only a shotgun makes you a very good listener. I was tossed between sleeping off shore in the boat during the night and hiding the boat with brush during the day. Supplies are enough to get you raided by bears at night and looters by day... and everyone is armed out here. That's why we need to get you loaded and us out of here."

"Us?" asks Anna.

"I didn't plan to walk back. I thought I'd join you and lend a hand getting you home. Besides, there's hardly any fuel left in the boat and bus service doesn't reach out here. Since Seattle is nobody's destination we can go to Jim & Rita's in Baja. I spoke with him from Ed's before the phones went out and they're OK. He has plenty of food, potable water, and fuel for the plane."

Jim and Rita Sanders are good people. Jim is a commercial rated pilot and does most of the flying for Dad and me. The company plane is a Pilatus PC-24 business jet. We've been pleased with its performance. Configured for eight plus cargo, it can land on short unimproved runways. It's perfect for oilfield work where destinations can get a bit leggy from regular airports.

We begin loading supplies for a long coastal sail to Mexico. Scott has done all right in the restock. He isn't a sailor but understands what works on a boat.

"Jason, how's your potable water?"

"Between the de-sal unit and rain catchment, we're full."

"Good, cuz Sitka city water stopped after three days and people began drinking anything they could with little or no filtering. There's lots of sick people and plenty aren't going to make it. We met some folks sailing out as we entered the East Channel, they said you can't trust anyone. It's life or death for many and they aren't choosy over who they take from."

Anna is an organizer and stores supplies in every locker and spare space on board Intrepid. Everything is stowed as good as it's going to get.

Then Scott says: "Well that's everything we need to get to Jim and Rita's."

"Everything?" asks Anna, with a smirk. Anna has a spray of freckles across her cheeks and nose that makes her look pixie-like when she smiles.

"Oh, that's right. One more thing." And from under the only seat in his open hull boat, Scott pulls out a package. "Five pounds of someone's favorite chocolate."

"Big brother, you thought of everything!" and with that, Anna gives him a big bear hug, planting a kiss on Scott's cheek. For the moment, Anna is able to escape the sadness she feels for countless millions who failed to prepare. It is only for a moment though.

There was plenty of warning. Even at O.S.I. we sponsored preparedness conferences and formed a local preparedness group that met once a month sharing skills of independent living. It made a difference for some but others pushed it off, choosing to believe the services they depended on would always be there. Today, those skills are being put to the test but for many, it's too late to start learning.

The sun has gone down hours ago and a cool breeze has Anna and me looking for jackets. Scott is about to untie his boat and let it drift.

"Won't be needing this anymore. I hope whoever finds it can make use of it. It's about out of fuel anyway. Jason, it would be safer if we weren't here come daylight. Can we head out to open water?"

"Good idea, but don't cast off the skiff just yet. We can do that after we've entered the channel. The tide ebbed about half an hour ago and we should be able to ride the current to reach the channel. We can motor after that without drawing too much attention. I'll need you to watch the sounder while I navigate the bay and Anna; I need you up front to watch for floaters."

Scott and I drape Intrepid's port side with the dark canvas tarps he used to cover the supplies in the skiff. It's a gamble but we don't have enough canvas for both sides. There is no way to conceal our mast but this will at least break up the outline of the hull on one side. I throw a sea anchor off the bow. Sea anchors are like a small parachute. They can be used to slow the wind's drift effect against the hull or can be used to pull a boat in a current. Everything is quiet. All you can hear are waves lapping at the hull and an occasional gunshot coming from the direction of Sitka. There are no lights anywhere and I am not about to use Intrepid's running lights. The sea anchor is catching the tidal current and towing us out to deeper water where we will run the motor again. Hopefully, the sea anchor will find the center of the channel and keep us from running aground. The mouth of Coogan Bay is only about 800 feet wide. Without a moon and thick clouds blanketing starlight, tonight's sky is black as ink. Except for a slight pull from the sea anchor, we can hardly tell Intrepid is moving. Normally, sailboat drive units are quiet enough to go unnoticed but without electricity city noises are gone so even the soft purr of a Yanmar diesel can be heard a long way off. For now, it's a free ride on the current as we three remain quiet... listening, watching, and praying.

Scott whispers, "Somehow, this reminds me of when we had to sneak out of North Africa."

I respond, "Yeah, I was just thinking of that. Let's hope this goes down easier. I don't like being shot at."

Do I ever remember that day. It was an event that

changes who you are forever. Scott and I were working an oil production problem in Tunisia but keeping an eye on civil unrest forming in neighboring Algeria. We should have been watching over our shoulder because the birth of the Arab Spring rose right at our feet. We left everything and made our way to the airport with just passports and the clothes we were given by our Tunisian host. Scott looked ridiculous in a Jebba and Barnous. The Jebba is a near floor length Tunisian man's robe and the Barnous is a poncho like outer covering with a hood. I'm sure I looked equally strange but it did help us blend in as we passed through the crowds. Scott left his laptop but executed a program he designed to completely erase and repeatedly overwrite his memory files until someone turns it off. Not even the NSA could retrieve data after that. Anything else we left could be easily replaced and payment for the job was in advance so it was time to say adios and get out of Dodge. At Carthage International Airport we were some of the last to get in before authorities blocked the entrances. Gunshots were getting closer and a bullet hit the glass above us once we got inside. We boarded the first jet headed north, just before they closed the gate. I think the crew knew we were aboard because we taxied and took off quickly before the plane could be stopped and searched for Westerners. We learned that others were not as lucky. Sitting quietly at Intrepid's helm is a far cry from the noise and hostility of Tunisia but the feeling in my gut is strangely the same.

With only a few hundred feet to the channel, a light paints us on our port side. It's low on the waterline and appears to avoid Intrepid. Maybe the canvas is working its magic but the light does find and remain on Scott's skiff in tow. Anna is first to spot it.

In a very loud whisper, "Jason! There's a light!" Anna is normally a calm person but fear is obvious in her voice.

Leaning toward Scott, I whisper, "Pull the skiff up, lash the wheel and turn it around. We'll use it for decoy."

The light is gone but there are voices from shore. Scott pulls the skiff by the tow rope and secures it close behind Intrepid. He jumps to the skiff and ties a rope to the stern; the other end is tied to Intrepid. Cutting the tow rope allows the skiff to swap ends and I pull the skiff's stern up close.

More voices come from shore and what sounds like an aluminum boat being dragged across rocks. A group of men are either hunting the island near the mouth of Coogan Bay or they are looking for Scott's camp and got close, but now they are coming after us.

Trying to speak soft enough not to be heard from the shore, I ask, "Scott, do the running lights work on that thing?"

"I don't know. I never used them, but we'll find out."

Scott starts the motor on the skiff and pulls the knob for the running lights. They light!

Scott puts his hand on the shift control and looks toward me.

"Get ready Jason."

We feel the skiff kick into drive as it pulls against Intrepid's sea anchor, bringing us to a stop. As soon as Scott jumps aboard, I cut the stern line and let the skiff go. It keeps a true course down Coogan Bay but will this trick work?

The sea anchor slowly gains toward sea again as we sit breathlessly listening for any sound. The sound of the skiff's motor is fading but the voices are growing louder. They do not sound friendly. Splashes indicate oars but where are they going?

Finally, a light breaks the darkness. It is from the rowboat but focuses on the skiff. They are trying to head off the skiff in mid channel and evidently have missed seeing Intrepid. We all give a collective sigh and resume our escape to the sea. I start the drive unit as we turn into the Eastern Channel. Anna pulls in the sea anchor as Scott and I remove the canvas but after that episode, none of us sleep.

Scott says, "I don't think I like Sitka's new hospitality. Let's go find somewhere else to visit."

Still watching for other boats; Anna replies. "I'm with you big brother. How about Mexico?"

# Southbound:

Dawn breaks with Intrepid under full sail and heading further out to sea. We avoid the Inside Passage in preference for safer open water. I keep the AIS transponder turned off. It is doubtful we will see any cargo ships for a while and I prefer that no one be signaled of our presence. Intrepid's radar is seldom turned on and only then for a sweep or two.

Coastal seas are rough right now and the sky is gray and low. Gentle rains pass over us from time to time but the sun isn't coming out.

Anna comes up to the helm and hands me a cup of coffee. Sitting here, as the sun rises to only brighten the clouds, Anna speaks softly. "How do you think your parents are doing?"

Anna is very close to Mom and Dad but especially close to my Mom. I answer, "I'm sure they're at camp and have probably brought others with them from work.

One thing Mom and Dad took seriously was having an exit plan. Dad was the motivation behind all the preparedness conferences at O.S.I. A lot of people thought they were about surviving in third world countries but Dad knew our infrastructure was fragile enough to sink America to third world status overnight. I'm sure Mom and Dad are OK."

Anna replies, "I'm sure they are but I'll feel better after we hear from them. I guess we knew this would happen someday but I'm expecting to wake up from this bad dream I'm having. It's hard to believe how fast everything fell apart."

"I know the feeling," I answer, "We're lucky to have some distance out here but I can't imagine what's going on in cities right now. Camp is our best hope to ride this out."

She asks, "How long do you think it will last? When will it end?"

I take a moment to answer because it's not a happy thought. "Everything unravels quickly. Within four to ten days violence peaks and people do unimaginable things to stay alive. Many will fall to bad water and spoiled food. It's worsened because hospitals won't have room. After the first thirty days, most urban dwellers will be gone. They will have left early or died. Some will have stored food but not enough. They will make it longer; mostly in the suburbs or rural areas. Few have prepared well enough to last but some communities will hold out. Small agricultural towns won't do too bad. Ninety days is a milestone. Those who make it that far have a chance as long as they stay away from hot zones."

"Hot zones?" she asks, "What are they?"

"Hot zones are any former concentration of people, like urban areas. The system will be overwhelmed and between bodies that aren't buried and sewage backups, the risk of disease will escalate in those areas. Even ground water will be polluted. Next are the spent fuel rod pools around nuclear power plants. With no electric power to run the pumps, the pools heat up and begin to boil off. Once the rods are exposed they spread radiation to the air and anything within two hundred miles downwind will be affected. I have a map of the locations and prevailing winds for most of the southwest. After that, we need to watch our water source to avoid typhus, cholera, and typhoid. In all, we're looking at major isolation for about three months and general isolation for the next few years. Even then, the world is going to look like a ghost town."

Anna's eyes are full. "Why didn't people listen? We knew this was coming. The warnings were all there."

I put my arm around Anna. "I don't know. Probably the same reason people don't wear their seat belts. They think it will never happen to them. It's always someone else's problem."

Scott comes up from the cabin after Anna clears the narrow ladder. "Seas are kinda rough today." Scott's voice doesn't conceal his nervousness very well and he doesn't have his sea legs under him yet. His focus is on keeping a breakfast of Pilot crackers down.

"A bit; but they can get much worse. Intrepid is a strong boat and she can handle a lot. Once we get further out to sea, it might calm down." I don't feel this is the time to tell Scott that this stretch of water is known as a ship graveyard. Frequent storms rise fast and available protected ports are off the many rivers that deposit sand bars at their ocean mouth. Those sand bars create terrible waves and shallow entries. Plenty of boats have been lost trying to navigate these in good weather. Bad weather makes them almost impossible to cross and a compromised boat doesn't have much of a chance. For now, we have steady wind and it is blowing the right direction. We are making good time.

Scott is easy to read. We have worked as a team on many projects but our friendship is more than professional. We think alike and have been through a lot together. After our narrow escape from North Africa in 2010, Scott became as much a brother as he is a friend. Both of us like to hunt and we've made frequent trips to our family property near Big Bend, TX. We just call it camp. Until then, Scott had no idea that elk ranged so far south. Right now, Big Bend is where all three of us would rather be. Even still, a boat on the open water is as close to your own country as it gets. We have our own water, food, shelter, and can go where we choose. Eventually, however, every boat has to make port and when we do, there's no telling what we'll find.

Two days out; Intrepid turns due south. We are

approximately a hundred and seventy-five miles off the coast of British Columbia and still have good wind. Scott is beginning to be more comfortable with Intrepid's steady roll and the seas have settled down some. The sun even comes out occasionally.

Anna pops up from the cabin: "Dinner anyone?"

"I think I could eat a horse. Got any horse down there?" Scott has been eating Pilot crackers the last two days. Now he is hungry.

I set the AutoHelm and join them for beef stew and dinner rolls. The rolls are a treat as fresh bread doesn't last long and it's a long way between stores when you're at sea.

"Ahhh... You're a great cook, Anna." Scott is only half joking.

"When you're on the boat, heating up canned stew is about as gourmet as it gets. Get me to a proper kitchen and I'll fix you something good." Anna replies.

"Actually, I mean it. I know this is just canned stew but somehow it tastes better out here." Scott isn't just trying to get out of trouble.

I begin to say, but don't get to finish. "Everything tastes better at sea. Must be the fresh air..."

"Or the hunger." Quips Anna. She leans over and looks her brother closely in the eyes. "You haven't eaten anything but crackers for two days. I bet dog food would taste good by now."

We are all laughing and it is a real good laugh. The laughter is better than what caused it in this case. Stress and the huge wad of social change that each of us has had to digest over the past few days, make this laughter special. It is therapeutic and has been a long time coming. Alone on the open ocean, we feel safe....for now.

As the humor wears down, Anna voices a question that addresses no one in particular. It is clear that at least part of her thinking is parked on what has happened.

"I've read that an EMP will stop everything electronic. Cars, watches, radios... but Scotty's boat engine ran, our radios work, and everything works on Intrepid except what depends on signals from satellites. How is that?"

I answer first: "The atmosphere protected us from most of the EMP and what did get through only damaged equipment connected to long wires, like wire antennas and power lines. Newer equipment has some EMP protection built in. The only EMP that can do what you heard about is a military grade Gama device and even it can only shut down electronics for about fifteen to twenty miles."

"I guess it doesn't matter much in the long run." Scott adds. "With the grid down, we can't refine oil or get it distributed to vehicles that could run otherwise. Even if we could, what would we use to buy it? Welcome to a whole new world."

"I guess we're not in Kansas anymore, Toto." Anna's

comment is funny but no one laughs just the same.

Anna's eyes begin to well up and a tear rolls down her cheek. I reach over and take her hand. With a squeeze I ask, "What are you thinking about?"

Anna looks up and says, "Everything. I'm frightened. What of our friends; our house; the horses? Will there be anything to go back to?"

I move around the table, sit next to Anna, and hold her close. "I'm not sure. It's not in our hands. Maybe some of our friends made it to the ranch and can make use of what we stored. In any event, we've done the best we could to nudge people toward preparedness. I just never thought it would come like this. I don't think anyone could have seen this coming but we all knew it would come, some day. If it helps any, I don't feel too courageous right now, either."

The three of us sit and poke at our dinner, not saying much but thinking about friends, family, and that our lives have been turned upside down so quickly.

Sailing is busy and enjoyable when sails are full and you're making good headway, but when you have to wait for wind, it helps to have some books and a board game or two. Off the coast of southern Oregon, we reach that place. Scott tries fishing but we are too far off the coast for that. Anna and I are suddenly awakened in the forward V birth by a thunderous splash that shakes the boat. I scramble aft to the cockpit. Anna pops up through the hatch over our berth to see what is going on. Scott is already on deck and has seen the whole thing.

"Jason! Did you see that? It was AMAZING!" I'm reassured that Scott doesn't seem too upset at what has broken a really good sleep.

"See what?" I am just coming up the ladder from below deck.

Anna's head and shoulders are through the forward hatch. "I saw the water churning but nothing else. What was it?"

Just then a Gray Whale breaches about 100 feet off starboard. With everyone's mouth gaping, a single word proceeds from all of us...

"WOAH!"

Anna is most surprised. "What are they doing here? The Gray's don't migrate for another two months at least."

Scott has the answer. "There is a group of about forty or so whales that stay here and don't migrate but I've only read about it and never seen one this close. That was awesome! I didn't know they came this far out."

Then as an afterthought, Anna asks. "Did anyone get any pictures of that?"

"Pictures!" I say. "We've been missing a lot of pictures. Why don't we think about the camera until it's too late?"

"Well at least you have the log book. That can paint a picture in words I guess." Scott has a positive way of looking at things. Anna has the same trait and it is one of the many things I love her for.

The whale never comes back and that is about the only activity on the water today. Anna and I have a lot of combined sailing experience and we are both baffled at how calmly we took the whale incident. Whales have rammed sailboats before and something that large could have easily sunk Intrepid. Thankfully the wind picks up and before long, Intrepid is under sail again.

California is east but you can't see land from where we are. Daytime temperatures are getting warmer but Anna's sunny spot on the bow is vacant. Her heart is too full of thoughts for friends and family.

Nurses tend to move around. School friends can be anywhere and it seems that no matter where a medical conference is, Anna knows someone at the host city. These thoughts trouble her now because cities are hardest hit by these circumstances. Electric power is the life blood of a city and just like blood flow in a patient; you can't let it stop for long.

Some of her friends work in city hospitals but live out of town. Country living is a good diversion from the rush of urban life and many bought into the need for alternatives to the corner grocery store. A preparedness mindset comes naturally to country people; it's the city dwellers that take so much for granted. Stopping by a local store to bring home dinner can be a deadly practice when both the store and your pantry go empty.

# Baja Sur:

We're keeping a wide berth rounding the southern tip of the Baja Peninsula. Its official name is the Free and Sovereign State of Baja California Sur, but most call it Baja Sur. It is the thirty first sovereign state of Mexico and boasts an impressive large presence of American expatriates. For economic reasons and the beautiful tropical weather, many US citizens choose to live down here. I turn on the AIS transponder again. We are going to be visible from shore radar anyway and attempting to sneak in might get us confused with smugglers. This is Mexico and they play by different rules down here. There is also a real threat of piracy. Even during normal times, pleasure sailors have run into trouble in these southern waters. Especially now with so much unrest, a boat like Intrepid would make an attractive prize.

Scott is on the cabin deck, keeping watch with binoculars. His attention locks onto something to our starboard.

"Jason! I think I need my brown pants."

"What's up Scott?"   Anna notices the serious tone in my voice.

"We have visitors, coming fast in two boats, non-military. I think we have trouble." Scott's voice has that same serious tone and now Anna is listening to every word from below deck.

Two boats are approaching at full throttle and traveling together. Each appears to be carrying at least four men but it isn't obvious if they are armed. A sailboat has no chance of outrunning a power boat so we need a different plan. I open the port sail locker and move a catch to release a side panel, exposing a long gun with collapsible stock.

"How's this instead of brown pants?" I hand Scott what looks like an AR-15 but bigger. It is an FN SCAR 17 in .308 NATO.

"MUCH mo betta! Where did THIS come from?" Scott is pleased to have some respectable firepower but he's not looking forward to the possibility of using it on people. There isn't much time so Scott begins setting up his firing position.

"Your Dad never left things half done. You can't call the police in international waters. I have a little extra punch down here too." Scott looks over his shoulder to see me with an M79 grenade launcher, modified with a folding stock.

"Good golly miss molly! Dad did have some toys, didn't he? How come you knew about this stuff and Dad never told me?" Scott sounds more confused than upset.

"Had you ever taken the boat out, I'm sure he would have told you. It's not like this stuff makes for good dinner conversation." Without another word, we turn our attention to the two boats. "Don't shoot unless we have to. Open up if you see weapons but not until. We may discourage their plans before things have to get ugly."

Suddenly, both boats turn away from each other and head back the way they came.

"Jason, are you seeing this? Why did they bail like that? They couldn't have seen we were armed, not yet, they weren't that close."

Anna sticks her head out of the hatch to the cabin and points aft. "I bet that's your answer."

Behind us, in the distance, a boat is coming very quickly. Only a military 'fast boat' moves this fast in these waters and it is coming straight for Intrepid. We don't have much time before it will be on us.

"Scott, hand me the rifle. We don't want to upset the locals with these."

Scott hands me the .308, keeping it low, and I pack both it and the grenade launcher back into the sail locker and behind the cover panel. With the spare sail put back, nothing looks out of place.

A call in Spanish comes over the marine VHF hailing channel for us to stop and prepare for boarding. Anna responds as she speaks pretty good Spanish, while Scott and I drop the sails. The tone of the reply from the Mexican military speaks volumes for the advantage of speaking the native language but Anna's soft voice couldn't have hurt either.

The "Armada de Mexico" patrol boat is impressive. It is very fast and just less than fifty feet at the waterline. As we help place fenders and tie up, an officer comes aboard with two armed soldiers. Two additional soldiers with sub-machine guns remain on their boat but directly above us. The officer is courteous but leaves no doubt to his authority. We are in his jurisdiction. There is nothing we can do. If they have seen the weapons or find them in a search of the boat, we could be spending a long time in a Mexican prison. The rest of our lives depend on the decency of the officer in charge.

"May I see your passports and vessel registration?" We are pleased by his nearly accent free English and I think he is a bit proud of his command of it.

Anticipating his request we each have our passports ready, including my Canadian version, and Intrepid's registration.

The officer's commands are no nonsense. "Are there any others on board besides yourselves?"

I answer, "No, we three are all."

The officer continues, "I must ask you to remain here while my men search for contraband."

Anna comes up to the cockpit as two soldiers begin searching every compartment, including the engine and bilge. They are very thorough. If they find our guns, we are done.

Anna sits on the sail locker as the officer reviews our sail log. Eye contact and the smiles she makes with the two soldiers are flirtatious and something I don't like but this is no time to start a conflict.

One of the soldiers asks Anna to rise as he opens the sail locker. He pulls the extra sails aside and then closes the hatch and smiles back at Anna as he stands next to her. Anna returns his smile and sits back on the sail locker.

After a lengthy review, the officer returns our log and gives a command in Spanish to the armed soldiers who return to their boat, awaiting his return. Anna later tells us he told the men that we were not of concern and they could go back to their boat. Intrepid has a fair size cockpit but four of us on deck make it cramped. Our relief has to be obvious but the commander doesn't react to it.

"May I offer you some tea?" Anna asks.

"Thank you for your hospitality but I must decline." The officer's demeanor is definitely softening to Anna's charm.

"I am Lieutenant Commander Antonio Garza, I assume

it was your feminine voice we heard speaking Spanish on the radio?"

Anna replies with her best pixie smile, "Sí, mi nombre es Anna Connors." which brings a generous smile to the officer's face and another wave of relief to each of us.

"When I heard your very correct Spanish with such an accent, I was sure you were either American or Canadian. We don't speak such good Spanish in Mexico." With that, everyone courteously laughs at his humor.

"I'm Jason Connors and this is Scott Iverson, we are pleased to meet you." As everyone shakes hands the conversation flows more smoothly.

"When you first appeared on our radar, your identification beacon was not functioning however we began to register you as you entered our waters. That was appropriate on your part. We have seen some smuggling and even piracy these past weeks. Just the same, we must investigate every incoming vessel. Since you are Canadian with a Canadian registered vessel, you are welcome to visit our country but please use good caution."

I hope to get some news. "We've been at sea for nearly two months with only one stop for supplies in Alaska. Can you tell us what has happened? When we left Hawaii, everything was fine."

Lt. Commander Garza's voice becomes a bit somber.

"It's very bad. Failure of the US dollar has created chaos for all sides. As people became more desperate, violence began at border crossings forcing them to close. It is strange today that it is the Americans who are sneaking across the border into Mexico and not the other way around. I feel sorry for these people. They are hungry and only seeking someplace to live but we have no resource for so many. When the Mexican military enforced the borders, shooting started and for a time it was very dangerous. It's better now with no more shooting but our government had to restrict entry by Americans. This is why we must inspect your papers. A few weeks after trouble began; all communication and even the Internet became silent. Nothing works, not even cell phones. Now some phones work but reception is not good. All electric power from the states is also off. We only have a few generation plants working. It was thought to be retaliation from the Americans because the border closed but our engineers said we were experiencing trouble also. We heard later that it was from an atom bomb which was detonated in space. Two were launched, one from the east coast and one from the west coast. Both from off shore."

"Have there been any updates from the states?" I try not to sound overly concerned but am hungry for news concerning my family.

"We have heard nothing since the electric went out. I would not go there, it is probably not safe. Thank you again for your hospitality but I must go now. I wish you a safe journey."

Scott hasn't said a word yet but as he shakes Commander Garza's hand he says, "Thank you for your kindness and assistance. We are grateful for your presence and protection as we visit your good country."

With that, Anna and I shake his hand and say our goodbye's. We untie and waste no time getting Intrepid under sail. As the Mexican boat speeds away, Anna sinks down and sits where she is.

"I didn't think we were going to make it through that and I don't know which scared me more; the pirates or the Mexican court system." None of us are laughing, not even a smile.

I don't even question Anna's flirting with the soldiers. She did it for good reason and it worked.

Scott keeps a good eye from the cabin deck while I man the helm, Anna is spending extra time in the galley fixing a better than normal dinner. I figure it is her way to spool off tension from our encounter with the Mexican military. The galley doesn't rock as much in the gulf coastal waters and she can finally use it for more than heating something. Intrepid's galley features a propane stove and oven. Many sailboats use alcohol stoves for safety concerns but LP sensors, leak detectors, and burner ignition has come a long way. The bottom line is that Intrepid has a better than expected oven and Anna is putting it to use. Dinner will be special tonight.

Anna has many talents and one of them is instinctive

cooking. She holds command of food and seasoning; she never needs a cookbook, and seldom requires measurements. Ingredients are added by handful, palmful, and pinch. She can make a cardboard box taste good. The smell of Anna's cooking is fantastic, driving us crazy on the deck and cockpit.

"Dinner!!!!" Anna doesn't have to say it twice.

I am down the steps first because I already have the snaffle lines connected to the helm. Scott is right behind me.

At the table are three place settings but NO food. Anna sits smiling as she begins to explain...."Before we start dinner, there is a matter that must be addressed."

Both Scott and I are bewildered as Anna continues, looking directly at me:

"When Scott saw the pirates coming, he asked you to hand him his brown pants. You understood what he meant and there will be no dinner served until I get the full explanation for the obvious "boy code" between you two."

Scott howls, "We've been PLAYED, Jason!!! I've seen this before!"

I start laughing to tears and surrender saying, "And she's won!!! We give up! I will tell you the joke as my HARD EARNED DINNER is held hostage."

Scott continues laughing as I explain. "There was a valiant French sea captain who led a ship of buccaneers. When they prepared for battle against a British ship, the brave captain would say, 'Prepare for battle and bring me my RED shirt.' One day he was asked the significance of his red shirt to which he replied... 'If I am injured in fighting, my men will not see my wound and fight bravely.' That next day the lookout shouted, 'Captain, I see six British ship of the line, they bear down on us and we are alone against them.' The brave captain then said, 'Prepare for battle, and bring me my BROWN pants'."

Scott and I roll with laughter as though this was the first time we had heard the joke. Anna's response is different; she just rolls her eyes and says... "That's it? Just a silly joke? You men!"

And with that, we all enjoy a fabulous dinner. This is probably the first good meal we felt like eating since we left Sitka. Scott and I keep laughing at the joke while Anna occasionally interjects...

"It's NOT that funny."

# Loreto:

Jim and Rita Sanders are close family friends and Jim is the designated pilot for the company plane which is shared between our various oil businesses. It looks impressive when we step off the 'Corporate Jet' but it is practical too. Most of the places we have to go are not located next to commercial airports. When there is a problem requiring vital freight getting to a site that Fed-Ex doesn't even know exists, the corporation's Pilatus PC-24 can land on unimproved runways as short as 2700 feet and has a range of over 2200 miles. Add the dedicated side cargo hatch to the cargo bay and you have an ideal oilfield corporate jet. Rita chose Pegasus as its name and everyone thought it was great so it became official.

Jim and Rita have a condo in Houston but their home is in Loreto, Baja Sur. Separated from Mexico by the Gulf of California, the only way to get here without crossing into the US, is by air or boat. A lot of U.S. expatriates have moved to the Baja but property ownership is reserved for Mexican citizens. That's where Rita comes in. Rita is of Spanish descent, Mexican born, and carries dual citizenship. The property is in her name and Jim calls himself her hired hand. The lower cost of keeping the plane here makes it convenient as a base of air operations for Jim and the company.

Our visit with the Armada de Mexico was two days ago and Carmen Island is coming to port so I call Jim on the hailing channel. "Pegasus, Pegasus, Pegasus, this is Intrepid. Pegasus, Pegasus, Pegasus, Intrepid calling." There is no response.

Then Scott remembers. "Try channel nine. Sixteen is monitored by everyone and Jim doesn't like to hail on that one."

I switch the marine radio from channel sixteen to nine. "Pegasus, Pegasus, Pegasus, this is Intrepid. Do you copy?"

After a brief delay comes an answer. "Loud and clear Intrepid. Is that you Jason? Glad you made it in one piece. What's your location?" Jim's voice is welcomed as it means our long cruise is about to end.

"We're approaching Carmen. Where should we meet you?" I am unmistakably energized.

"Come right into the marina. I have arranged a temporary slip for Intrepid. I'll be waiting for you. Pegasus out." Jim is short on words when it comes to marine radio. That seems strange to me because Rita says he regularly stays up all night, talking on ham radio.

The marina is west of the southern tip of Carmen Island. It's naturally protected and has very good security.

Anna loves sitting on the bow deck to read but not even a good book can divert her thoughts from how strange our world has become. She makes her way back to the helm after hearing Jim on the radio.

"It will be great to see Jim & Rita again. I can hardly believe it has been two months since we left Hawaii." Anna speaks 'matter-of-factly' and may have been more celebratory for ending such a great cruise, but in her heart of hearts, she senses a foreboding that perhaps our adventure is just beginning.

Jim is at the end of the floating marina dock and directs me to the slip. After helping with lines and fenders, he comes aboard.

"You must have had an easy passage. The boat looks good but you all look like you could use a rest. Welcome to Mexico!" Jim shakes both our hands but gives Anna a hug as he tells her in a loud whisper and a wink, "Don't let Jason know that I'm your second flame. Jason, the marina is keyed entry with good security. Just grab your day bags and come to the house to freshen up. Rita has dinner ready and we can catch up."

A day bag carries a change of clothes and whatever a

boater needs to use a marina guest facility for shower/shave and general clean-up. It is a refreshing change from the cramped head on a sailboat. After fifty-five days on Intrepid, leaving her with bag in hand feels strange but not as strange as learning to walk again on solid ground.

Jim & Rita's home is truly beautiful; a Tuscan style with openness that makes you feel cool and refreshed even on hot days. Rita is waiting for us in a white blouse and colorful ankle length skirt that reveals she is wearing no shoes. Her style is simple but elegant and it explains her character perfectly. Rita is what you might call calm under fire. Nothing seems to rattle her. Even now with the world in tatters, she's preparing a gracious meal and entertaining friends as though nothing is amiss.

Rita's greeting says everything, "Welcome! I'm so glad you could come. Sit down and relax but first I need a hug." Rita takes Anna's hands in hers, looks into her eyes with a smile and asks, "And has that old man been flirting with you again?"

Giving Rita a hug, Anna responds, "Would you expect anything else?"

Rita gives Jason and Scott a hug and offers them a seat. "Sit, I have some tea."

She doesn't have to ask if we want any; Rita's tea is to die for. It really isn't only tea; the pitcher is full of sliced kiwi, peaches, and cherries, with a strong dark tea poured over and left to blend flavors. I call it

Heaven's Nectar.

Jim sits in his favorite chair; plainly marked by his guitar in easy reach. An accomplished musician, Jim can sit and play from his heart without printed music. Rita says printed music is for musicians who play from their head but not their heart. In any case, listening to Jim play is soothing and makes this hacienda a relaxing home.

Anna and Rita disappear to the kitchen for talk and to share their love of cooking as first Scott and then I take showers, shave, and get cleaned up.

Rita is what some call a deep soul. She can read your heart simply by looking into your eyes but she never pries; she never has to.

"Your cruise must have been wonderful. You two are so busy; it must have been a good change."

"Oh, Rita, it was! At least the first leg. For a whole month, it was the two of us with no interruption; I didn't want it to end. Well, besides a few rain squalls that broke up the routine, even the weather left us alone most of the time. The trip from Sitka was full of questions and we couldn't wait to get here."

Rita stops and takes Anna's hands as she often does when she is going to say something especially important. "Right now, things are very bad in the States but everything is in control and we are well. We must tend to what we can and let God take care of everything."

Dinner is exquisite as usual and everyone helps wash and put away the dishes. There is a real peace in the house. In work or at rest, no matter the task, everyone enjoys each other's company. There is much to talk about with Jim, but for today, it's time to recoup.

Evening, on the veranda with Anna in my arms, we sit in the overstuffed wicker recliner. Anna comments, "You know, I've always liked the Baja and really love Jim & Rita but this visit is different. I feel a bit guilty that we are comfortable while people we know may be hurting. It's unsettling."

Scott has just stepped out to see the stars and comments, "Unsettling? You mean because our money is trash, the government is hiding, and cities are in flames; you feel something amiss?" Scott's attempt at humor would have been funny if it were not so real. With the cruise complete, our minds are free to realize how drastically the world has changed in a few short weeks. Each of us has been successful in business with full schedules that reach at least five years out. Now, those plans can be tossed. It is certain that appointments will be kept but what those will be and who they will involve is unknown. What we assumed our future to be must have been written on an Etch-a-Sketch and something or someone has given it a good shake.

# Making Plans:

"Sleeping I n a bed that doesn't roll with the sea takes a bit of getting used to, doesn't it?" My comment finds no response. Anna's spot beside me is empty and she isn't fixing her hair in the guest bathroom. Rita and Anna awoke with the sun and snuck off to create a breakfast to die for... or from, if you aren't careful. Why Jim does not weigh four hundred pounds is puzzling. Teamed with Anna, no hunger can survive

Ingredients from the refrigerator explain without words that quiche is on the menu. Anna cuts fresh fruit into a bowl as a compliment dish and makes a yogurt/sweet cream sauce to coat the fruit. Rita pours a thawed puree of purple fruit into a glass pitcher with sliced oranges and kiwi, the slight curious look on Anna's face triggers the few words Rita actually shares about this meal.

With a smile, Rita simply says, "Cactus fruit and guava."

Delighted, Anna smiles and gives a, "Yum!"

That is all they speak regarding food this morning. They are both intuitive cooks and take ques from each other like sisters but they do talk about other things; mostly camp and how life has changed.

"I have some things I would like to give you that will help you at camp and I have a gift for you to give to Cynthia, if you wouldn't mind taking it to her for me."

"Rita, you have given me so much already.    Your friendship and opening your home to us means more than you know."

Rita takes Anna's hands, looking deeply into her eyes, "It is no trouble for us.    We enjoy having good company and kindred spirits are a taste of Heaven. We get so few visitors since the border has closed.    At least we are far enough from it to be safe here.    Jim learns of many bad things happening in the States, from the radio.    He doesn't tell me about all of it but I see in his eyes that it must be really bad.    I'm glad for your mother that she is safe in Canada, and for Matt and Cynthia that camp is isolated.    You will be safe there too.    For now, we are here, and you are here, and life is good.    I think our quiche is ready, let's have some food."

Rita pulls Anna close for a quick hug and they carry their creations to a receptive table.    Kitchen aromas work better than an alarm clock and conversation, already active at the table, stops except for the ooohs, and aaahs, of a perfect meal.

Anna holds a passion for cooking and enjoys serving great food. One of Anna's friends 'of the more liberated persuasion' once commented that I had Anna 'bare foot and kitchen bound' to which Anna fired back that she was in the kitchen because she wanted to be there and if that ever changed, she would hire a cook! The look in Anna's green eyes bracketed with red hair conveyed the foolishness of crossing that little Viking. Her friend never offered opinions about cooking again.

With the dishes washed and put away by grateful men, Jim joins us back at the table to provide updates and discuss options.

My first question is, "Jim, what have you heard about my folks? Are they OK?"

Jim is floored and apologetic for neglecting to tell me about my folks right away. "Jason, I'm so sorry for not telling you. Your folks are fine. I completely missed how isolated you've been since this whole thing started. Your Dad and I knew there would be what he called a "fecal/fan convergence" following news of the collapse. The EMP was a surprise but everything else has progressed according to typical social meltdown. Your Dad and Mom flew out of Houston with Rita, me, and a few others that same day. We touched down at JF, unloaded a Ranger ATV, and your folks headed to camp with the others while Rita and I came here. We keep radio contact three times a week. You'll be able to talk with them tonight. I don't know what I was thinking that I didn't tell you all the details right away."

Relief floods over me. "I'm just glad to know they're OK.  I gotta tell you, when you didn't talk about them right off, I expected the worst but in my heart, I still knew they were alright.  I guess that's why Rita says you're spending nights on the radio."

"We keep good contact.  Your folks have organized quite an operation up there.  The camp is completely cut off from what's left of the country.  The desert is lethal to cross on foot except in winter.  That's why the border patrol is light near Big Bend.  We can get in there by plane and I can get supplies from here in Mexico by drawing from the corporate Mexican bank accounts.  Your Dad set up accounts to keep some of the proceeds of jobs down here so we could purchase future material and maintain the plane with pre-taxed money.  I also do a little bartering for cargo services to some remote Mexican communities.  Legit I might add. I'm no drug runner."  Jim has an understanding smile.

"I guess you three will be wanting to head to camp; and Jason, your folks will be very glad to see you.  I have Pegasus already loaded with supplies they need up there and a Polaris diesel Ranger with extra fuel for you to get from JF to camp.  JF is the designation of an obscure grass landing strip that is no longer listed on charts.  I've been running supplies there on several trips but randomly rotate landings at other locations. This Ranger only has two seats so one of you is going to have to ride "ghetto" but it beats walking.  Anna, there's an emergency Med/Surg kit already there but we're sending additional pharmaceuticals for stock. Another request was for a couple rolls of black poly pipe.  It's light so we can lash it on the roof of the

Ranger. All we have to figure now is when you want to leave."

Scott speaks up, "I got ghetto!"

"We'll take turns." I reply. "It sounds like there are more at camp than Mom & Dad. How many more?"

Jim has a proud sparkle in his eye as he says, "They have nearly fifty by now. Quite a little outpost from what I hear."

"FIFTY! That place isn't built for that. How is Dad doing it?"

"Jason, you won't recognize the camp from what your Dad says. We've flown in materials and tools and that group is handy. You know some of them. I'll let your Dad give you the grand tour when you get there but brace yourself to be highly impressed."

By the way Jim talks of the camp; you would think it was his favorite son.

"Holy crimole!" Scott says, "No doubt the place is big enough but where do they all sleep? I mean: one cabin; a kitchen; work shed; and an outhouse. I wonder who's sleeping there." With a chuckle from all three of us, Anna responds,

"Well, if I know your Mom & Dad, they have everything worked out and running like a clock. When do we go?"

Jim has everything organized. "We need to get you

back down to Intrepid. You'll want some things to take with you and she needs to be made ready for haul-out. This is a good time to clean her bottom and check her lines and sail. The marina will start Monday after I get back from taking you to camp."

My head is swimming laps around my heart. Dad taught me that a man can only deal with so much at one time and trying to think about too many things, opens the door to mistakes. This principle has saved my neck and career many times in the oilfield.

Dad used to tell me; 'When you're up to your neck in alligators, it's hard to remember your objective was to drain the swamp.' I guess we've had a few alligators to deal with lately. Everybody has to die someday but I'm not ready to give up my folks and I'm glad I don't have to today. Dad has been my role model and hero all my life. I can't remember not wanting to be just like him. He teaches by example what a man should be and how that man should be tough when it counts but tender hearted otherwise.

Dad knows how to read people and told me once that when a man acts tough all the time, he's trying to prove something that isn't true; usually it's that he's not scared. Mom and I have never doubted his devotion to us and even when away on some remote project, he always calls and never misses a birthday or anniversary. He taught me his secret but made me swear never to tell that he has all Mom's birthday, anniversary, and significant holidays, set for automatic delivery by his florist. It was actually their suggestion after his many calls and one near miss. The florist even has Sally's number, Dad's secretary, so they can call to make sure Mom is not on a trip herself and they send him copies of the beautifully written notes they include. Usually, Dad is ahead of the game to tell them what to put in the card but if he gets busy chasing alligators, the florist has his back. Now that plan works for me too.

Mom describes themselves as, 'Matthew and Cynthia Connors, the proud parents of a successful son who is carrying on the family business.' Dad goes by Matt but Mom is never called Cindy. She said it gives away telemarketers as they always use nicknames. Dad has recently taken an advisory role with the corporation as he migrates to retirement. Their health is good and both keep active lives but sixty-four candles are showing their burden on Dad's birthday cake. He has earned and is enjoying more time with Mom and now with Anna and me too.

Anna tenderly reaches from under my arm, rests her hand on my bicep and leans onto my shoulder.

"Jason? You OK?"

As well as Dad taught me how to read people, Anna is better. She knows her husband is sorting things out and her support is always there for me.

I pull her close, kiss her cheek, and say, "It's alright. I was thinking about Mom & Dad and how good it will be to see them again."

At times like this, Anna's faith shines, "I'm glad they're OK. I was praying for them on the way here from Sitka but didn't want to bring up something else to worry about that we have no control over. God is good no matter what but it is great knowing that he's taking care of what we can't."

# Contact:

Most of the day we spend unloading Intrepid, sorting what should stay and what will go with us to camp. By evening Jim shows us what he calls his ham shack. It is a small den between the master bedroom and guest rooms. The den is made smaller by shelves on three walls filled with radios and electronic test equipment.

"Our power down here in the Baja, isn't reliable but at least it isn't tied to the Western Grid. We're on a local power system and the southernmost point of the Western Grid is north of here. When the grid failed, our system was repaired and back up in two days. Of course, it goes down about every other week so we learn to deal with it. All my radios are powered by battery and kept charged by commercial power when available or by the turbine on our roof like yours on Intrepid. We're protected from most storms but being ready for anything is a way of life in the Baja. When you need it most, the phones will be out... radio is a good backup and only dependent on the laws of nature and providence itself."

Jim connects an antenna cable and turns on the radio. The blue and orange lights of the radio dials give the room an impressive glow. Listening as he scans a narrow band of frequencies he says, "I don't think the band is open, we'll have to wait for the sun to go down a bit more sp the D layer can dissipate."

Anna asks, "Jim, what's a D layer?"

Jim motions us further into the room as he closes the door. On the back of the door is a chart with a representation of the earth, mountains, antennas, and lines going up and down. Jim is in his favorite realm... explaining technical things.

"Radio signals generally travel what we call 'line of sight.' That is, until it bumps into something and stops. Now long ago, it was discovered that signals were getting further than the horizon by bouncing off layers of the ionosphere."

"Is that what they call skip?" Scott asks.

"That's what the CB crowd incorrectly calls skip but I have to explain propagation before I can get to what skip actually is," he says. "Most radio signals go in a straight line unless they are obstructed by solid objects. On the surface, the earth's horizon is about twenty seven miles away, after that signals start heading into space. This is called ground wave and with an antenna on a good tower you can't reach more than about fifty miles. Then there is sky wave. These are signals that reflect off various layers of the ionosphere and come back to earth; perhaps thousands of miles away. The area between the limits of ground wave and the beginning of sky wave is called the skip zone. It's the area that is skipped by traditional radio propagation."

Scott seems to light up a bit, "So what the CB crowd calls skip is really sky wave."

"Now you got it!" Pleased that Scott catches on, Jim continues, "Now different frequencies bounce off different layers at different times of the day. The layers change their distance from the earth as the atmosphere expands and contracts according to the sun rising and setting. That's the reason a lot of hams stay up late to catch the reflective layers while they are closer to earth. Am I going too fast?"

Anna answers, "I'm not catching all of it but enough to get where you're going. As the atmosphere cools, the layer we need is getting closer and that's what we want?"

Jim's face gives way to a puzzled look as he explains further. "Sort of and sort of not but it will come to you in a minute. Jason, your Dad is in a narrow canyon at camp. The mountain walls block radio reception except what comes down to them at a steep angle, besides that, they are in our skip zone. What we need to do is send our signal straight up (or as close to straight up as we can) and have it bounce off the right layer to come down into that canyon to your Dad's receiver. We can do this by what's called near vertical incident sky wave, or NVIS. Getting back to Anna's question; there is a layer that forms by the effect of the sun's rays called a D layer. It absorbs radio waves and acts like an obstruction during the day. Only high angle signals get through which limits range. We need to let the sun go down so the D layer will dissipate as the F layer moves closer. So, in the end, we're waiting for the atmosphere to collapse so we can use the 'F' layer of the ionosphere for a wider angle and bounce our signal further. It sounds confusing but in the end, our signal can go farther at night so we stay up to make contact."

We all look confused but tell Jim that we understand enough to make sense of the need to make radio contact at night.

Jim moves back to the radio, "Let's try it again." The radio sounds much different as Jim scans the frequencies. "I think we might be able to reach camp. Let's give it a try."

"CQ, CQ, CQ, this is X-ray Foxtrot One Foxtrot November Foxtrot CQ, CQ, CQ."

Jim waits about ten seconds and keys the radio again.

"CQ, CQ, CQ, this is X-ray Foxtrot One Foxtrot November Foxtrot CQ, CQ, CQ."

Still there is no reply. As Jim consults a chart, he adjusts the radio to another frequency and sends his call again, this time there is a reply.

"XF1-FNF, this is Kilo Five Oscar Sierra India,

do you copy?"

It's the camp!

"Roger K5OSI, I read you loud and clear. Is Matt there? I have someone who I'm sure he would like to speak with very much."

Jim hands me the mic and I wait for a reply.

"Jim, this is Matt, are the kids there?"

I squeeze the mic and speak.

"Dad, we're here and will be headed your way tomorrow. It's real good to hear your voice, you have no idea how good you sound right now."

My voice has a bit of tremor to it and Dad's reply seems to have the same. Anna is smiling as tears begin to roll.

"We're fine son, I'm glad you guys are safe. We're praying for you, Anna, and Scott, that you have safe travel. I'm going to give your Mom the mic before she comes apart. Love you son."

"Jason, this is Mom. I've been worried sick over you and Anna in that little boat... Scott too. How is Anna?"

Mom's voice is coming through tears.

"We're all fine here Mom. Jim's making things ready for us to get there soon. Anna and Scott are real fine too. Here's Anna."

"Hi Mom!"

Anna and Mom are as close as Anna is to her real Mom and she never felt right not to call her Mom as well.

"I'm SO glad to hear that you're safe. I've been praying for you every night."

Anna's tears are still flowing as I hand her a tissue.

Mom's voice is excited and happy.

"Us too dear. That is, we've been praying for you three also... and Rita & Jim. I wish I could reach through this speaker and hug your neck. I can hardly wait to see you."

Anna wipes her tears again and blows her nose as she hands the mic to Scott.

"Scott here, I'm feeling out of place, being the only one not bawling on this end. I understand you've made some improvements to the camp. I can hardly wait to see what you've done."

"Matt here; we've made some major improvements. Wait 'till you see the place. Was Jim able to lay hands on some inch and a half poly pipe?"

Scott hands the mic to Jim as the conversation turns to the business of supplies and tomorrow's trip.

Anna and I go to the veranda as Scott says he has some last minute packing to do. Rita gives Anna a consoling hug as she hands each of us a hot cup of another amazing tea. The stars dazzle like diamonds on black velvet. A cool breeze carries the gentle fragrance of jasmine from plants that Rita has everywhere. How can the world be so messed up when this place is so perfect?

Even with the rest of the country in shambles, hearing from Mom and Dad and knowing they are OK, takes an enormous weight from us.

Anna cuddles in my arms on the wicker lounge we have claimed as our own for a time.

"Jason, I remember the first time you took me to meet your parents. I was really nervous. "

"It was at the company picnic, wasn't it?" I say.

"YES IT WAS, but you only told me it was a picnic. You said nothing about it being a company-wide picnic. I was expecting a small quiet family gathering."

I'm almost laughing as I recall the details as Anna continues to tell it.

"It was at Lazy Acres, near Tomball and when we got there, the place was packed with people. You and I were holding a picnic basket between us and when I saw the crowd I asked you how we were going to find your family among all those people."

I finish the story for her. "And I said, 'That IS my family.' The look on your face was priceless. I only wish I had a camera to catch your expression."

Softly punching me in the gut, Anna continues but with a big grin. "You were SO mean!"

Anna turns and cuddles back into my arms. "But that was when I first met your Mom. She and your Dad came to meet us and I'll never forget what she said. 'Hello, you must be Anna. I'm Cynthia and this is my best friend, Matt; welcome.' Then she held my hand and walked us to their picnic table and I've had a second Mom ever since. It's always been special to me that your parents see themselves as best friends first and their marriage follows. That's never left me."

"Mom and Dad have always been real close. I guess I grew up thinking every family was that way. At least it's the way they ought to be."

Anna looks up at me while patting the arm of the lounge chair. "Ya know? We need to get us one of these."

I bust out laughing, "You are amazing!"

# Flight:

Jim has probably not slept as he tends final preparation for a pre-dawn flight across the border into Texas. With fuel tanks topped off, it gives Jim a margin of nearly 500 air miles for the round trip. There is no airport fuel truck there; he has to bring it all. Pegasus has a dedicated cargo bay and in it is a Polaris diesel Ranger ATV. Stuffed into the back of the passenger cabin is an ATV cargo trailer that increases load hauling by 1500 pounds. Finally, supplies are packed in the space remaining, including several rolls of black poly pipe. There are only two passenger seats left without cargo stacked in them and a net holding it down.

Jim drives back to pick us up for the short trip to the airport. Rita is not going but has packed a lunch basket for us and another for Jim.

Rita takes Anna aside as she places in her arms a soft bundle in brown paper tied with string, "This is a special package I would like for you to give Cynthia.  It is a gift from me."  There is a sincerity and fullness in Rita's eyes that imparts a unique quality to this gift and Anna will guard it well.

Hugs are shared as darkness is challenged by the faintest hint of sunlight on the horizon.

Scott is pleased that all but two passenger seats are filled; his will be the co-pilot's.  Pegasus is a dream to ride but the view from up front is beyond words.  We taxi to the end of the runway and with a quick radio authorization, engines spool up and Pegasus takes flight.

"Jim, this is really cool.  I've never been in Pegasus' jump seat.  How long is it to camp?"

"Well Scott, that all depends on how things go.  If we're lucky, we'll be there in just over two hours.  If not, it could get interesting."  Jim's voice implies this is not going to be a routine flight.

Scott's voice lowers as he turns to Jim, "What does "interesting" mean?"

Jim has a sly grin.  "Since the border closed and relations sorta fell apart, if you will, getting from here to there became a process of... let's say discretion."  Jim is trying to be subtle but is enjoying Scott's apprehension.

"Discretion?  I'm assuming we are jumping the border without a flight plan or clearance.  Won't the authorities of involved governments take this rather personal?" Now Scott is being subtle.

"Oh, it's not like these aren't OUR countries anyway. Governments are supposed to be working FOR us aren't they? AND, I don't plan on causing them any excitement by letting them know we're there. Remember I told you the border security wasn't strong around Big Bend?"

Scott just nods to respond.

"Well that goes for US radar as well. Our transponder range is only about 110 miles, the nearest commercial airport to pick us up is much farther than that, and the radar around the border is scattered by mountains. If we cross real low, they won't even know we're there. There's also a good chance U.S. civil radar is still off line and the military is probably looking for something bigger than a single low flying corporate jet."

Scott is squirming. "Jim, you just took the fun right out of this trip. What are our chances of getting in and you out without incident?"

"This is not my first rodeo Scott. This supply mission is a milk run. We'll drop off the radar right over a small airstrip here in Mexico that's just long enough for us to land, but instead of landing, we make like I'm going around for another attempt and then turn north to JF. Easy-Squeezy!" Jim is like a kid with a new toy. He is enjoying every minute of this kind of flying. "JF is an unmarked airstrip that isn't on maps anymore. It's so well concealed that if you don't know it's there, you can't even see it from the air. It will look like we're just landing in a field. When we land, we'll have to unload fast and leave quick. I can't stick around to help you get set up for the drive to camp. I briefed Jason already. Maps, compass, and landmark pictures are in a roll strapped to the ceiling of the Ranger's roof. Radar isn't going to pick us up but locals will know we're there. Pegasus is too big a target to let her sit still too long."

"Target?" Now Scott is really uncomfortable.

Jim begins his approach to the decoy airstrip and as he drops below radar detection, he turns north as he said. Scott is wide eyed and has forgotten what he thought about the co-pilot seat being really cool. Jim is truly a great pilot but the hills are close enough for a burro's ears to wipe the belly of the plane.

You can't tell when we actually crossed the border but it seems a short time before Jim makes a low pass to check the airstrip, then landing gear comes down and Pegasus is braking to a stop.

Jim keeps the engines at idle as the doors all open. Anna and I begin unloading boxes and bundles as Jim and Scott unload the Ranger and its trailer.

"Scott; tools to put the wheels back on the trailer are in the box on the front of the trailer." With Jim's help, the Ranger is unloaded in record time. It is obvious Jim has done this before. "There's tie straps in the toolbox too. God bless you guys; give my love to your folks, Jason."

With a quick round of handshakes for the guys and a hug with a kiss to the cheek for Anna, Jim says his goodbyes and warns them to stay clear of the exhaust. Doors close and Jim is taxiing back to the end of the runway. We move any remaining supplies off to the side of the runway as Jim and Pegasus come toward us, fast. Pegasus lifts off quickly without her cargo, and in no time we are alone on a grass strip, in the middle of nowhere. It is very quiet.

The world looks deceptively calm as I contemplate the change our lives have taken and how the nation is changed. To start with, we just had to sneak into our own country. Violence, hunger, and disease rage in cities across the land; yet this spot is quiet. I can see why old west outlaws came here. It is isolated and almost beautiful but one wrong move and it can become an unmarked grave that no one will ever find. Anna is my greatest treasure on earth and Scott is my best friend. Anna trusts me to provide for and protect her but the thought of failing her lays heavy on my mind. Now, here in this field, I feel vulnerable and powerless to protect either of them. In this deceitfully peaceful place, the mercy of God is our only hope. This is where fear and faith meet together.

I break the silence, "Let's get this rig together and packed. No doubt we didn't get here unnoticed."

The trailer wheels mount easily and packing is simplified by Anna's gift for arrangement. Scott says the stacked rolls of poly pipe on the roof make the Ranger look like an antique refrigerator.

As we start to laugh, Anna says just one word:

"DUST!"

She points in the direction of what certainly is an approaching vehicle. There isn't enough time to run and if we try, our own dust trail will be equally obvious and easy to follow. I don't want to lead anyone to camp if these are unfriendly. I just have time to unzip the bag I carried from Intrepid, slide a magazine into the .308 and release the bolt. I am prepared to talk nice but I'll keep a big stick handy.

# Challenge:

It is a good decision to not attempt outrunning the approaching truck. It's obviously built for this terrain and has way more power than our Ranger, even without our loaded trailer. The truck is a deer lease vehicle modified especially for hunting. Two men are riding in the cab and two more on seats mounted in the box. Above the cab are a cargo tray and another elevated seat that with a screen, serves as a blind. All four occupants look like they mean business.

The truck pulls parallel to our loaded Ranger but on the far side of the grass strip. We keep the Ranger between us and the truck. A bearded man opens the passenger door and using the truck as cover, speaks in a loud and clear voice.

"We don't get many strangers out here; much less so well provided. I'm going to have to ask you your names and intentions."

His associates in the truck keep their hands clearly below the doors and truck bed sides. I am sure they are armed and at the ready. I respond equally loud and clear.

"I'm Jason Connors; this is my wife Anna and her brother Scott. We're taking medicine and supplies to my father Matthew Connors. Is there a problem?"

At this range, I feel confident I can take out the two men in the back of the truck with a side arm but bringing the .308 on line will be slower. I don't feel ready for this and thoughts of this being how we will die are overshadowing my inner cry for God's protection. There's a hollow feeling in my gut.

After a slight hesitation the bearded man replies. "Would that be the same as Matt Connors?" And with a big grin, "The orneriest cuss of a man I ever met! You must be Matt and Cynthia's son. I'm Travis McCann and these are my sons; Willie, Pete, and Greg. Your Dad and me go back a long way in West Texas oil."

A sigh would be one of the biggest understatements ever penned.

Travis McCann is a friend of my Dad's and his words unlock a lot of caution. With genuine smiles the men in the truck disembark and join their dad as they walk over to shake hands with Scott and me. A tip of the hat to Anna makes her feel quite special but it will take a while to recover from the tension of this moment.

"Please excuse our caution. The blackout has shut down most business but drug runners are still at it. We investigate and run off most outsiders who don't have reasonable business here and everybody knows everybody in the Big Bend."

Sighs of relief favor both sides and after the cordial greeting, I reach over and zip up the bag I had opened but not before Travis, Pete's son, catches a glimpse of the .308. "Oooh, that's down right purty. Mind showing it off?"

Normally there would be some caution flags here, but I have heard Dad speak often of Travis McCann. Dad says he is a man you can trust and that men like him are hard to find. Besides, he and his sons apparently have left their firearms in their truck.

I unzip the bag, pull out the SCAR 17, drop the magazine, and cycle the bolt to empty the chamber.

"Beautiful!! Remarks Pete, can I see it. Willie and Greg also seem highly interested as I let them all handle the rifle.

Then Travis speaks, "Well boys, break out your hardware, looks like we're having us a gun show." Pete hands me back the .308 and with big smiles the boys put their right hands up in a show of peace and with their left hand, pull pistols from their backs. The guns are upside down in their hands so as not to alarm us. I have to admit that for a second, I didn't know what to make of it. As they lay out an impressive spread of Smith & Wesson 40's and a Kimber 45, Scott and I grin and similarly remove our matched pair of Sig 40's that Jim had given us when we loaded the last of the cargo the night before. Anna just stands there amazed with wide eyes. As all us guys grin and admire each other's iron, it is Travis who thinks to get the last laugh. He is packing a Dan Wesson revolver inside his denim jacket and reminds the boys as he lays it on the Ranger's deck,

"Never leave yourself without an exit plan."

Now it is Anna's turn. She clears her throat loudly, places her foot on the Ranger's tire, and pulls up the cuff of her jeans. From a boot holster she calmly removes the Ruger SP-101 38 special revolver that Rita had given her the night before. As she lays it on the deck next to Travis' Dan Wesson, Travis just says,

"Well I'll be dipped. Will ya look at that!"

All laugh 'til we can hardly breathe. Travis has been bested by a pretty little redhead but none is more surprised and proud than me. We probably all need the laugh to help cleanse the pile of adrenaline in our systems.

Travis continues the introduction. "Me and my boys don't live at your dad's camp but we have a place a bit north of your property. We drop by from time to time and are headed there now."

Holstering our hardware set a tone that we are well armed for most things that can go wrong regarding people. In the truck is an AR, a deer rifle, and an extended magazine shotgun but nothing really special. Travis takes another look at Anna's Ruger pistol sitting on the deck of the Ranger and says once again, "I'll be dipped."

"You can follow us to your dad's camp but watch the dust and don't eat too much of it. They always have a good feed for visitors and friends. You know the way from here?"

I nod and keep a good distance while we traverse the dirt roads. The Dust helps you appreciate surfaced roads.

Big Bend is a unique place. In the middle of some of the most inhospitable land that God created, stands a small range of mountains with canyons and valleys hosting a bounty of vegetation and wildlife. Desperadoes from the old west hid in these holes to cool their trail from posse and bounty hunters. It's rumored that Jesse James came here after narrowly escaping capture while working with the Younger Brothers in Minnesota. It's easy to see that if someone wanted to disappear, this would be the place to do it.

From a child, I have been here countless times. The family ranch is a hundred and ten acres adjoining Big Bend National Park. Sweet springs of water exist if you know where to look but trees are scarce. Gardening can be challenging but Mom has managed to work with the soil to coax it into producing a fair produce plot. I'm not much into working dirt. My interest is hunting. Mule deer, Aoudad sheep, a few Elk, Javelina, Quail, Rabbit, and Dove, which are just some of the game available. Edible plants grow in abundance with no reason to go hungry for those who know what to look for. Big Bend is a good place with a boundary of misery protecting it.

Over the years, I've invited many to enjoy hunting and

relax at the cabin on our ranch. Scott has joined me several times. There is no electricity and though other property owners have found ways to run power to their rustic hideaways, remaining off-grid somehow helps the serenity. Returning from a few days at the cabin makes you feel more rested than visiting other places for weeks. It is paradise hidden in the rocks. I can hardly wait to get there but this visit is going to be nothing like before. This isn't a vacation.

Anna is driving and I am sitting on a pile of tied down cargo in back. Leaning forward I ask Anna, "What did Jim say when he kissed you goodbye?"

With a big smile, Anna replies, "Why Jason, are you jealous?"

"No, just curious." I have no fear of Anna's commitment but I'm curious just the same.

"He told me to try to make it without him. I swear if I ever responded to one of his advances, I'm sure he would run and never stop. Besides, Rita would skin him alive."

It's assuring that Anna never hides things from me. Even Jim's playful antics are always expected but never taken for more than from a good friend.

The Big Bend is prone to the rise and fall of draught. Many have tried to settle here, only to move on to more hospitable land. Passing abandoned buildings as we get closer to camp, more and more of them appear to be at least partially disassembled.

# Camp:

Scott is in the right seat of the Ranger with Anna still driving. In childish fashion, I pat Scott on the shoulder...

"Are we there yet?    Are we there yet?    How much longer?    I gotta pee."

If laughter is medicine, we are healed but we will need a lot more of it to spill off today's stress.

Travis drives directly to camp.  He obviously knows where he's going because the secluded canyon entrance is well concealed.  Just before he rounds the last corner and the camp comes into view, he begins honking the horn.    There are nearly twenty people gathering to meet us as we pull into what looks like the same canyon but definitely not the same camp.

Scott is amazed, "Jason, will you look at this?  It looks like a city!  You can hardly find the old cabin and kitchen. WOW!"

Anna and I spot Mom and Dad and bolt out of the Ranger, leaving Scott behind. "That's right, leave ol' Scott with the strangers. I can bumble through on my own." Scott loves playing the 'poor, poor me' routine.

Several men from camp introduced themselves to Scott as they thank him for bringing supplies. They quickly unload the cargo and take it in various directions, depending on what each package is labeled. Only our personal bags and the package marked 'to Cynthia from Rita' are left in the Ranger.

Hugs and kisses mingled with tears are the recipe of the moment. Calling this a joyful time is a supreme understatement.

Mom, wiping her tears says, "You look marvelous, both of you! I want to hear all about everything since you left Hawaii. We only tracked one day of your trip before coming to camp and have been here ever since. Jim and Rita kept us updated with your progress and messages until the EMP but nothing after that."

Dad has his arm around my shoulder, "Son, it's good to have you here. I knew you would take care of yourself but when things went dark it got scary all the same. I see you've met up with Travis. He's a good man but don't tell him I said so."

"I heard that!" Travis shakes Dad's hand and as his arm comes free from my shoulder, he gives Travis a hug too. Travis replies, "Shouldn't we save the last dance for the ladies?" Dad pushes him back as they laugh. It is a good, good day.

Mom and Anna are still arm in arm as Mom loudly calls, "Lunch is almost ready, let's head to the kitchen! There's certainly room for our welcomed guests too. Travis, Willie, Pete, Greg, you will be staying for lunch, won't you?" She never has to ask twice when offering a good meal.

The old kitchen shack is barely discernible by the new wing that swallowed it up. Fifty people hardly fill the dining area with picnic table seating. Glassless, shuttered windows form a row on each of the two-foot-thick stone and adobe walls. The end wall has a door and the far end is the kitchen. Inside is remarkably cooler than outside and the floors look like concrete. This is the community building and the largest in camp.

We can't believe the expansion to the old camp.

"Dad, how did you do all this? Where did you get materials? Pegasus couldn't have brought in all this." My questions are piling up faster than Dad can answer.

Dad begins chuckling, "All in time, son. I want to show you everything but for now, you've been traveling a good way and it's time to eat and get you settled in."

Anna sits between Mom and me, while Scott and Dad sit on the opposite side of the table. People begin filing into the seating area picking up their plate and utensils as they come in. Large serving dishes of food are placed on pass through shelves from the kitchen area behind what used to be the outside wall of the old building.  Efficiency is everywhere.

Mom picks up a big bowl of rice with meat and mixed vegetables while Dad collects a basket of what looks like biscuits.   It looks appetizing but the vegetables don't resemble corn or peas or green beans.  The meat is dark and Scott correctly guesses venison.  The bread is somewhat darker than whole wheat with a sweet nutty flavor and a lot like cornbread.  Mom explains the bread is Milo bread and an enjoyed staple around the camp.

Several people from camp come up to the table, introduce themselves, and welcome us.   Everyone apparently knows who we are and that we are expected.  I know our presence increases the burden on limited food supplies but their welcome is genuine.

Mom explains to Anna, "We're learning to adapt our diet to indigenous resource.  We had what Matt likes to call our 'deep larder' and stored as much as three year's food for ten people.  That was for the two of us, you and Jason, Jim and Rita, and up to four more.  We had no idea our group would grow to this many.  Our new group would eat through everything we had in a little over seven months.  So, Matt got all the heads together and we began coming up with solutions.  All the food was gone from local grocery stores, and the regular silo grains, like wheat and rice, were raided quickly but for some reason, they passed up the Milo.  Did you know that most of the world eats Milo as a food source?  Only in America is it considered livestock feed.  It's dark, sweet, and you can use it the same as you would use cornmeal.  The men made trips at night to bring it back here and gathered a large supply until it became too dangerous to be on the roads. We don't travel more than we have to, these days."

Dinner is delicious and filling. As we finish, Dad says, "We need to get you weary travelers to where you can freshen up. Let's get your bags and I'll show you to your cabins? We can show you the rest of the camp and talk later. It sure is good to have you here; and I want to hear all about your journey."

We chat while taking our empty dishes to the wash station, clean the plates, utensils, and cups, and put them back on the community rack. Everyone busses and cleans their own, which makes living with so many, much easier.

Dad is proud of the camp and what it has become.

I am blown away at how many new buildings share the grounds around the old camp. "Dad, these buildings, they're adobe, right? How did you do it, I mean... where... what...?"

Dad is enjoying my bewilderment. It takes a lot to catch me speechless.

"Fantastic, isn't it? And I didn't come up with the ideas either. The walls are stacked stone with adobe stucco. When we first got here, there were only eight of us: your mom and me; Fred and Irene Livingston; Harry and Rachel Taylor; Sam Elliott, and his girlfriend Stephanie."

Dad remembers those first days like they were

yesterday:

# Retrospect:

[Matt's account of the first days
after the financial collapse.]

[Radio Message] We interrupt regular broadcasting to bring you this special announcement from the office of the President of the United States. Please stand by.

"Ladies and gentlemen, I bring you the President."

"It is my sad duty to inform you, our American Public, that after long deliberation and bi-partisan effort, we have not been able to secure necessary financing to support the U.S. treasury and make further payments against the national debt. In simple terms, America has defaulted on our debt. I join with congress in asking for calm and order as we continue to seek answers to meet the needs of so many......" [audio fades off].

The phone immediately rings in my office.

"Matt? Jim here.  Are you listening to this?"

"Yeah, I have it on right now.  This is it.  Get the plane ready and load the bug-out pallets.  I'll get things ready on this end and meet you at the hangar."

I call Cynthia, "Hi, it's me.  Did you have the news on?... Well, the president just announced the feds have defaulted on the debt.  This is not a joke.  We need to go to camp.  I'll be there to pick you up in an hour after getting some things in order here... yeah, I know it's bad.... I'm sure they'll be OK.  Jason's a smart man and will know where to come.... Love you too."

My next call is to Fred Livingston, plant operations:

"Fred, Matt.... Yeah, I heard.  Look, things are going to melt down fast.  Can you get Irene here and your stuff to the plane in about two hours?  We're going to camp until we see how this plays out.  ...OK, see you there."

As I hang up, the phone immediately rings.

"Matt.  Yeah, Harry, I heard.  Can you and Rachel meet us at the plane in about two hours?  We're bugging out and I'd like you two to be with us. .... Good.  See you there."

Hanging up the phone again, I dial the outside office.

"Sally, I'm going to shut operations down.  Have security get ready to lock it up.  I'm sending folks home to be with their families.  ...You too.  ...Thanks.  ...No, we'll be fine.  Look, if things get bad for you folks, get to my house.  You know the codes.  ...Be safe."

I dial the number code to tie my phone to the company intercom system, "Good morning. This is Matt Connors. As many of you already know, the president just announced the country is in default on the national debt. This is a serious event affecting the stability of the nation and the viability of the dollar. We are closing down operations to allow each of you to be with your families at this time. When normalization returns, we will attempt to resume operations and each of you will retain your current positions. God bless you all, you are free to head home. Be safe."

I go to my office safe and open it for perhaps the last time, at least for a while. From it, I remove a small backpack and a case. The pack contains emergency gear and the case holds firearms. On the way to my truck, I pass an O.S.I. engineer, Gary Wagoner.

"Gary, when you get things organized head to camp with your folks. You'll have two or three days before things get really out of hand. Here, take this. I have another in the truck and it might come in handy." I toss him the pack.

Gary replies, "Thanks Matt, I'm headed for home and then to pick up Mom and Dad. We'll see you there. Thanks again."

"One more thing," I add, "top off your tanks here, there won't be any stations open between here and camp." Gary has been to camp before and it is good that most company trucks carry auxiliary transfer tanks in the bed. Six hundred miles is a long way between gas stations.

Traffic is unusually light as I drive home. As much as I estimated how social degradation would play out, I am amazed at the slow response. Do others think this is a drill? Can the masses be so naïve to what is sure to follow? In any event, I am pleased with light traffic in Houston this mid-morning.

Cynthia is waiting for me when I get home. We have planned for this with boxes pre-packed for storage in our safe room, and others to go with us. The safe room isn't as much a vault as it is a storm and fire resistant room with a hidden entrance through a walk-in closet. Even if you know where it is, it would be difficult to find its entrance.  It is a good place to put photo albums, and the things that can't easily be replaced. As I meet Cynthia, her face is already covered in tears.

"Oh, Matt." Cynthia wraps her arms around me and weeps. "This is awful. Everything is falling apart and people are going to suffer. What about the kids? We can't even reach them. I don't know that I can bear it."

I sit down with her and take her hands in mine. "We'll be OK. The kids are in the safest place they could be and we'll be in the next safest place until they get to us. I'm not sure how but Jason is resourceful and Anna is strong. They will know where we've gone and they'll make it. God has put us in just the right place and His timing is perfect. If we trust Him, we'll be OK." I'm even a bit taken at my courageous words and apparent conviction but inside, I'm scared. This is bad, real bad.

Cynthia takes confidence in my assurance. "This morning, in my devotions, I read across Nahum 1:7 and it jumped out at me."

*"The Lord is good, a stronghold in the day of trouble, and he knoweth them that trust in him."*

"I didn't realize how much I needed that today but God did."

Our truck is loaded in fifteen minutes and we are headed to the airport near Tomball. Cynthia understands now why I've had us practice loading the truck for an event like this. In case of fire, flood, riot, or storm, we pack the truck the same, with the same prepared containers. Practice has been like a fire drill but this time, it is no drill. Streets are not too busy but traffic is starting to grow. We make it to the airport and park near the company hangar. Jim has the plane already loaded, fueled, and warming up. On a business trip a few years ago, we were delayed six hours because the airport fuel truck had run dry. It became Jim's practice to top off fuel tanks soon after he lands. Our cargo fits easily. Irene and Cynthia hug, cry, and talk about each of their extended families while Jim and I initiate exit strategy.

"Matt, we may have some trouble getting a U.S. flight plan. I expect the FAA to ground all air traffic so right after you called I filed my flight plan with Mexico, over the internet, it will be in effect in about an hour. We'll file our FAA flight plan after we're airborne. Good thing this isn't a controlled airport. Ignorance is a wonderful excuse."

I smile and say, "You're a good man, Charlie Brown. Have you heard from the others?"

Jim answers, "Harry should be here real soon. He lives

close. Fred has further to go and I don't know about Sam. Cell phones are down with all circuits busy so we'll have to wait as long as we can."

A horn honks and Harry Taylor's truck pulls up next to the hangar. Rachel is in the passenger seat. Rachel runs up to Cynthia and Rita while Harry begins loading their belongings to the plane. Jim and I give him a hand.

"Have any trouble?" I ask.

"Not much but we nearly got T-boned at a light. It's starting." Harry refers to the disregard of civil order when people panic.

Fred and Irene Livingston pull in next with Sam Elliott following. Sam is single but brings his girlfriend, Stephanie Sweeny. With everything loaded, everyone gets on board and Jim begins to taxi. Without a control tower, Jim taxies to the end of the runway and electronically files his FAA flight plan. We no sooner become airborne when local air traffic control announces closure of all airports and the grounding of all flights. Jim continues due south. Within minutes, we are approaching the Gulf coast and gaining speed.

As Jim expected, air traffic control calls us directly over radio with an order to return to our point of origin. Jim ignores the first contact attempt as he sees the water pass beneath us. On the second call,

"Air traffic Houston this is Nancy-OSI, please repeat last transmission."

Jim is stalling.

"Nancy-OSI, Houston. Please be advised, FAA has issued a national directive grounding all civil and domestic flights until further notice. Please return to your point of departure."

"Air traffic Houston, this is Nancy-OSI, we will begin our turn."

Jim begins a very wide turn to the west. However, the apex of that turn crosses the twelve-mile boundary of international airspace at which Jim radios a message to Air traffic control, Houston.

"Air traffic Houston this is Nancy-OSI, please be advised we are no longer in your airspace and will continue our approved ANS flight plan to our base of operations in Mexico as it will be easier than further complicating your flight jurisdiction."

Without waiting for a response, Jim switches frequency to Airspace Navigation Services (ANS). ANS is the Mexican version of air traffic control. Rita is seated in the co-pilot spot and comments to her husband.

"They aren't going to like that." Rita's smile says a lot about her understanding of international politics.

Jim replies, "I didn't think they would but unless I miss my guess, there won't be any administration to answer to in the near future. If there is, we can claim compliance with their intent by leaving their airspace. Moving our base of air operations to Baja was a good decision."

Cynthia, Irene, Rachel, and Stephanie, sit together and share their concerns. They all shed tears intermittently as they talk. Most have lived long enough to draw on experience but Stephanie is still in her twenties. She looks very troubled.

Rachel Taylor tries to calm her by asking about her family. "Stephanie, where are you from?"

Stephanie pulls herself together as she answers, "My family is in Colorado, that's where I grew up. We have a vacation cabin up in the mountains. It's kept well stocked so we don't have to pack much when we go. I'm hoping that's where they are going. I couldn't reach them by phone. All circuits went busy within seconds of the announcement. Getting home was impossible so coming with Sam seemed my best option but I sure wish I knew that my family is OK."

Cynthia puts her hand over Stephanie's hand and says, "I'm sure they will be fine. I'm guessing they're most worried over you right now."

Jim has a lot of experience flying through Mexican airspace and the ANS is familiar with his flight patterns. Nothing is unusual except that he requests a stop at a small strip in central northern Mexico. The diversion is granted. Fred and I squeeze up to the pilot cabin as Jim explains the next part of the plan.

"There's a small strip north of Ocampo that I've done some work for. When we make approach, we'll be off ANS radar and they will expect we landed. I'm going to turn off the transponder and make like I was buzzing the strip to say hello, then we'll divert to JF and off-load. You'll have to get to camp from there. Rita and I will take the plane on to Baja."

I take it from there, "Pat is coming with Gary and his family. He's bringing his radio gear so we hope to have some communication. If you don't hear from us within two weeks, fly over and look for smoke."

Smoke refers to using smoke flares to signal green for OK and red for help.

Jim and Pat are both amateur radio operators and have discussed frequencies and methods to communicate from the camp to Baja. The original purpose was to provide communication during extended hunting trips but it will be especially valuable now.

# Making do:

<u>[Matt's account of the first days
after the financial collapse.]</u>

Jim makes his low pass at the airfield near Ocampo and switches off the aircraft beacon.

"For now, the ANS will think we landed and the U.S. won't see us, as long as we remain at low altitude." Jim's piloting is good but following the land contour makes for a wild ride. At least it doesn't last long before we are circling to land at one of our favorite spots. It never set well with me to land a multi-million-dollar aircraft on a grass strip but JF is an old military airstrip with the advantage of not being on current flight maps. We are on the ground at the southern tip of Big Bend National Park. Camp isn't far.

Jim and Rita drop us off at the airstrip and we use the Ranger to get four of us to camp and then return for loads of supplies we had on the plane and the remaining people.    Finally, we get everyone and everything transported and begin setting up camp.

Cynthia and I take one bedroom of the cabin while Fred and Irene take the other.  Harry and Rachel sleep on the futon sleeper sofa in the living room and Stephanie sleeps on a cot behind a privacy curtain.  Sam draws the short straw and takes up residence outside in a tent. Accommodations are rough but after the long hard day traveling, we are just glad to be here.  Sleep is so good but it comes slowly to weary souls concerned for loved ones.

Morning comes but with little motivation.  There is a lot to do but no energy to do it with.  Overwhelmed is a better description.  Have we made the right decision? Did we over-react?  I take a battery powered all-band radio to the top of the ridge, to try to get some news. We feel cut off from the world and aren't sure if that is a good thing.

The radio doesn't pick up any U.S. broadcasts and only a few foreign stations.    Night will provide better reception.

Breakfast is quiet considering we are all good friends. Smalltalk is made but most of us are thinking, wondering, praying, for those who aren't here at camp.

I don't even remember what we did that day.   Not much, I think.  It is all so different than we thought this would be like.  This is all new ground and we are surviving on prior guess work.  I hope we guessed right.

Evening and night come again as I make another trek up to the ridge with the radio.

[radio]"Today marks the second day following collapse of the U.S. dollar with wide spread instability felt in countries around the world. None quite so evident as in the United States itself where disturbances erupted almost immediately in poorer sections of major cities. All flights in and out of the U.S. are indefinitely suspended by authorities leaving many travelers stranded. The President and Congress have made appeal for calm during this difficult time as security forces appear to be doubling up around the White House and Capitol buildings.

Meanwhile, Arabs in the streets of Tehran are celebrating what they are calling the death of the great western evil......"

Though it isn't good news, it does affirm we made a good choice in coming to camp while travel was possible. I hope the others are OK.

I don't share details of what I picked up from the British news station but do tell them that things are destabilizing around the country and that we should stay put until order is restored.

The next day, around mid-day, we hear a truck rumble into our canyon. It's two trucks really. Bob and Lisa Isham are in the first truck with their three children Trevor, Hailey, and Amber. Bob brings a small cargo trailer with camping gear, Lisa's gardening tools, and four dairy goats. Behind them are Allen and Christi Duncan with their son Riley. Allen is a welder with OSI but left his work truck behind. He drove a different OSI truck but one without welding equipment which gives him more cargo space.

As he gets out, I ask, "Allen, glad you made it. Whose truck is this?"

Allen has been anticipating my inevitable question for over 500 miles and has an answer all prepared.

"Why, it's got your name on the door, it must be yours."

Then I spot what clearly are three bullet holes in the rear fender and ask, "And how did you manage to get holes in my truck?"

"Someone out here must not like you. I'm glad your friends are bad shots."

Later, with Christi and Riley out of ear shot, Allen tells me they were nearly ambushed outside of Hondo, east of San Antonio. They traveled side roads by night after that. Today was the end of last night's very slow drive.

"They came at us from an overpass. As we approached, I saw part of a truck parked on the far side and it didn't look good to me. We hadn't met up with Bob yet so being alone; I crossed the median and drove up the 'on ramp' on the other side. As soon as we crossed over... there they were, on the other side of the highway, waiting for us to pass through. When they saw we crossed on the wrong side ramps, they opened up on us. Sure glad they were lousy shots. We saw Bob a few hours later and we've been traveling together since. I just told Christi and Riley they were shooting to make us stop but not actually aiming at us. I guess I almost lied. They got close."

Our camp population doubles that day and as we think our limit has been met, the next day brings fourteen more. Among those are the Wagoner's with Pat's ham radio equipment. Gary thanks me for the emergency backpack I had given him when we left and returns it still intact. Better to have than need. I feel better that he had it with him.

How are we going to fit all these people in one tiny deer camp? People are sleeping in trucks, tents, and under tarps. We have to call a meeting of minds.

We meet in the evening as the heat of the day passes. As we talk of the challenges, twelve-year-old Brendon Wagoner says we're like the Pilgrims when they built Plymouth colony. They built one big house to fit everyone until each could build their own house later.

That is a good idea but how can we build it? Our cabin took several years of hauling materials on each trip, before it was done, and this is a small cabin.

It is Riley Duncan, also twelve years old, who comes to our rescue.

"Why not use mud like they do in Africa and Mexico?

Out of the mouths of babes! We have engineers and plant managers among us but the answer we needed comes from two twelve-year-old boys. We modify their building method but start a stacked stone structure with adobe plaster for stability.

With everyone lending a hand, it takes our minds away from thinking about family and friends. Being extra tired at the end of the day also helps but everyone has moments when sorrow gets the best of you, either by not knowing, or from knowing about trouble near one's home. We help each other and strength grows within our numbers.

Pat Wagoner unpacks and sets up his ham radio for an attempt at contacting Jim and Rita in Baja. He says reception is best at night and that he will try to make contact that evening.

Construction of the community building is coming along and the walls are nearly six feet high as a plan hatches to scavenge roofing from abandoned buildings near us. We grow to over forty but each new hand is appreciated because it makes the work go faster. That's better than seeing people as just more mouths to feed.

We don't start out this way. Some of our camp meetings give example to the fears and uncertainty we all share. An 'ace in the hole' is the fact that both the deep larder and the camp belong to Cynthia and me so we have final say over who stays and who doesn't. That helps but we need something more if we are going to keep these folks together. As more people arrive the question comes up regularly, when our 'lifeboat' will be full. I really grow to hate that analogy. Each of these people are friends, coworkers, and family. Which can we even think of sending to their inevitable death? On the other hand, can we survive out here with such a large group and limited resource? Without a miracle, the answer is no.

Cynthia finally brings understanding that each of us can grasp. She says, "Each of us has braved the elements, distance, and social breakdown to arrive here. None of us could have made it without God's help and intervention. Since all arrived by God's helping hand, we must trust that same hand to provide for our need. We should spend our time praying instead of complaining and He will take care of us."

I think I know why God says pastors should be men. If women like Cynthia begin to compete for those jobs, men might not have a chance. Cynthia sure lays it out strong to the group. Our problem solving sessions are very productive now.

Camp is a safer place but not much on comfort. Among the supplies people bring we cobble together some tents but we eat in shifts, sleep in shifts, bathe in shifts... well, you get the idea. It isn't going to last long the way we are going.

One problem is motor fuel. Most have empty tanks and now we need fuel to make foraging trips for building materials. It is perfect timing that Pat makes radio contact with Jim and arranges for a fuel delivery from Baja. Mexico still has a working economy, even without U.S. foreign aid. It's a struggling economy but Jim is able to barter legitimate air service for supplies and he brings us four drums of diesel #2 and a barrel pump. His business use of the plane to ferry cargo to small communities provides a perfect cover for his diversions to south Texas. By draining what is left in all the trucks, we have enough fuel to get one truck to where Jim can land the plane. Once we get fuel we use the Ranger as a scout vehicle to locate where we can scrounge roofing tin to cover the community building. A sense of accomplishment grows as we build and it helps us through the dark days knowing what our country must be going through.

There is a problem with our scavenged building materials. The arid climate in the Big Bend is tough on wood. All the wood we scrounge is so dried out that a nail splits it right in two. We have better luck tying boards together than nailing them. Good thing too because we have no nails. We make shutters and doors for the huts but any hope of a tight fit is futile. A cat can walk through a closed door. Good thing we don't have any cats.

We also scrounge for food. The longest we travel is to scout a group of grain silos. All of them are empty, except one. It holds grain sorghum; most people call it milo. There must be two thousand pounds of it. By night we begin trucking pickup loads to camp. It takes all night to make just one trip due to avoiding main roads and tactics to prevent being followed back to camp. That's where Travis and his sons save us. That man knows logistics. He knows how to cover our tracks and how to fend off attacks before they happen. I never understood what a 'rear guard' was, before, but I do now. There are still a few hundred pounds remaining when Willie and Greg meet us on the way back to warn us of a well-armed ambush waiting at the silos. We decide what we have is enough and leave the last of it.

Stephanie Sweeny is a Godsend to us. She spots edible

plants and food sources we never would have identified. Between discovering the bounty of milo and her finding wild food sources, our deep larder is effectively doubled; so much for the 'lifeboat' doctrine.

Recounting these days to Jason leads me to realize how stressful the unknown can be. Most believe it is difficulty that creates stress but we found adversity unifies our group. There is no time to play politics with people sleeping on the ground and there is too much work for anyone to do or manage it all by themselves. The women organize what supplies we have and add them to our 'deep larder.' Though, it doesn't seem so deep anymore.

Our first huts use tarps to keep rain from collapsing the roofs but we found a way to make cement and we've coated all those now. With rain so scarce, it doesn't get tested much.

# Huts:

[Back to Jason's perspective.]

I can see the weight of leadership that my Dad carries. As heavy as it is, it also seems to strengthen him, or is it God's grace that strengthens him to carry an even heavier load. Dad is still my role model.

Mom continues to walk arm in arm with Anna. She is very pleased to have her children close. Beyond the utility buildings are a curved line of uniform sized huts. They partially circle the community and utility buildings.

"Anna, I've been so excited to have you come. The huts are sparse but I found some curtains for your windows. Beds are another thing. Boards are scarce but from what the men have been able to scavenge from abandoned buildings, they make doors, shutters, and platforms that we loosely call beds. The beds take some getting used to."

Mom lifts the door latch to a hut. The floor is hard and smooth like the community building and the hut is an open room with a small table, a chair and a platform covered with a woven mat of long grass. The room is about ten feet by twelve with a small window at the front and another in back. It is enough room for sleeping but it's hardly a house. Adobe walls and a domed ceiling give protection from the sun and provides a cool feeling.

"Mom, this is better than I ..." Anna pauses to find the right word.

"Feared?" Mom laughs.

"No ... I mean, I didn't know what to expect but this is a nice little house." Anna can tell her cheeks are flushed but she is sincere and Mom knows it. Both women laugh. Anna walks to the bed and feels the grass mat.

"What is this?"

"It's something the younger women make. They aren't a store bought mattress but it beats sleeping on a board or the ground. There is so much work here that everyone does what they can. The children often help as much as grownups so we've taken to calling any child above the age of six, a younger man or woman. In this case, your mat was woven of Johnson grass, by the Palmer girls: Kristen, Kellie, and Kory. You'll meet them later."

The room grows dark as Dad and I step through the doorway. Mom looks up with a smile, "Well, you two must have taken the long way here."

I give Anna a kiss and apologetically say, "I'm so sorry I wasn't here to carry you over your threshold. Please forgive me."

Anna smiles and replies, "Just make sure it doesn't happen again." Then as she notices Scott isn't with us, "Where's Scott?"

No sooner does she ask then the sound of the Ranger's diesel grows closer and stops at the door. Scott's voice announces, "Movers are here! Need any of this stuff?"

We bring in our things along with the package from Rita. Anna sees it and says, "Mom, I almost forgot. Rita sent a gift for you; I think it's something special."

"She told me about it and it is very special. Please put it back in the Ranger and I'll get it later. Rita is an amazing woman, thanks for bringing it to me."

Mom stays to help Anna arrange their few things and then talk more as we find Scott a place to stay.

Taking the Ranger down a row of huts, Dad explains, "Scott, we house single men in bunkhouse style. We don't plan on staying here permanently and for the sake of efficiency, this works best for now. I hope you don't mind."

"I don't mind at all." Scott replies, "It will give me a chance to meet some of the other guys. How many to a hut? I see they are all about the same size."

Dad says, "Keeping all the huts the same size was a suggestion from one of our ladies. They call it cookie cutting and it simplifies making many of the same kind of structure. There's a team putting up a new hut at the end of the row. They started day before yesterday and should be done tomorrow by dinner. The young men and women love the last day because they get to play in the mud. We dig a shallow pit and line it with a tarp. Add the clay, sand, grass, and water, then turn the youngsters loose to stomp it into adobe. We add lime and mix the last coat by hand to keep the rain out."

"A hut can house as many as six but we like to keep it to four for now. The hut you'll be in has Randy Fowler, George Hardin, and John Stubbs. You'll be the fourth. They're good guys, I'm sure you'll enjoy their company."

I perk up at one of those names, "Is that the Randy Fowler from Houston? We graduated High School together at Lamar. How's he doing?"

"The very same Randy; you can ask him yourself at dinner. He's working at the pit but should be back around four."

Dad knows all the people and their schedules. He seems to hold a personal regard for each member at the camp. It is the same at our business. No matter where he goes, he knows everybody and calls them by name. It always amazes me how he does it.

"Here we are; there aren't any fancy curtains but the locals respect each other's personal space. Windows stay open most the time so we build them a little higher and work with it."

Joking with Scott, I ask, "Can I help you with your bags to your room, sir?"

Scott jokes, "I can handle it. You'll ask for a tip if I let you help." Scott takes his large single duffel bag into the hut and sets it on the empty bunk. "All moved in."

We drive back to the utility buildings where Dad continues the tour, "This first building is our communications center. It isn't manned during the day but it gets busy at night. We have a mobile HF radio that can work everything from the ten to eighty meter bands but we only use forty and eighty because that's all that can get out of this canyon."

Scott interjects, "Jim told us about that. It's NVIS, right?"

Dad replies, "I think you're right. That's the name the radio guys throw around. I'm not a ham operator but we have two in the group that are. They are a big help to us. I don't know what we would do without regular contact with Jim. He is our go-for guy and has been able to get us almost anything we need."

Dad continues, "For local communication we have plans for a small remote radio on the ridge-line that will receive and re-transmit our signals from down here to others in our group that are outside of the canyon. Pat Wagoner can explain all this better but he's rigged up a low power radio that uses a smart-phone or a PDA, I'm not real sure which, but it lets you send text messages on very low power. If we communicate with text messages the repeater radio can operate on low power and we'll be able to run it from a battery and solar charger. Like I said, Pat can explain all that better than I can. Communicating by text now requires us to send someone up to the canyon ridgeline to make each radio connection. When that repeater radio is working, we'll be able to stay down here and still talk outside the canyon."

Dad walks over to an area with many small boxes that have names on each. "This is where messages are passed. Like a post office, everyone has a box or slot and individual messages can be passed between the group members." Pointing to a large overhead board, "Group wide messages are tacked up here on this board."

There is a notice posting today's date and what dates we have radio contact with Jim. Another notice is a reminder of the cutoff for supply requests to Jim. There is another post that announces birthdays.

"Wow, Dad, you've thought of about everything."

"Not me, Jason. We have group meetings and this all came from them. It's amazing to watch."

# Water and Gardens:

Traveling outside the circle of huts, Dad takes us on a four wheeler trail past another small building and up an incline.

"You remember the spring where we get our water? When it was just us, it supplied more than enough, but with over five times the people there isn't a drop to waste. This is what we need the poly pipe for."

The Ranger comes to a stop near where a group of men are working. Some are digging a ditch while others are unrolling and splicing the pipe together.

Our plant operations foreman, Fred Livingston, and one of our civil engineers, Harry Taylor are here.

"Fred! Harry! How goes it? I see you two managed to do the light work while Ted, Mark, and Dennis got stuck with the back work."

"Hey Matt!" says Harry, "Well, someone has to

supervise and tell these guys which end of the shovel to hold." Everyone takes a short break, shake hands, and welcome Scott and me to camp.

Dad continues, "Looks like you're making progress. Would you mind explaining to Scott and Jason, what it is we're up to here?"

Fred speaks first, "Sure! The spring water runs all day and night so most of it runs right back into the ground. We run a pretty consistent bucket brigade to camp but it's a poor use of hard work. Someone mentioned they could put a garden hose to use here and the idea got momentum. We're building a spring box out of stone and will line it with some red clay we found. It should create a backwater reservoir. We'll run the poly pipe from here to camp and have low pressure water service to the kitchen, wash huts, and laundry. Waste water from each of those will then be sent to the garden. We won't be wasting much and nobody will have to tote buckets anymore."

Scott asks, "Can you bury it all the way?"

Harry adds, "Not all the way but we need to keep it buried or the sun will turn this pipe into a water heater. There are some rocky places to cross so we plan to pile material on it and bury it above ground. Most of it will get buried below. Would you like to help? I'm sure one of these boys would loan you his shovel."

"Not yet," says Dad, "we're giving them the grand tour today. They'll pick a place to help out later."

Then it dawns on me what those buildings are at each

end of the garden area. "Are those the wash huts and laundry we saw near the garden?"

"Yes, and we'll head there next. Fred, Harry, see you guys at dinner. It's looking good!" With that, we turn the Ranger around and head back down the hill.

The wash huts are much different than I expect. They have doors on four sides, each opening to a small private room with a shower stall. They are elevated by about four feet and the shower-like enclosures are over what look like shipping pallets.    Silver tarps are suspended beneath to catch water runoff. In the stall are a bucket of water and a smaller dipper can. The best you get is a splash bath but it will get the job done. More important is that every drop of waste water is collected and sent to the garden. Hanging on the wall is a small mirror to shave by. I am sure Anna will have some comments but she is one girl who knows how to make do with what is available.

Dad explains, "This took a while to get used to, especially for the ladies, but most have adapted to it. The breeze coming through the open eighteen inches between the roof and walls is a big help for now but we may have to tighten things up when the weather gets cool.    We built this with scavenged materials from derelict buildings in the area. It went to top priority after an embarrassing close call near the spring."

Scott and I chuckle with Dad as we imagine how those close calls could happen. Scott adds, "Depending on who was embarrassed, I can imagine how high on the list it became."

"Well, let's just say it went straight to the top and exceeded all other needs," Dad replies.

"Don't tell me it was Mom!" I gasp, but Dad only grins while Scott covers his eyes.

Anna and Mom don't take long to finish up at the hut and they continue conversation on their walk to the old cabin. Anna is curious how Mom and Dad dealt with some of the challenges.

"You must have been really surprised by all the unexpected people that showed up here. How did you handle it emotionally? I mean, everything you planned just went up in smoke."

Mom gives Anna's arm a little squeeze as she explains, "It wasn't easy. You're right about the plans. We always knew the economy was in trouble and that a crash was possible, even inevitable, but you're never really ready for it when it comes. In our best plans we counted on six people with a margin for up to four more, but fifty was way more than I thought possible. Some are accepting all the change better than others. Matt, Harry, Fred, and Pat, are the leadership council but they have earned the respect of the entire group. Work groups are designed like the 'small groups' we have at church. Each group has at least one very stable leader who can help the struggling ones with their concerns and fears. We all have plenty of those to go around."

Arriving at the old cabin, Mom invites Anna in. The cabin is not large by most standards but does have two bedrooms and a futon couch at one end of the single room that serves as kitchen, dining, and living room.

Mom continues, "Fred and Irene Livingston stay with us and have the other bedroom." With a smirk she said, "We old people need to stick together."

Anna asks, "Isn't Fred over plant operations? I think I met them once."

"That's them. Our largest family at camp is the Wagoner clan. Gary and Melinda have four children and they came with Pat and Marge Wagoner. They brought thirty laying hens and six dairy goats along with the rest of their trailer full of food and supplies. Everyone is welcome here but the eggs and dairy were especially welcome. After Harry and Rachel Taylor decided to move to the community building along with Stephanie Sweeny, we took in two of the single girls, Nicky & Jackie Chambers, you'll like them, they sleep on the futon in the living room. It's crowded but not bad and better than some of the huts with families of five. The Wagoner's are six but their two older boys stay in the single men's huts."

"Mom, did you ever think that you might have to turn someone away? I've read a lot about the preparedness mind and they explain the lifeboat decision where your lifeboat is full and one more will capsize the boat and all perish. I understand what they are saying but can't picture myself turning someone away who is seeking a safe haven."

"Matt and I partly prepared for that by coming here. We are far enough away from the masses that we didn't think anyone would find us. Then as they came, they were friends and people we knew. How could we turn them away? They had risked their lives just getting here so we determined that those who came were directed and delivered by God's grace. Who were we to turn them away? So, just like God provided for the widow of Zarephath to feed the prophet Elijah during a famine, we would trust the same God to feed us and His refugees. The process has been amazing!"

Scott, Dad, and I walk past the garden to a utility building on the far side. It is raised off the ground by the height of the fifty-five gallon drums, visible beneath the floor. Construction resembles more of a covered patio than a building. The walls are only half high making this laundry impressive.

Roxanne Bellows is in charge of laundry operations. She steps down from the washing area to greet her guests. Her soft brown hair compliments her deep brown eyes. Scott is speechless when he sees her. She has what his mother called a strong chin and she definitely carries herself as a competent worker.

"Hello, Mr. Connors, what can I do for you?"

"Roxanne, this is my son Jason and his brother-in-law Scott. Would you mind explaining your operation here?"

More than pleased to show their operation, she explains...

"I'd be glad to. We find hot water and a little detergent does most of the work. Getting the water hot isn't a problem with these solar heated barrels, we have lots of sunshine. Our problem is keeping them filled. The new water line will be a great help."

Roxanne walks them through their washing process. Two sets of three wash tubs arranged in a triangle pattern comprise their washing "machines." A hand crank wringer is moved between any two tubs. The first tub holds soapy water followed by two tubs of clean water for rinsing. Agitation is manual but plans for a wind driven agitator are coming. Lightly soiled clothing washes first, followed by heavy work clothes. From the soapy water, clothes go through the wringer into the first rinse tub and then to a second rinse before being hung to dry. When soapy water becomes too dirty it is drained into holding barrels to cool and eventually used to water the garden. Hot clean water is put in that tub as it becomes the new second rinse tub while more soap is added to the tub previously used for the first rinsing, to then become the first washing tub. This progression conserves the most water and allows for an efficient laundry process. Washed clothes are hung on a line to dry and then sorted by laundry mark. Clothes are marked by a laundry pen with the number of each person's box in the communication hut. We are impressed with the organization and process that Roxanne has developed.

Roxanne worked in billing for OSI along with Nicky and Jackie Chambers. All three women are quite attractive, in their twenties, and very capable at taking care of themselves and whatever business they are occupied with. When national default was announced, the three girls packed up what they had and headed for camp. They had been here once before when Mom organized a "girls retreat" for the women of OSI. Fortunately, Nicky had the coordinates saved in her GPS and they arrived before the EMP hit. Nicky now works in the camp communication center and Jackie, who has advanced first aid training, works at the medical hut. Having these ladies operate key functional areas of camp greatly improves the attention paid by the single adult men to their laundry, communication, and proper care of minor wounds.

A large garden plot stretches between the laundry and wash huts. Lisa Isham maintained a large garden at their home in the Hill Country, north of San Antonio, so it made sense to have her head up this work at camp. Lisa's husband Bob built homes as a general contractor but also serves as a game hunting guide, which is how we met him. Bob knew they could survive in the Big Bend area while the country mended and our camp was the first place they came. Mom and Dad insisted they stay.

Lisa's gardens are not traditional. The growing beds are raised with stone and mortar sides. Water is added to three inch PVC pipe that carries it past the surface soil to the base of each raised bed.

Dad greets Lisa by name and introduces Scott and me as he has been doing all day with everyone in camp. Then he asks Lisa to elaborate on this unique growing method.

Lisa explains, "These are called wicking beds. Sidewalls keep the dirt in and we line the bottoms with heavy black sheet plastic that my husband used for foundation liners. In each bed, we've put a piece of three inch PVC pipe from the bottom to the top, so we can get water down and create an aquifer. Eight inches of sand under a foot of soil is all that's needed in each bed. Water levels are kept between four and six inches under these beds in the sand layer. Natural wicking and the root structure of plants keep them watered from below with very little evaporation. Our garden is growing and we look to be producing for the kitchen in about two more weeks."

Dad thanks her for the tour and says he can hardly wait for the fresh salads.

At the Ranger again, we climb in and drive to the old cabin where we join up with Anna and Mom for dinner.

People filter into camp. Some of them must be working at the place Dad called 'the pit' because their clothes are very dirty. Some are covered with red dirt; others with much lighter colored dirt, and some aren't dirty at all but carry rifles or shotguns. A few have rabbits or birds they harvested. These go straight to the kitchen so the animals can be properly processed and cooked.

Everyone seems somewhat happy and genuinely glad to see each other. Many go to the communication building to check for messages while others grab fresh clothes and head to the wash hut to clean up before dinner. Water buckets are loaded onto carts and wheeled from the spring to the wash hut and kitchen. It is apparent the new water line will be a blessing for all, but especially for those who port water by bucket and cart.

Camp is coming alive. I hear my name called from behind and turn to see who it is.

"Jason Connors! I heard you made it to camp." It's Randy Fowler.

We exchange a firm handshake and hug between long friends.

"Randy! How long has it been? Three years since the twentieth class reunion? Haven't you found a woman to put up with you yet?"

"Not yet. I'm saving myself and being selective. Not just ANY pretty face gets THIS handsome beast. I heard you did though. I'd have attended the wedding but you got married where only an Eskimo could drop in. North of the Arctic Circle; right?"

"Not that far north. Anna, this is my High School buddy, Randy Fowler. Randy, this is Anna Connors, formerly Anna Iverson."

"Anna, I'm very pleased to meet you. My condolence for your choice of husbands."

Anna is quick to pick up on the banter of old friends and is very capable to dish it back, "Well, I caught him fair and after looking him over, decided that he cleaned up pretty good. It's nice to meet you, Randy. Jason speaks of you often; mostly in a respectable manner."

"The pleasure is all mine; Anna. I can tell that Jason has met his match; you are as beautiful as you are quick witted. Congratulations to you both. Please excuse me to go wash for dinner. Jason, I'm looking forward to catching up. See you both soon." Randy proceeds to his hut. Scott excuses himself to do a little exploring near the camp and to help draw water. He seems interested in something.

# Dinner meeting:

At dinner, we are joined by Fred and Irene Livingston. Dad does the introductions.

"Fred and Irene Livingston, you know Jason and this is his lovely wife Anna, and her brother Scott Iverson. Jason, Anna, Scott; this is Fred and Irene Livingston. You boys met Fred up at the spring. Fred has run plant operations at OSI for fourteen years and we couldn't have done as well without him."

"Matt, those are kind words that I hope to live up to. Jason, your dad and I go a long way back. He's a good man and a pleasure to work with." Fred turns to Matt with a smile, "Does that secure my next raise?"

As everyone either smiles or laughs, dinner is plated up. In a big bowl is something that looks like a cross between chili and stew. Vegetables, meat, and beans are served in a bowl with more milo biscuits. Since ice is not available, a pitcher of cool tea complements the meal. The tea tastes like chamomile with a hint of lemon. Scott tastes it and has to ask...

"What's this tea made of? It's really good."

Irene answer's, "Scott, I asked the same question. Lisa Isham says our garden isn't producing yet so it has to be wild herbs. Then I asked Stephanie and Christi, they run the kitchen, and they told me that Lupe Ramos and the Palmer girls pick herbs and things like lemon flowers for teas and seasonings. They are good at finding it and run across plenty as they pick Johnson grass for making sleeping mats. A lot of the seasonings we use are local herbs and picked by our girls."

Scott asks, "How do the girls know what plants NOT to pick? Aren't some plants poisonous?" Scott has a bit of concern showing on his face.

"Good point. Stephanie Sweeny is a dietician and minored in botany. She checks everything with a plant identification guide and sometimes sends things to the medical hut. She has been teaching the girls what to look for. I'm pretty sure your tea is safe." Irene's assurance relieves Scott's concern but his attention turns to the meat in the main dish.

"Complements to the chef; you eat well." Scott is accustomed to eating unusual foods and not at all squeamish but his curiosity is peaked. "I can't make out what meat this is. It's very good but not venison or beef. What is it?"

Fred speaks up. "I think it's the last of the Aoudad, the boys shot last week."

"Aoudad!" I say. "Scott and I have chased those nearly every time we've come out here but never got a clean shot at one. Who's the great hunter?"

"You would expect Bob Isham," says Dad, "But you'd be wrong. It was Paul Sayer. He was checking out fishing holes and walked right up to this big Aoudad doe. I guess it didn't see him. Paul took it with his sidearm from fifty feet. He has bragging rights this week."

Most have finished eating but those that have bused their dishes are returned to their seats. Dad stands and gets the attention of the group.

"Before we start, I'd like to introduce, with great pleasure..."

"AND Relief," adds Harry Taylor, as everyone chuckles.

"And relief." Repeats Dad, "My son Jason, his pretty wife Anna, and her brother Scott Iverson." Dad doesn't have to ask that they make us welcome. Applause begins almost before he finishes our introduction.

Fred speaks up, "Jason, Anna, and Scott, I can assure you that your parent's prayers, as well as the rest of us, have been with you as you journeyed here. Your radio call this week was a tension reliever for the whole camp. We're glad you're here and that our prayers have been answered. On behalf of the whole camp; welcome!"

We rise and mouth "Thank you" but our voices are

drowned by applause.

Dad speaks to the group again.    "I know we're all waiting for the new water line..."

Roxanne Bellows lets out a loud..., "Wah-Hoo!!" and is joined by laughter.

"...and none quiet as anxious as Roxanne. Fred, how's it coming?"

Fred stands and gives an update.    "Ted, Mark, and Dennis are making great progress on laying the line and we're near complete on the retaining wall for the retention pool.    We'll begin sealing it with clay tomorrow if Randy has enough gathered.    We are on schedule to have water down to the garden area by the weekend, and into the kitchen, laundry, and wash huts by early next week."

Roxanne asks, "Does that mean we can draw water from the new line this weekend and not have to bring it from the spring?"

"Good question, Roxanne, but this brings up a problem we need to address.    When we seal the bottom of the retention pool, the red clay is going to muddy up the water pretty good.    We'll do the walls first and the bottom on Friday.  We have to let that settle by itself to get a proper seal so the plan for now is to temporarily suspend the laundry and go on water rationing while the pool fills and clears itself.    As soon as the water clears, we'll be able to use the new line."

Roxanne suggests, "We can scrub out the wash tubs to

hold reserve water and top off the barrels we have."

Suggestions come easily as the group develops several ways to accommodate the water shortage. There are no complaints, just assistance and cooperation. Some are comical but one meant for humor turns into a great idea. It is a comment made by John Stubbs.

"If Randy and George smell too bad on the way home, I'll do everyone a favor and shove 'em in the creek that runs by the pit."

Laughter fills the room but it is Melinda Wagoner's comment that starts them in the right direction.

"I might run a bunch of the children and young men and women up there for their baths. That would save some water."

Kathy Palmer adds, "We all could jump in and cool off while we washed the clothes on our backs."

Then with two words, a plan is born. It comes from Roxanne:

"POOL-PARTY!"

Dad leans over and can be seen talking with Fred, Harry, Irene, Rachel, and Mom. They are all smiling as Dad stands with his hands raised.

"We've all been working pretty hard without a break or complaint. I think it would be a great idea to shut down for a day and throw ourselves in the creek on Saturday. What say you?"

A mix of cheers and applause make it official. Calling this a pool party is accepted, even though it is at a small creek and not a pool. Hardly a water resort, the creek is within walking distance, a safe place, and we can make this a fun event. Perhaps it is the diversion or that the group needs something... anything to celebrate, but the talk everyone shares as we walk home from dinner is all about Saturday's pool party.

Anna and I retrieve our day bags that we carried on Intrepid, and head for the wash huts. Anna holds my hand as we speak of the changes our lives have taken.

Anna's soft voice shows no regret but it is full of amazement. "Who would have guessed we would be here right now? Or that the camp would be so filled with people and working like a small city?"

Concern for how the changes might be affecting Anna, I ask, "Do you wish we were back home? I mean, you never bargained for this when we agreed to sail your Dad's boat to Seattle."

Anna stops and looks up into my eyes. This is a serious moment with her heart completely exposed.

"Jason, I love being with you and I love you. I was more at home with you on the boat than at our house in Houston. I guess our home will never be defined by an address or a place. Home is where WE are and right now, it's here. Our life will always be an adventure but as long as I'm with you, I'm good with it. We didn't plan this but we do have to roll with it, so far, I think we're doing pretty well. Think of the stories we'll share after we've grown old together?"

Anna then gives me all the confirmation I need as she wraps her arms around my neck and kisses me like she did that first time at the altar. All my apprehensions flood away with Anna's passion for living the instant.

"Hey, you guys! Get a room!" It's Scott. He is heading for the wash huts with his day bag in hand and flip-flops on his feet. As he passes us and hurries on, he shouts over his shoulder, "I get the first stall!"

But Scott is wrong. When he gets to the wash huts, there is a line of about six people waiting for an empty room. Showers, if you could call them that, don't take too long but eight stalls have to be shared among nearly a dozen families and about equal number of single people. Cooperation is important. Diversity of work helps as those working at the pits or other dirty jobs choose to wash up before dinner. Those working in the kitchen, laundry, and a few others, choose to wash in the morning. The rest stand in line as the sun sets. It became a social gathering and waiting isn't a bother. At the front of each line are barrels of water and buckets for each person in turn to fill and take with them into the wash hut. Of course the girls take longer but as each surrenders to the simplicity and ease of shorter hair styles, hair care becomes easier and takes less time.

Scott, ever the clown, has borrowed a pair of pink bunny slippers from Roxanne and when he emerges from the wash hut, he has a towel wrapped in a turban around his head, the bunny slippers on his feet (though they hardly fit) and his day bag over his arm like a purse. The whole camp hears the laughter but most wonder what they missed seeing.

# Finding their place:

Anna and I don't sleep well tonight. These mats are going to take some time getting used to. At least a breeze keeps the air moving. As the sun begins to chase away the darkness, I kiss Anna awake.

"You have to get uuuuuuuuup. It's morning and they won't keep breakfast waiting for you."

"What time is it?" Anna's response is with closed eyes that don't want to wake up.

"Seven o'clock comes twice a day and it's here right now for you." I enjoy waking up my 'NOT a morning person' wife.

Anna cannot conceal her smile as the corners of her mouth begin to curl upward. "I think I'll wait for it to come around again."

Reaching over with a single outstretched finger I begin moving it towards Anna's ribs.

Anticipating what will come, Anna brakes into uncontrolled laughter as she grabs my hands defensively. "NO! I'm up! I'm up!"

Breakfast begins at seven and customarily the pit and field crews eat first. Way more work can be done before the heat of the day and it helps to get them going first.

When we get to the community building, some mats are still occupied with smaller children but most are stacked against the back wall and those who don't have a hut are already up. Anna feels bad that we were assigned a hut while others are still sleeping in the community building and says something to me about it.

Kathy Palmer comes in with us and overhears Anna's remarks to me.

"Good morning! I'm Kathy Palmer. My husband, Brent is already off to work but my three daughters are Kristen, Kelly and Kory. I'm glad to meet you in person."

"Oh, it's good to meet you too." Anna turns to Kathy. "I've heard a lot of good things about your busy girls. You have good reason to be proud of them."

"We are; thank you. I couldn't help hearing your concern for being assigned a hut while others share the community building. I don't mean to be nosey but I want you to know that your hut was one of the first built and we've been waiting for you to come fill it since the beginning. This is your family's camp and we are the guests. We all are grateful for the Connors' opening up their place to us and you're not being here was such a burden for Matt and Cynthia; we just love those two. We decided to build your hut first, after the community building. Everyone needs hope to lean on when life gets tough and your hut became a monument of hope for us because you were on your way here. In some ways, our wait for you to arrive represented the hopes we all have concerning loved ones on our hearts and minds. Your arrival answered our prayers and it's a joy for us to see that special hut is no longer vacant."

Anna's tears begin leaking down her freckled cheeks as she hugs Kathy. All she can muster to say is, "You people are awesome! "

Breakfast is special this morning. Thanks to the Wagoner's thirty chickens, fried eggs accompany pancakes today. The pancakes are light but filling with that same nutty flavor and dark color that give away milo as a main ingredient. They are really good. Syrup is in a pitcher but not syrup like you might be used to, it is more of a sauce. A combination of apple sauce, peaches, and some wild fruit, with a little extra sugar, and it makes a great pancake topping. Cooking the fruit-mash boils away tartness and blends the flavors. Getting used to this will not be a problem.

People are eating and chatting as the door opens. Scott walks in and many stop eating, stand, and applaud. Scott grins and takes a complimentary bow, still hamming it up over last night's shenanigans at the wash hut. Roxanne is sitting with Nicky and Jackie Chambers but waves for Scott to join them at their table. He picks up a plate, cup of hot tea, and utensils, and walks to where Roxanne scoots over, making him a place next to her.

Anna, comments, "Well, big brother seems to have hit it off with the locals."

Quietly, I add, "And pretty ones too." We both smile understandingly as we finish our tea together.

After breakfast we walk over to the old cabin where Mom and Dad meet us on the porch. Mom wants to show us the livestock.

As Mom walks, she explains why the livestock is so close to the cabin. "Predators are plentiful in these hills and we've seen cougar, bobcat, and numbers of eagles and hawks. We can't provide feed to keep the stock penned up so we let them free range during the day and penned up at night. The hens keep a watch on the sky. One will give an alarm and they all take cover. The hawks may get a few but they won't get many. Cougar and bobcat are a different matter. If they attack, we won't have chickens in the morning and they will cart off a goat every week if we don't stop it. Next to the cabin, we can hear the goats and they get noisy when they sense a predator. Matt has a shotgun next to our bed and he wakes really easy. We haven't lost a bird or goat yet."

"The goats aren't here right now. Robert and Brendon Wagoner are our shepherds. They take them out to graze and find food by day and bring them back here before dinner. Robert keeps a shotgun and Brendon has a slingshot for lesser trouble."

Mom walks over to the chicken pen and opens the door letting them out. Most of the birds run out to begin scratching for food but some stay behind for their turn in the nesting boxes.

Anna smiles as she says, "I guess they have to wait in line too."

Dad asks, "What are your plans for today?"

Anna says she wants to look over the medical hut while I have arranged for a tour of the pit. We visit a bit longer and make our way to our respective tasks.

Three small buildings lay between the community building and cabin but inside the outer circle of huts. Communications is furthest from the old cabin; Headquarters lay in the middle and Medical is closest. If sparse is a good description of the medical hut, this is sparser. A cot is collapsed against the far wall with a chair in front and to the middle of the floor. Next to the chair is a small end table and to the right of the room is a counter made of boards with shelves behind. On the shelves are bundles of weeds and a few bottles of various 'over the counter' medicines. On the end of the counter is a good sized Aloe plant, missing the ends of several of its leaves.

"Welcome to the camp hospital. Anna, I'm Jackie Chambers. I've been working here because of my first aid training and because I know how to put Band-Aids on boo-boos. I am sure glad to see you arrive. We can really use your RN skills."

Anna's first impression of Jackie is good and it only

grows better with time. She is a stunning brunette but her most attractive feature is the look of purity in her eyes. She radiates compassion that is sure to calm the most nervous patient. In a different way, Jackie is like Rita. Anna feels naturally comfortable around her and she knows that working with Jackie is going to be easy.

"I'm glad to meet you Jackie. I've heard a lot of good things about your care already. You've done a good job. As for RN skills, let's hope we can stick to Band-Aids and boo-boos. That will suit me just fine."

Jackie reaches for a package, "There's a box here that Jim sent for you. I didn't open it because I think it's medicine and I wouldn't know how to use it so I left it sealed." Jackie lifts a medium sized box from behind the counter and sets it on top for Anna to open.

"Well, let's see what Jim sent us. Do you have a knife on you?"

Jackie reaches behind the counter and brings out a pair of scissors.

"Works for me." Anna opens the box. Inside, under bubble wrap, are boxes and bottles of medicine along with supplies of syringes, needles, bandages, and ointments. Looks like we're in business, Jackie."

"How do you know what medicine to use? Do they make you memorize all that in nursing school?"

Anna carries a side bag with a strap from her opposite shoulder. In it she carries a stethoscope, blood pressure cuff, latex exam gloves, personal items, and two books that she removes to show Jackie.

"I have a copy of the 'Nursing Drug Reference' and 'Where There Is No Doctor.' Between these two we can determine what problem we're dealing with how best to treat it. It's not as good as my library back home but it fits in my bag. It looks like we have some pretty good antibiotics. Jim did a good job. I do have a problem with our location though. We're in a great spot for wound care and general care but what if we get a contagion? Keeping a sick person here could infect the whole camp. We could really use an isolation hut. Keeping an illness from spreading can be the best way to beat it."

"Can we treat sick people at their huts?" offers Jackie.

"We could but that would spread whatever they had to others in the hut and they could spread it further before symptoms appeared." Anna appreciates Jackie's willingness to offer suggestions. "What we need is an isolated hut with a couple of beds, at least. It needs to be down wind and away from camp, have its own outhouse, and have food and medicine delivered at a half-way station."

"What's a half-way station?" Jackie asks.

"That's where a person brings food or supplies to a drop off point and leaves it there for the care giver to come retrieve after that person leaves. It isolates contact so germs can't spread."

"Wow, I hope we don't need to do that very often."

Anna replies, "We shouldn't, but we need to be ready to, or the whole camp could get sick all at once. As close as we all live, it's a possibility we need to guard against."

Jackie smiles, "Now I'm really glad you're here. I would not have thought of that."

Wanting to know Jackie better, Anna asks, "Are you from the Houston area?"

Jackie smiles again, pleased that Anna shows interest in knowing more about 'who she is', more than 'what she does.'

"I'm not originally from the Houston area but I've lived there with my sister Nicky for about three years. We're originally from a tiny little town called Short Pump, Virginia. There's not but one street there and Dad used to say it had "Welcome to Short Pump" on both sides of the same sign. It is definitely rural Virginia. It's about twenty-five minutes outside of Richmond."

Anna is even more curious now, "I love small communities. I'm from a place in northern Alberta that is much like your Short Pump. It's called Trout Lake. So how did you and Nicky get to Houston?"

"My Mom died of cancer when I was eight so Dad raised us by himself for three years before he remarried," she says. "It took a while for me to accept Jennifer but she was exactly what I needed. When Nicky graduated college, she wanted to see more of the world and randomly picked the Houston area to search for jobs. She got on with O.S.I. and a year later, I graduated and followed her. She got me my job. Dad and Jennifer moved to western Montana after Nicky and I left. They live in a rural area and should be OK but I still worry about them."

Anna asks, partly for Jackie's sake and partly for her own longings for home. "Do you ever miss Short Pump?"

Jackie takes a contemplative deep breath as she answers. "Yes, I do sometimes, mostly in winter. The leaves change to brilliant colors in the fall and nothing compares to a fresh blanket of snow. I try to explain what tubing is and people down here can only imagine floating down a river."

Excited by the sudden memory, Anna replies. "TUBING!! Oh, I remember that. No sled ever matched it for fun. Up at Trout Lake, we made runs that were sometimes a hundred yards long!"

Anna and Jackie are connecting with a fast friendship. Their memories of home become a glue that binds their hearts as more than friends and more like sisters.

# The Pit:

Following the trail out of camp and on to the end of the narrow canyon entrance, it bends to the left. About two hundred yards further, it crosses a small creek where in two days the camp will gather for the 'pool party.' The trail continues on the other side of the creek into a very shallow canyon, more like a deep indentation in the hill, where about eight men are working. Randy looks up and comes over.

"Glad you could make it to see our operation.

Then I ask, "Randy, how's your family?  Have you heard anything?"

Randy's countenance grows quiet. "I don't know.  My folks are pretty up in years and my sister and her family live right in downtown Houston.  They never bought into any sort of preparedness so this caught them with little to no resources.  The phones jammed up before I could call either of them.  I'd love to be surprised but fear the worst, thanks for asking anyway. I mean it."

Putting my hand on Randy's shoulder, I say, "Randy, I'm sorry. Anna and I will keep them in our prayers. Don't give up hope. You never know."

Randy says thanks, takes a deep breath, and then seems to want some diversion so he resumes explaining his operation.

"This is where most of our building materials come from…. Well, except for the stone and what the scavengers bring in from the field, but this is where we process clay, mineral sand, make lime, and even make charcoal."

I look around in amazement. On one side of the pit are two big kilns that look like stone chimneys built against the pit wall. Men are filling one of the chimneys with coal and limestone. Once full, fire is put to the bottom opening and tinder catches the stack burning. Smoke from the fire follows the pit wall and dissipates over the ridge. It would be very difficult to follow that smoke anywhere.

Randy explains, "We get this coal from a vein we found a little way from here. It doesn't provide much but we can use wood or charcoal if we drop the percentage of limestone to fuel. This stack will burn hot all day. Tomorrow we'll start pulling out the burned limestone. Here's a piece we burned yesterday, watch what happens when I pour water on it."

I watch as Randy dribbles water from a soup can onto a

burnt piece of limestone. At first it appears the water was only absorbed into the limestone but then it begins to sizzle and steam as the limestone falls apart.

"We make a pretty good mortar out of this. The burnt limestone is quicklime. We crush it to powder and mix it with sand to make mortar. The crusher was found at what looked like an abandoned blacksmith operation. It's really ingenious." Randy walks over to the crusher so I can get a better look at it.

The crusher is very simple. A steel beam has a piece of drill pipe welded perpendicular to make a hinge point. At the far end is a counter weight made from an old engine block. At the near end is about a two-foot section of eight-inch pipe, vertically welded with an end cap to act as a hammer. The eight-inch pipe is filled with scraps of metal and nails to make it heavier. A car spring causes the beam to rebound as it pounds the soft burned limestone into powder. The crusher can be operated with one hand pulling a rope connected to the beam.

"Well Randy, I doubt OSHA would approve but this thing is cool. How did you move it here?"

"We used the Wagoner's truck and trailer back when it was safer to move around. It still took a lot of hands to take it apart and get it here but it's the core of our whole operation. I think it was designed as a blacksmith's drop hammer but it works really well on limestone."

"What other stuff do you make? You mentioned clay processing and mineral sand; what's that?" I am impressed with all they do at this pit.

Randy enjoys showing their work. "Red clay is everywhere around here but raw clay is either too heavy to haul in large quantity or too weak to make pottery with. We do two things with it. For the water box reservoir, they need a lot of clay to seal it. We take raw clay and pound it to powder after it's dry."

"Do you use the crusher for that?" I asked.

"We can do that by hand. The clay is soft and turns to powder without a lot of effort. Drying out the clay removes most of the weight and as a powder; it's easy to work with. We'll be able to deliver all the clay for Fred and Harry in about three trips in the Ranger. Now to make clay ready for pottery, we burn some raw clay as 'mud pies' with the limestone. After they're fired, we crush them into what looks like coarse sand, called grog, and blend it back into some clean, raw, clay. The grog acts like aggregate in concrete and gives strength to the clay to use for pottery. We're not producing much pottery yet but several people are learning to work with it for the future."

"I guess you can fire the pottery here too." I add, "What's mineral sand?"

"I didn't understand it at first but Stephanie Sweeny, she's a dietician who works in the kitchen, she picked out some green looking limestone and asked me if I could crush some for the garden. She says that crushed limestone adds a lot of minerals to the soil. Must be working; the garden looks great but I better not break a tooth on a tomato." Randy's grin is obvious.

Dad taught me the importance of work being manned by people who like what they do.

"How are your guys holding up? Do you all like working out here? I bet it gets hot and it's obviously dirty work."

Randy replies, "We were just talking about that yesterday. It's hot everywhere and working around the kilns can make it worse, but as to the fires, we light 'em and forget 'em. Our work is a lot of lifting and hauling but the physical aspect of our work is sort of rewarding in itself. The guys said they would rather work out here than closer to camp. Working the pit is good. We're OK. But thanks for asking. It's nice to know we're not forgotten."

Almost as soon as Randy speaks, Brent Palmer and Allen Duncan come by with a field dressed Javelina tied to a pole between them. Brent is one of the gifted hunters who help provide for the kitchen. This female Javelina was snared last night. He said it had been feeding on cactus and roots and didn't smell strong. It should be good eating but he wasn't headed back to camp and it won't wait 'til he does.

"I guess I'm going to have to impose on you fellas to consume the evidence again."

George Hardin and John Stubbs come right over, thank Brent for the lunch and say they know just what to do with it. They also tell them to stop by in about four hours if they are hungry. Brent has to decline but says he will another time.

Randy comments, looking rather coy. "As you may have gathered, life out here in the pit can have its advantages."

I gain a new appreciation for these 'hard working slaves of the pit' and can't help notice how quickly they get the meat mounted onto a very handy impromptu rotisserie with charcoal and mesquite already laid out to work magic. This isn't these guys first try doing this.

After the Javelina is taken care of the hunters notice me, "Hello Jason, glad to see you. I'm Brent Palmer and this is Allen Duncan. We saw you last night at dinner but didn't get around to proper introductions. We're heading out to an abandoned building that was spotted last night and could use a third hand if you don't have plans."

We shake hands and I respond, "Glad to meet you Brent; Allen. There must be hundreds of abandoned old buildings and shacks out here, what draws you to this one?"

Allen answers: "Last night after dinner, there was a new moon so I took a walk with my son Riley and the Wagoner's son, Robert. We took the east trail up to the ridge to see the stars without the hills in the way. We also keep a lookout for camp lights that might indicate predators in the area. That's when we noticed a light, not much bigger than a candle flame or a flashlight, coming from the northeast. I mentioned it to Brent and he said there's only about one place it could be coming from and now we're going to check it out. You could help us with back-up."

My caution flag goes up. "Shouldn't we bring more people for backup? What if there are unfriendlies down there?"

Brent says, "I appreciate the caution. I've hunted that part and know the lay of the area. There's a dry wash to give us good cover to approach unnoticed. We can get within fifty feet of that shack in complete cover. We've been glassing the area from the ridge and seen no activity but we need to get a closer look. If we see no sign from the wash, I'll work my way around and peak in the broken window on the shaded side. No shadow, no reflection. If I get into trouble, you two will have my back from good cover. I have an AR-15 and a shotgun that I keep on every hunt and both Allan and I keep a sidearm."

I was carrying the Sig 40 that Jim had given me, in case I came on a snake or other unpleasant wildlife.

Brent continues, "Bringing more than three men makes it difficult to approach un-detected and bringing more will make it difficult to be discrete. If there are unfriendlies, we need to know about them."

Brent's plan and logic are solid and gives me a better feel to the mission. Part of Brent's job as a hunter is to also work reconnaissance. This fit that role precisely. We tell Randy, who knows of the shack, if we are not back in three hours; he is to bring help from camp. All is set.

# Not Alone:

Following the ravine provides good cover and allows us to reach the shack in just over half an hour. We watch for nearly an hour longer with no sound or movement detected. Brent hands me the AR-15 while Allen holds the shotgun. Birdshot is replaced with alternating loads of buckshot and solid slugs. If trouble comes, it isn't going to be pretty.

Brent circles around the back of the building and comes to the northeast wall. The setting sun casts long shadows for Brent to move among without being lit up by the sun or casting a shadow himself. He sees only one set of footprints leading to the shack. Slowly, pistol drawn, Brent peers into the shack's interior. I can hear him speaking softly into the shack. Holstering his pistol he calls for us to come quickly.

"Bring some water!" Brent goes to the door and pushes it open with his shoulder. Inside, a man lies curled up on an old door, long since fallen from its hinges.

He is alive but barely able to sip water. The remains of a votive candle on a badly chipped saucer must have been the source of the light that Allen saw from the ridge the night before. Both the angle and timing had to have been perfect for him to see it from the ridge.

Brent turns to me, "We need to get this man to camp. He won't live long out here. If we alternate carrying him, we can get him there pretty fast."

Allen has an idea, "Why not use that door like a stretcher and lash a pole to the front. With two of us on front and one on back, we can still rotate positions but we'll get there faster."

We find a length of galvanized water pipe and tie it to the underside of the door beneath the man's shoulders. Allen and I start up front with Brent holding the door in back. The only problem is that whoever is in back can't see where he's walking so the guys in front have to steer for unobstructed ground. With all three facing forward, we make good time. Rotating positions helps us keep going while a dried bush, dragging behind us, covers our tracks.

Passing by the pit, Randy sends George Hardin ahead to prepare the camp to receive the sick man. We stop twice along the way to give him sips of water and he appears to be improving.

At the medical hut, Anna is ready. She takes his pulse, puts a blood pressure cuff on him, and pulls the skin on the back of his hand by pinching it and letting it go. Next she grabs an IR thermometer and takes his temperature through his ear canal. The man is now unresponsive.

Anna goes into what I call her Viking mode. She quits being sweet and kind and starts barking orders like a drill sergeant. She's not mean spirited; she simply sets aside politeness if favor of efficiency. When a life is on the line, she doesn't take time for feelings. You do what she says and don't bother her with lengthy explanations, she'll make nice when there's time for it. Right now, her patient needs a Viking.

Anna barks short orders. "Clothes, off. Start with the boots. Jackie, I need a sheet."

Jackie covers the man with a sheet as Anna removes his shirt. She smells the unmistakable odor of infection and has to make sure it isn't from a snake bite.

Allen and I get the right boot off easily but working to get his left boot from a swollen foot is apparently taking too long. Anna doesn't even turn to us from her head to toe examination.

"If you can't pull that off, cut it off! Jackie, get them some scissors."

Allen holds the man's leg down and I give another strong pull on the left boot. The boot comes off as Jackie hands me the scissors. I feel some accomplishment as boot stores are no longer open for business. But I get no praise from the Viking.

"Get his pants off," comes her next order. The odor from his left foot is obvious but she continues her head to toe exam. She isn't going to miss anything.

Watching her work sends mixed emotions. If I were hurt, my health would be in capable hands, even if those hands are attached to Nurse-zilla.

Anna completes her exam and barks more orders.

"I hope we're in time. What he needs is an IV. Jackie, do we have distilled water?"

Running back to the counter, Jackie reaches way to the back corner. "Better! We have two bottles of IV fluid. It says 0.45% Sodium Chloride. They have a pack with tubing and stuff with it."

"That's perfect. The tubing is the administration kit. Give it to me." Anna busily sets up the I.V. as she asks Jackie, "Where did this stuff come from? How did it get here?"

"It was in a pack of medical supplies that were here when I arrived. I don't know who had it but Cynthia gave them to me to store here when the medical hut was built."

"Well, Jackie, whoever it was, may have saved this man's life today."

Getting the I.V. started was a challenge with the man's dehydrated condition. His veins are nearly collapsed but Anna manages to get the I.V. going.

With the I.V. started, she goes to the shelf where she and Jackie have organized the antibiotics; looking for one in particular.

"There it is, Doxycycline. Let's hope this works. This is going to be tough on him if he has liver or kidney problems but it's the best we have and he can't tell us his medical history."

"Jackie, I need a soaking pan with a quart of sterile water."

Jackie goes looking under the counter again. She looks like a prairie dog; always ducking down and popping back up from behind the counter but the tone of Anna's voice conveys this is serious and no time for laughs.

Jackie soon has a pan with a quart of clean water. A gallon jug of boiled water is kept at the medical hut for use in cleaning wounds. Anna adds a teaspoon of baking soda and 95ml of bleach to the pan of water. She is making Dakin's solution to help cleanse the horribly infected blister on the man's left foot. This is where the odor is coming from and Anna needs to clean and debride the wound.

As Anna lays out a small surgical kit, Allen and I ask if Anna needs us to stay and are grateful to leave. This doesn't look like something fun to watch.

An hour later, the man comes conscious but he's very weak. He is able to tell us his name is Carlos but little else. Not wanting to use the last IV bag, Anna and Jackie continue giving Carlos water by sips as his condition continues to improve. They take turns staying with Carlos through the night. I stay up with Anna for the first shift and George Hardin sticks around so Jackie won't have to be alone on the second shift. Carlos sleeps peacefully so Jackie appreciates

George being here for company.

In the morning, Anna and I come to relieve Jackie and George. After an hour, Carlos wakes up and is able to talk.

"Hello Carlos, do you remember me?  My name is Anna and I've been caring for you since you got here. Do you know how you got to the shack where we found you?"

"Si... yes, I remember you.  I drove until my truck broke then I walked."

"Carlos, I'm Jason, Anna's husband.  I was part of the team that found you and carried you here.  Where did you come from?"

Carlos thought a moment, "Fort Stockton."

"Fort Stockton?  That's over a hundred miles from here through some really bad country.  How long were you walking?"

"My truck broke a couple days ago.  I walked for two days before finding the shack."

Anna asks, "Did you have any water with you?"

"I had a water jug but only one," he says.  "When it was gone, I dropped it somewhere."

"When did you drop it?" I ask.

"At the end of the first day.  I was going to save some for the next day but was too thirsty that night."

Anna can't believe what she is hearing, "You mean you walked all day yesterday, without any water?"

He says, "I had to; I had no more water to drink."

Switching subjects, I ask, "Tell me why you left Fort Stockton. Why did you come south, to here?"

"I was going to Mexico. Things are better there. It is bad up here. People are dying, killing each other, there's nothing to eat, water is sometimes bad and makes people sick. I had to go. It would be better to die in the desert than to stay."

Anna is amazed to hear that things could be so bad. "Isn't the government helping? What about FEMA, or the police, or the military?"

"When the electric stopped, the police went home to their families. FEMA never came and nobody knows what the Army is doing. There is no help and all the stores are smashed up. I had to find a safe place. It is no good up there."

Anna looks at his wound, checks his temperature, and gives Carlos another shot of antibiotic. She gives me a look and I follow her outside.

"He's still burning up. His temp should be coming down with hydration but the infection is spreading. I'm afraid he's going septic." As Anna looks up at me, I see fear in her eyes for the first time since Carlos arrived. "Jason, I'm just not good enough to save him. I don't have a hospital, or a lab, or the drugs I need to fight this thing."

Anna is being really hard on herself. I hold her close for a while, and ask her some questions.

"Anna, if Carlos was admitted to a hospital, what would the process be?"

Anna looks up at me with welling eyes, "They would have done all I did but also taken blood. They would have identified the specific infection he has and they would use an I.V. antibiotic."

I take her hand, "And how would they have determined what infection he had?"

"From the lab results. They would have sent the sample to the lab...." and then Anna sees what I am getting at. "But I don't have a lab and I don't have the I.V. antibiotics."

"My point exactly. Without a lab, you found the infection and used the best resources available to treat it. You did a good job and are still a great nurse."

Anna puts her arms around my shoulders for a hug, "and that's why I love you so much."

Anna continues to try all she can to save Carlos but nothing seems to help.

The result now depends on how strong the infection is and how much strength Carlos has to fight it. The Viking goes back to its lair and Anna is again her sweet compassionate self and all of us have a renewed appreciation for the power that rests within her.

Carlos' fever keeps rising and no matter what Anna does, it isn't going to stop the inevitable. There is just too much infection for him to survive out here.

I sit with him for the three more days that he lives. As he drifts in and out of consciousness, I learn his name is Carlos Varga; that he has only one brother still living in Mexico, and that he has never met a more beautiful woman than Anna Connors. I certainly agree with him.

"You married the right one, Jason. Anna is soft heart and strong spirit. God has blessed you both with each other."

Anna continues to be hard on herself but is coming out of it slowly. She keeps going over everything she has done but has yet to find glaring error. My Dad once told me there are two rules in life. The first rule is that everyone dies and good people sometimes die young. The second rule is that there is nothing you can do to change rule number one. Anna is a good nurse who gets caught between those two rules.

The 'Pool Party' is unanimously postponed. It would be difficult to unwind with thoughts and prayers focused on Carlos recovering. Work is still suspended for Saturday and re-directed toward conserving water and prayer for Carlos. A constant vigil is held in the HQ hut. Volunteers come and pray for a while and then are relieved by another, then another.

The reservoir is sealed and the red clay settles out. Clear water is delivered to the wash hut, laundry, and kitchen. It is the single best improvement to life in camp. The bucket brigade is retired with honors but the 'Pool Party' will wait.

Carlos comes in and out of consciousness but shares his faith in God and that the journey he thought was to find a safer place in Mexico will be to Heaven instead where he will be safe always.

As Carlos breaths his last, I am holding his hand. There are tears of joy and sadness both, but not grief. Anna and Jackie have worked tirelessly and are for now, beyond tears. They will come later.

The funeral is attended by all the camp. George finds a limestone slab that takes a chisel well, Carlos is buried at a beautiful place where wild flowers grow. He had only one request; that no dates be placed on his grave. He said, "Only my destination is important."


CARLOS VARGA

NOW RESTING
IN GOD'S CARE.

# Pool Party:

Saturday comes again and with it the camp 'Pool Party!'

As hard as everyone works, we play harder. Kristen, Kelly, and Kory Palmer, apply their weaving skill to making grass hats. Some look like Sombrero's, Panama hats, Cowboy hats, and even a dunce hat. Every head has a hat. Sunscreen isn't abundant but sleeved shirts and long pants keep the sun off during peak hours.

Our kitchen staff prepares food that can be carried to the creek and Bob Isham teams with Brent Palmer to catch another Javelina. Roasting 'pig' on a spit by the creek adds to the party atmosphere. Javelina isn't really a pig but the creek wasn't really a pool either. The party is pure success.

With the 'pig' eaten, the roasting fire is now a campfire. Ramón Ramos plays guitar as the sun sets. Ramón arrived at camp with his wife, Imelda, and three children; Thomas, Lupe, and Zach.  His pickup camper was on fumes when they pulled into camp but it did provide one less needed hut.   Under a starlit sky with stomachs full and bodies both rested and played-out, sweet music fills the air.    Some tunes are joined by singing and others bring memories of better times. All who listen take time to search within ourselves to find solace in something.   Loss has touched each life but there is a spirit of hope among us.  Mixed with tears, this hope is strong.  Nothing like the wishful hope for better times, it is a sure hope that regardless of future events, we are going to be OK.

I sit on a sandy spot with my back against a smooth rock and Anna cuddles against me.    Anna speaks softly, so as not to interrupt Ramón's guitar playing.

"This may sound strange but I don't think I've ever been this much at peace.   Even on Intrepid, it was peaceful but our destination was always ahead of us. Here, we don't know when it will be over or what the future will bring.   Our life is just for today and we'll deal with tomorrow when it gets here."

I give Anna a squeeze hug, "I know what you mean. Lately, I've been thinking about what matters and what doesn't.   Most of my life has been busy doing what doesn't matter in the end, and racing to a finish line that moves away as fast as I run.  Carlos helped me get some focus.  Did you know he held a master degree in mechanical engineering?  He had opportunity to make good money but passed it up for jobs that paid him just enough to meet his needs.  He told me, when a job offers you more money, it is buying something.  That something is your mind, your will, and your emotions. They want you to think for them, be loyal to them, and look happy as you work for them. He said we seldom own possessions but possessions can own us. They become our masters; compelling us to work to pay for them and demanding our time to care for them."

Anna sits up and is listening intently, "Wow, Carlos was also a philosopher. He had quite an effect on you."

I smile, "A good effect too. Life is way too short to waste it on what doesn't matter. You matter, we matter, and people matter, but career empires? They don't matter. I think I'm learning contentment with much less than I needed before."

Anna responds, "Maybe that's why I feel more at peace here. Here my work is important to others but not for a paycheck that's usually spent before I get it."

Across the creek from the campfire sit several others along with Roxanne and Scott. Somewhere during the evening, Roxanne's hand finds its way into Scott's and remains. They are enjoying soft music and the dancing light of a campfire while the stars twinkle so brightly you can almost touch one.

For Roxanne and Scott, talk is a cheap second to the communication their hearts share as they sit among friends, hand in hand. Roxanne's heart remains full with concern for her family, but she is grateful for Scott's friendship and support. Perhaps, in time, there will be room for more.

"CQ – CQ – CQ – This is Kilo Five Oscar Sierra India –

CQ – CQ – CQ"

Pat Wagoner is in the communication hut. This is one of the scheduled radio contacts where Jim passes on the news collected from other hams in different parts of the country. The canyon hideaway has its advantages but being able to contact distant ham operators isn't one of them. All our news comes from Jim who is dedicated to keeping us informed.

"K5-OSI, X-ray Foxtrot One Foxtrot November Foxtrot, I read you loud and clear."

Jim's voice punches through the static. Pat adjusts the squelch to eliminate the background noise.

Pat replies,

"Sorry I'm a bit late this evening. The camp took a day off to splash around the creek and let off a little steam. It's been a great day and it did a lot of good."

"Roger that, I'm sure it was needed by all. Please pass our condolences for the passing of Carlos. Rita and I were praying right along with you all. Are you alone with the radio tonight?"

"Yes, Jim, I'm afraid it's just me tonight. Everyone is at the campfire. They haven't looked this rested since we got here."

"That's good, Pat. I didn't want to spoil things with what's going on up country but thought you should know just the same."

Jim's voice has a more serious tone.

Pat plugs in the headphones and puts them on.

"It's clear on this side, Jim. I've switched to headphones just the same. Go ahead."

"What you told me from Carlos was just part of it. There isn't a metropolitan area or large city that has answered a CQ in over a month. Some have relocated but most have just gone silent and we suspect the worst. Most urban areas went to riot right after the money failed. A lot of cities went dark even before the EMP because of fire related outages and utility workers refusing to go near the riots. Outages caused sewer and water systems to quit. Urban streets flooded with raw sewage and what water there was, became polluted. There isn't a city of any size in the country that's safe to live in."

"Got that, Jim. Where did most people go?"

"Some fled right away and got clear but after two days the exit roads became hopelessly jammed. Cars were abandoned and the only way out was on foot. Hospitals had emergency power for a couple of days but elderly people were dying as their oxygen ran out others from violence. It was too much for the coroner's office and funeral homes to handle. Pat, they are just leaving the dead in their homes and in the street. I've never heard anything like it."

"That's real bad, Jim. Didn't the military try to help? What about FEMA?"

"They didn't do squat. In their best day they would show up too late and do too little. They never had a plan for a national problem like this. Communities are on their own this time."

"Roger that. Are there any groups still standing?"

Pat is hoping for some good news.

"We're still hearing reports coming from small rural towns in out of the way places. Some of these saw trouble coming and cut service lines from the grid after it went down. They're running on local power. There's one city that bought a diesel-electric locomotive for a static display. What few knew was that it was functional and now provides emergency power to the whole town. Some towns are still kicking but no big ones."

"What about violence? How far has that spread?"

"It was concentrated in the urban areas at first. Martial law was declared and a lot of looters were shot. They couldn't control the inner cities but did keep them contained. After the EMP all control was lost. Without communication they couldn't remain organized. After that, it was every man for himself. Shooting continued and even the rioters had to hide. That slowed the spread."

"Is it still going on?"

"Not much now. It's been ten weeks or more since food and water were wiped clean from stores. No deliveries since and people are starving. Not many of even the toughest gangs are left. Those with food and water are well armed but it's not over yet."

"What do you mean; not over yet?"

Pat is listening intently.

"Reports are that you can smell the stink of death from miles outside city limits. Typhoid and Cholera are expected to start spreading in about another month. Perhaps a bit longer in the northern states but it will hit them in the spring. This will be just like Haiti except much worse."

Pat's voice reflects the sobering thought of all the people he knows that never prepared and never gave serious thought to warnings given for decades. His only consolation is the small group at camp. By God's help, they will survive.

"We should be OK here. We're over a hundred miles from a town of any size and isolated by desert. How long do you think we need to stay put?"

"Best guess is another eight months but that puts you into May and past safe travel across the desert. Looks more like this time next year."

"I'll advise leaders here. I know this wasn't good news, Jim. I'm sure it was as hard to deliver as it was to receive but thanks all the same. Give Rita our love. If there are any more supplies we need, I'm sure they'll be ready for next contact. Stay safe. XF1-FNF, K5-OSI, seventy-three my friend, K5-OSI clear on your final."

"K5-OSI, XF1-FNF. God bless. We're praying for you all. XF1-FNF, seventy-three, I'm clear."

# Darkness Calls:

Finishing touches are nearly complete on the isolation hut. It is downwind and has its own latrine and water barrel. A natural flat topped rock serves as the base for a drop point where food, medicine, and supplies are placed for pickup after the delivery person is gone. Without a local drugstore, camp has a limited supply of medicine. They can't treat everyone at once for colds or flu. Even the slightest symptoms are treated quickly and the isolation hut is completed just in time.

Anna and I are at breakfast as George Hardin comes by our table. "Anna; John coughed all night and didn't feel like coming to breakfast. Would you mind checking on him?" George must be worried about John, as he would normally use this opportunity to go see Jackie.

"I'll check on him right away. Thanks for letting me know." Anna is almost done with her breakfast. I tell her not to worry about her dishes; I will take care of them.  She takes one more drink of her tea as she rises to go by the medical hut for her bag.

John Stubbs shares a hut with George Hardin and Scott. The others are already off to their work but Anna can hear John's cough from just outside the medical hut.  It doesn't sound good.

"John, it's Anna.  Are you decent?  Can I come in?"

John answers, "Yeah, come on in."  He is pale and looking rough.

"George stopped by and asked me to have a look at you.  I understand you didn't sleep well.  What's wrong?"

"Weak, coughing, head-ache, I feel bad."

Anna takes John's temperature, heart rate, and blood pressure; then looks in his ears, eyes, and nose. "Your blood pressure is OK, heart rate is a bit high, no sign of sinus or ear infection.  I'm going to take you to isolation to be on the safe side.  Can you walk?"

Pat Wagoner installs a bonus to the isolation hut. Among the assets that Matt and Cynthia stored with the food in the 'deep larder' is a spool of communication field wire.  Pat hooks up an auxiliary computer speaker at each end of the field wire between the medical and isolation huts.  Using it like a child's "tin can and string telephone" it allows Anna and Jackie to talk to each other like a voice powered phone.

"Jackie?  Can you hear me?  We're here."  Anna isn't

sure how well the speakers will work since they hadn't had time to play with them yet.

"Yes, Anna. These are going to work well. I can hear you fine. How's our patient?"

"He's pretty uncomfortable. I'll need some Acetaminophen, Ibuprofen, and Mucinex DM. I'll also need the kitchen to provide some tea and juice if they have it."

"Got it. Let John know that he's getting a new sleeping mat. We're burning his old one and cleaning the hut with a scrub-down."

John hears Jackie over the speaker and replies, "And I just got that mat broken in."

"He heard you Jackie. I think he's going to pull through. His sense of humor is still in good shape. Tell Jason I won't be home for dinner... or breakfast... or lunch." The girls are somewhat joking back and forth but the isolation hut is not a fun place to be for the sick person but especially for the caregiver.

The hut has a patient cot and another for the caregiver with a partition wall between. Partitioning provides privacy but more importantly it allows for some isolation of the caregiver from constant contact with possible contagions. A small table serves as desk and storage. About ten yards from the door is a water barrel that is kept full and a big flat rock where supplies and food are dropped off.

John responds well to meds and his fever subsides by

the next evening. George and Scott hold an 'exorcism' fire and carry John's sleeping mat to a ceremonial blaze. Roxanne and Jackie help the guys wash down surfaces in the hut with a vinegar solution from the kitchen.

George jokingly says, "If this place doesn't air out, I'll be dreaming of pickles all night."

Day three comes and goes with no return of John's fever so it is agreed to let him return to camp. Anna is glad to head home as well. Her first stop is the wash hut.

The following day, Jackie and Anna review what they now call their practice drill. It is the first use of the isolation hut and it gives them some ideas to improve how they will use it in the future. An updated medicine list was prepared and sent to Jim and Rita when John first got sick. They decide, if possible, to increase stock on hand because it typically takes Jim a few weeks to find the meds and another week or more to plan a flight. If a viral outbreak happens, those meds need to be on hand right away.

"Anna, that's the third time you've checked your temp this morning. Is something wrong?"

"I don't know. Maybe I'm just tired and not myself after spending three days in ISO. I'm not running a temp but every now and then, I feel kinda punkish." Anna, replies.

Checking inventory and expiration dates on sensitive medicines takes up most of the morning but Anna and

Jackie enjoy their time together.

Anna enjoys the girl time with Jackie too. "I see George stopping by a lot. He's a nice guy."

Jackie brightens up, "Yes he is. I think he might like me."

Anna's first thought is "YA THINK!!" but softens her answer with "That would be safe to assume. Do you like him?"

Jackie's response is enthusiastic to say the least. "Well, he's smart; handsome; strong; kind; considerate, AND eligible."

Anna can't help but laugh. "I'll take that as a yes. But be careful of your heart. Are you falling in love with him?"

After a moment of soul searching, Jackie answers. "I think so... but camp isn't the real world and I'm not sure what to do. It's exciting to meet someone like George and have him be interested in me, but knowing if he's the right one is a hard question to answer."

Feeling more like a big sister, Anna gives some sound advice. "It's easy to fall in love out here; all alone with the stars and away from the rest of the world. What we don't know is how long it will last or what we might find when we go back. Make sure of lasting decisions. They are 'for better OR for worse' and either is possible. If you discover that George IS the right one, having him with you will make facing that future a lot less intimidating. Just be as sure as you can, before turning your heart loose."

"Lunch anyone?"  I enter the hut with George behind me.  Anna loves it when I come to get her for meals. Anna says that my care of the little things assures her of my love and commitment.  She meets me with a kiss and a hug before heading to lunch.  Behind us are George and Jackie, hand in hand.

# Incoming:

We have lunch with Mom and Dad and talk over camp activities and coming events. Dad gives us an update. "Jim is planning a supply run later this week. Do you need to add anything? Our last communication before he leaves will be tonight."

I say, "We need some wire to make more snares but I think it's on the list already. We plan to be there anyway. I wouldn't miss Jim's ten o'clock news." I look to Anna for input.

"Our med list update was sent already. I don't know how much he can fill this soon but every bit helps. Mom, thanks for your notes and the gifts you sent for John in isolation. I know the gifts were from the children but thanks to you for organizing them. It really brightened his day and I think it helped him feel better."

"It was my pleasure," Mom replies. "I'm glad they helped John, but I think it was good nursing that helped most. I can only imagine where that would have gone if it was flu."

Camp life keeps everyone busy but meals are always a good time to catch up. Lunch continues with small talk and that night we meet again at the communication hut. Gathering to listen to Jim's news update is the camp's only link to what happens outside our canyon hideaway. Without that link, imaginations and ignorance can feed bad decisions. Having Jim and Rita is also an emotional anchor. We are not alone or cut off and each radio contact instills another dose of hope for a camp of survivors.

Travis McCann and his sons, Willie, Pete, and Greg, come to visit. They came for dinner but stayed for the contact with Jim. Travis has his own shortwave radio and listens to every contact but he can't transmit and comes to camp from time to time on contact dates.

"XF1FNF, we copy, go ahead Jim."

Pat turns the volume up so all can hear.

"Good evening everyone. I have some good news for some of you. HF propagation has been smiling on us this week and I was able to reach Ed Iverson for nearly fifteen clear minutes up in Alberta."

Anna lets out a squeal of excitement as both Scott and I lean closer to hear.

"Anna and Scott, your mom is doing well. She and the

family send their love and want you to know that Parliament was able to organize some relief to their area. They are stocked and ready for winter but said to tell you that their first snow has already come."

"That's good news, Jim. Anna can hardly contain herself over here. That means a lot; back to you."

"News from the lower forty-eight is spotty. What I do get is often low power text mode. Still no grid power but violence is isolated to non-existent. Those with food and water are hunkered down and staying put. Potable water is the new gold standard with food a close second. The good news is that there are people out there. The cities are empty but out in the remote areas, people are holding on."

"Jim, this is Matt, on behalf of all here at camp, we're sending you and Rita our thanks for all the time and late night hours to keep us informed. It means a lot to everyone here. Were you able to handle many of the list items?"

"Thanks Matt; we love each and every one of you. I wish we could bring you all here with us. As for the list, I was able to get your copper device fabricated by a local craftsman. It looks like he's done a great job. He even shined it up for you. Tell Anna and Jackie that there's a package coming for them with all but item seven and item nine. They will likely fill, next time. List two; items three and seven are short. List four; item eight is short. All other lists are either full or partial."

Though NVIS transmissions are difficult to trace, lists are always sent by text and referenced by number. Openly communicating incoming supplies is an invitation for trouble from anyone with the ability to intercept those messages. Caution is the rule and a practice we strictly follow.

"Got that, Jim. No adds. Is there any more?"

"Is Travis there?"

Pat hands the mic to Travis who is standing close.

"Hello my old friend; Travis here."

"Rita says she's sending you and the boys some cookies... and before all you hungry folks at camp flood the hut with drool... she's also sending supplies for making cookies to Stephanie and Christi."

Travis has a big smile,

"Kiss that woman for me, Jim. She's sweeter than the chocolate chips."

Jim replies,

"How are you holding out? Can I make an 'add' for you and the boys?"

"Thanks for asking, Jim. We can use some number four from the standard list and some seven if you can spare it."

"Will do. See you zero nine hundred at LZ 5. K5OSI, XF1FNF clear."

Pat already has the modem turned on to catch the following PSK31 data that Jim always sends. It contains the real time and landing location but is never the same as the voice message. The modem drives a tablet computer and a message appears on the screen as text begins rolling up the screen.

Travis and Jim are watching as several different batches of data fill the screen.

Travis asks Jim, "Got your Julian calendar handy?"

I am curious and stay to watch. "What does the Julian date have to do with the message?"

Pat answers, "Jim sends several combinations of dates, times, and landing locations. Only one is real, the rest are decoys. Each has a four-digit number assigned. The first three digits are a Julian day and the forth is the last digit of its corresponding calendar day. We ignore data where the Julian day does not agree with the calendar day. There are four batches of delivery data where the Julian date and calendar day agree, two are odd Julian dates and two are even. Today's calendar date is an odd number so we discard the first and third batch. Since we are in the first half of the month, the first batch of remaining data is the one we want. Jim will be landing at T-3, on Saturday at about seven in the morning. All he needs now is our confirmation."

Travis keys a single two letter response on the tablet computer and copies it several times before hitting send. The letters are W C for 'will comply.' Fresh supplies will be here soon.

# T-3:

With just enough moonlight to slowly navigate the dirt road out of camp. More of a trail than a road but the Ranger has no difficulty. Scott and I are to continue east on 170 and meet up with Travis, Willie, Pete, and Greg, just short of Terlingua. The diesel's purr at low speed makes for a quite ride, as long as we don't hit bumps to make the empty cargo trailer boom like a drum. A soft glow at the horizon is gaining on the night sky. Daylight is coming.

About a mile short of town, a single blink from a flashlight signals we have found Travis. Scott slows to a stop and we get out and shake hands while making final plans.

Travis speaks in almost a whisper. "Good to see you boys, any trouble?"

Both Scott and I shake our heads 'no.'

"OK then, T-3 is code for an actual airstrip that's past Terlingua a way. We don't want to attract attention so we'll take a couple ranch roads on the way in and take the highway coming back. If anyone hears us, they'll think we're hunting game. Terlingua isn't but a few buildings and an old ghost town so one-time passing by shouldn't hurt. I brought my trailer and between the two of us, we should have plenty of room to make this in one trip. Just follow us and watch the dust."

We give a nod and start back to the Ranger. Willie stops me and hands me a small walkie-talkie radio.

Willie is a big man, not fat but big. Like his dad, Willie sports a beard but unlike his dad, Willie's is black and bushy. Willie's first impression might intimidate some but a kinder man will be difficult to find.

"This radio is all set on preset number one," he says. "It's tuned down to only one watt but that should be plenty for as close as we'll be. Only use it if you need it and keep conversations discreet and short."

Willie smiles and looks at me. "Did you bring the .308?"

I smile back with… "Wouldn't leave home without it but let's hope we don't need it."

Willie walks back to the truck, nodding in agreement but leaves with the words, "Still, it's better to have it than need it."

Following a pickup and trailer over ranch roads is not easy in the dim light of an imminent sunrise. Scott stays back far enough to keep from eating the small amount of dust that Travis is kicking up, however, keeping an eye on him; the road; and watching for spooked game, is a full time task. We arrive at the edge of the airstrip clearing by six thirty.

Travis signals us to stop where the brush meets the grass. He glasses the area with binoculars, listening, and watching intently. Then he sees it. A pickup truck is parked off the taxiway, near a small hangar. He scopes it with his rifle on highest magnification but sees no occupant. None the less, it has to be cleared and we don't have time enough to do it right. Travis steps back toward the Ranger and motions everyone together.

"There's a truck down there and I don't know if anyone's in it. They may be waiting for the plane. It's too far to recon properly in the time remaining so we have to get bold. Here's my plan. Scott, you and Greg take the Ranger right down there like you've been hunting. Take the shotgun with you. Keep an eye on that truck but not too obvious. Drive right down the runway, not the taxiway. If there's anyone in that truck, they'll break cover when you go by. If they're armed, we'll have you covered from here. I guess the range to be about a hundred and fifty yards so it won't be difficult to give you good cover. I don't like it but I'm open for suggestions if anybody has a better idea."

We all agree that nobody likes it but it is the best plan available. Scott and Greg get in the Ranger and head for the runway. The empty cargo trailer bounces on the cleared grass area beside the runway and rumbles like a drum. If anyone is in that truck, they certainly hear them coming.

Greg asks Scott, "You ever done anything like this before?"

"Never," Scott replies. "I've had to leave a country pretty quick but never had to troll for lead."

"Me neither. It may be necessary but it ain't comfortable." Greg is afraid but not backing out. His Dad's words keep coming back to him.

*'Courage is not the absence of fear; courage is the presence of duty in the face of fear.'*

Scott is ready to floor the accelerator if anything starts. As they pass the truck, he sees no movement.

"Good!" He says quietly, "It looks abandoned.

Travis, Jason, and Willie, each have high power rifles zeroed on the truck. One wrong move will cause some serious consequence, but none is merited. The truck appears empty.

Travis keys the radio.

"Scott, no activity from up here; how about you?"

"No sign here. What's next?" Scott is relieved.

Travis answers. "Double back on the taxiway and take a closer look. We can't let Pegasus in without an all-clear."

Daylight is coming fast. Scott drives by the truck while

Greg stands in the back to get a good look in the cab. It is empty.

As Scott says the two words, "**All clear.**" the sound of turbines grows closer. Jim is here. Travis, Jason, Willie, and Pete, jump in the truck and head for the airstrip. Pegasus makes a low, downwind pass to check the strip and then turns for a landing. Jim is accustomed to making landings at dawn or dusk with no aircraft lights. He brings Pegasus down and turns around in less space than a lot of smaller planes. As he taxies back to takeoff position, the Ranger and truck converge.

The door opens and Travis boards, "Good to see you, Jim. Any trouble this trip?"

"Smooth as ever." Jim replies. "I'm beginning to think I may have some protection going on."

"Like Angels, you think? We count on 'em." Travis claims that men make him careful but God keeps him safe.

Scott and I are right outside the cargo door and as it opens we see Jim. I speak first,

"What a lovely face!"

Jim acts embarrassed as he says, "Oh, you say that to all us good lookin' guys."

Laughing as we unfold and attach load ramps; Jim gives the orders.

"We have a heavy so back your truck up here."

Greg gets in the truck and backs up to the cargo bay as Jim and Travis lift the ramps to end in the trailer bed. A steel barrel is unstrapped, tipped on its side, and rolled down the ramps as the two men let out ropes that control its progress. With the barrel in the trailer, Greg blocks it in place and straps it down for the ride. The rest of the cargo is easier. Boxes and bundles mostly but there is one rather strange looking copper device with tubes connecting to it. It is about five feet tall and has a tag with Dad's name on it.

"Be careful with that thing," says Jim, "That's a special order." Jim reaches for a small package and hands it to Travis, "Rita wanted me to make sure you got this."

Travis thanks him and tucks the box under his arm for very special keeping.

Only the box marked for Anna and Jackie is labeled 'fragile.' In typical form, among quick handshakes and 'God's speed,' Jim and the plane head down the runway. The last supplies are loaded and both vehicles head down the runway toward the highway and home. As we pass the abandoned truck, Greg notices something. A young girl of about three years comes running out of the hangar building with a woman chasing after her. They don't get ten feet out of the building before Greg sees them and tells his dad to stop. The terrified woman runs back into the hangar with the child and shuts the door.

# The Hangar:

"Did you see that?" asks Greg. "Was I seeing things?"

Willie is in the driver seat and looks through the opening where a back window used to be. "If you were, so was I. They were just about back in the door when I caught sight. What do we do now?"

The Ranger has pulled alongside the truck and both are stopped.

Travis would normally keep moving. That would be the safe thing to do. But this time, he doesn't feel right about it.

"We can't leave 'em till we know they're OK. But we have to keep smart. Willie, you and Scott stay here and keep an eye out for any sign of trouble. If you see anything wrong, and I mean ANYTHING, you hightail it back to camp and bring help. We can't afford to risk these supplies... especially those chocolate chip cookies."

Travis' humor takes the edge off the moment.

"Jason and Pete, if you'll go around the back of the building, Greg and I will go to the front. Be careful, we don't want to shoot any women or children but I don't want any of us to stop lead either."

Travis takes the shotgun but we leave all the rifles with Scott and Willie. If we need more than side-arms, we'll need more help anyway.

Approaching the hangar is easy but there is absolutely no cover. I am glad to at least be close to the building. One of the hangar doors is open by about four feet at the bottom. The rest are closed. Pete lies down to the side of the door to look inside. I do the same from the opposite end. Nothing is obvious and the girl and lady are nowhere to be seen.

Travis or Greg must have opened the man-door on the other side because light shines across the floor and I can make out a single child's toy about twenty feet from the far door. It's one of those push toy ducks with rubber feet attached to the wheels that go flap-flap-flap when you push it. Travis is calling from the other side of the hangar.

"Hello?  Do you understand English?  We won't hurt you.  ¿Hola? ¿Entiendes a Inglés? Nos no referimos a ningún daño. Do you need help?"

I am surprised to hear Travis calling out this way. His voice is so disarming; I'm thinking *'I'm ready to answer him myself.'*

Then comes a woman's voice that sounds very frightened. "Can you help us? Please don't hurt us. We're over here."

Travis opens the door wide so he can see where her voice is coming from. When he steps into the hangar the woman lets out a short scream when she sees him. Travis realizes it is the shotgun she fears and immediately puts it down.

"I'm not here to hurt you. Tell me how I can help." Travis is slowly walking toward a place in the corner of the hangar, barely out of sight from where Greg and I are.

"My husband is sick; can you help us?" The lady pulls back a blanket she has draped over some boxes to reveal a pale looking man lying on some packing material. He doesn't look good.

Travis comes close and looks at the man, then turns to the lady. She has stepped into the light.

"Ma'am, my name is Travis McCann. I live near here. What's your name?"

She replies, "I'm Becky Spencer, this is my husband Chris, my daughter is Gina, she's three.

Becky is a young woman in her twenties; she has long light brown hair pulled back in a pony-tail. Her husband looks to be in his early thirties, but it is hard to tell with him being so sick. Gina must be hiding because there is no sign of her.

Travis has a commanding presence but a soothing voice as he talks with her.

"Becky, I don't want you to get alarmed but I have others with me that I would like to join us. Three are my sons and two are also good men. Would it be OK for me to call them here to help?"

Becky fearfully nods 'yes' and Travis speaks a little louder. "Jason, Pete, Greg, it's all right. Come on in and meet these folks. We need to give them a hand."

Greg comes in first; he is holstering his pistol as he clears the door. Pete and I holster our weapons and walk toward Travis.

"Becky Spenser, I'd like you to meet my sons, Pete and Greg, and our good friend Jason Connors. My third son, Willie, and another man, Scott Iverson, are watching the vehicles. "

Becky nods a greeting but it is obvious she has been under a lot of stress and appears weak.

I greet her also, "I'm glad to meet you, Becky. Is that your truck outside?"

"Yes," she answers, "we drove here from our home in Lubbock but couldn't find gas to go further. It was almost out of gas when we found this place. You're the first people we've seen in days."

"When did your husband get sick?" asks Greg.

"About two days ago. He's worse today. Maybe God sent Gina to find you. I was too afraid that you might be bad people."

"Excuse me Becky, but I need to clear something with Jason before we can discuss options to help you."

Travis steps aside with me and speaks quietly for only a moment while I nod in agreement. Travis again speaks to Becky.

"Ma'am, we need to get your family to a safer place and your husband to some medical attention. My cabin is small and just big enough for me and my sons but friends of mine have a camp where they can help you better. Would you come with us? The plane will have drawn attention to this place and we can't stay here."

Becky agrees and as she calls little Gina out from hiding, Greg calls on the radio for Scott and Willie to drive over to the hangar. With Chris secure, Becky seated, Gina in her lap, and what little food and supplies they have, we head back to camp. Just as we start to move, Greg says, "Stop a minute! We forgot something."

Greg bolts from the truck and runs to the hangar door. In less than a minute, he returns on a dead run with Gina's little push toy duck in his hands. Gina's smile was the first we see from her as Greg hands it to her but as time goes by, it's not her last.

There is little conversation as our full attention scans the road for possible hiding places that might be used for an ambush. We arrive at camp by noon with no incident or further complication. The Spencer family is taken directly to the ISO hut and it is Jackie's turn to be caregiver. Jackie has learned a lot from Anna in their few weeks together and with Anna on the other end of the make-shift intercom, she is quite capable.

"Becky, I'm Jackie Chambers and along with Anna Connors, we handle medical here at camp. I'll be here with you and your family until Chris is better and showing no sign of fever for twenty-four hours. It's isolation but nothing personal, I'm right here with you." Jackie's smile is comforting.

"We've started an IV to get Chris' hydration back to where it should be. He was really dehydrated. I'm glad we got to him when we did. Were you out of water?"

Becky's answer fills in more of their story. "We were out of almost everything. We had some flour and some bacon, a few cans of soup and we ate the last of the beans the night before. We left Lubbock with two cases of bottled water and some milk jugs that Chris filled from the water heater but that didn't last long. I think Chris was saving his share of the water for Gina and me."

While Chris sleeps, Jackie gets to know Becky better. "Do you and Chris have family out here?"

Becky replies, "I have a sister. My parents both died two years ago in a crash but my sister is married and her husband is serving in the Coast Guard up in Alaska. We haven't heard from them since the blackout but I think they're OK. Chris's parents live on a small farm in Iowa. They don't farm much anymore but Chris's brother and his wife live next to them and farm both their lands. We thought about going there but didn't have the gas to go that far; how about your family?"

Jackie's response is a bit slow in coming, "Well, my sister is here with me at camp. She runs the communications hut. ...My Mom passed away to cancer when I was eight and Dad raised us by himself for three years until he met and married my step-mom. I never thought anyone could take Mom's place but in time, I was really glad she came into our lives. I'll always miss my Mom but Jennifer helped Nicky and I through the tough years of growing up. We used to live in rural Virginia but she and Dad moved to Montana after I left for Houston and we haven't heard from them since before the blackout. A day doesn't go by that I don't think of how they're getting along in all this."

As it turns out, Chris is suffering from a rather serious stage of dehydration that followed a stomach virus. The medical supplies Jim sent contain several units of saline and administration kits. After two units, Chris' temperature comes down and he is hungry. Both good signs.

# Supplies:

Excitement runs high when supplies come off the vehicles. You could believe it was Christmas. Two large bags of flour, two more of sugar, one of salt, four bags of layer pellets that didn't belong in the kitchen, and an industrial size bag of candy coated chocolate bits. The chocolate chips are a copy of mini M&M's that don't need refrigeration to keep from melting together. Another pouch contains butter that is impossible to keep from melting but in the pouch it doesn't matter. Among all the food stuff are ample ingredients to make chocolate chip cookies as Rita promised. If Rita ran for president, she would win a landslide vote from this camp.

Dad comes to the kitchen with his 'specially ordered' device. With Stephanie, Christi, and their workers looking, he explains.

"You know how we've learned to make our own vinegar because we use so much? With this we can distill our own high grade alcohol for the medical hut AND for making extracts here in the kitchen. This is a reflux still. It's different than what's called a 'pot still' and it's way more efficient. What we'll need from you is to collect fruit peals and cores along with any flour or grain that you would normally toss out. We can make a mash out of that and then distill the alcohol."

Stephanie slaps her knee and says, "Well, granny git yer jug! Wee's in the moonshine bizness."

After a good laugh, Christi replies, "This will be useful. We can get vanilla bean by the bushel but extract is another story. We used to make our own extract with Vodka but that resource is gone. Having pure alcohol will work even better."

At the communications hut, a party is going on. They have a box of batteries for Pat and a stack of notepads with pens for Nicky. There are some bearings for Harry to complete the wind powered agitator for the laundry and a big package for Jackie and Anna that they have already opened to retrieve saline packs. They decide to sort the rest of the medical things after the Spencer family is released from ISO.

Travis, Willie, Pete, and Greg have three items. One is a wonderful smelling box from Rita. They decline to open it in camp but everyone knows it's the cookies. It is a highly guarded box. Next is another box of batteries and last is the steel drum of diesel. They need thirty gallons and the drum holds fifty-five so they go by the camp fuel drum and transfer twenty-five gallons to help the camp's fuel needs. Whenever they run low, the camp always helps them out. Paybacks are good business.

Rita is always looking out for them. In every package she includes sunscreen, body lotion, toothpaste, combs & brushes, or some other thing she thinks they can use. If you needed something and forget to put it on the list, Rita might just send it anyway. She is uncanny about knowing what you need.

Anna calls on the intercom to check on their patient. "Jackie, how are things today?"

Jackie moves closer to the speaker so she can be heard. "Better today, Anna. Are you ready for stats?"

"I'm ready. Go ahead."

"Chris' BP; 130 over 75. Heart; 57. Temp; 98.9. Becky and Gina are normal temps."

"That sounds good. I think we'll spring you guys out tomorrow by lunch if nothing shows up before then. Do you need anything we can send over?"

"How about some toys for Gina. She's sorta restless over here."

"I'll bet she is. I'll look around and see what we have. Keep strong."

Chris and Becky look much better after some food and water. Lots of water. Even little Gina drinks plenty. Jackie knows re-hydration is gaining when Chris asks where the restroom is.

Jackie is about to answer but Becky speaks up. "I'll

show you. Gina and I have already made the trip twice today."

Jackie asks, "How do you feel? You were pretty dehydrated and may still feel a bit wobbly."

"I think I can make it." Replies Chris.

Becky puts her arm around his side as Chris puts his arm over Becky's shoulder. Chris moves a bit slow but accomplishes the ten yards to the outhouse and back again.

"Mission accomplished." says Chris as they return. He sits on the cot as Jackie takes his pulse, blood pressure, and looks at the whites of his eyes.

"That's a milestone. Your kidneys are working and you should be finding your strength coming back. I think your family is going to have you around for a good while, as long as you don't do something like THIS again."

As Chris contemplated their recent events, he looks a bit amazed. "I didn't see this coming. I was cutting my water rations for Becky and Gina but thought I was handling it OK. I was tired but didn't want to eat anyway so I slept the time away. Next thing; I'm here. Where is here?"

Jackie smiles, "We're a rag-tag group of friends, coworkers, and associates that were invited here or had come here in the past. This camp is near Big Bend National Park. We're rather isolated by the desert and further by a steep canyon but it's a good place to be right now. I've been talking with Becky but I'd like to hear about you and what led to your getting down here where we found you. We don't get much local news."

Chris scoots back to lean against the wall and begins. "I'm recently separated from the Army. I hadn't even received my last paperwork in the mail before there was no mail. On my last tour, Becky got into this preparedness stuff and joined a small group up in Lubbock. I came home to find the whole commissary in our living-room." Chris shows his first good smile as he exaggerates the story. "She did a good thing and just in time. That was one week before the bottom fell out and money was no good."

Becky has inner strength, as most military wives either have or develop. She has learned to manage their home while Chris was deployed and she can think independently but she still looks to Chris for leadership and he is her anchor.

Becky explains, "With Chris away, a friend of ours gave me a book titled:

## 11th Hour Preparedness
## Making Choices While We Can

It's about living a more self-sufficient lifestyle. With Chris separating soon, it seemed like a good idea. We had no idea how long it might take to transition to civilian life. I stocked up on groceries and stored some recommended staples and canned goods. That helped in the short term but we burned through it a lot faster than I thought we would."

Chris continues, "It was a big help and we wouldn't be here without what she did. We live outside of Lubbock proper and managed to avoid the stealing and looting after things turned ugly. Our place must have looked too small to the looters but the new subdivision up the road got hit real hard. There was a lot of shooting and dead looters but it didn't stop more from trying. I knew it wasn't safe. The last straw for me was when my neighbor's wife took her own life. She was on a lot of medication and couldn't get them refilled. When she ran out, I guess the withdrawal effects were more than she could take. Her husband was beside himself with grief. I had to get Becky and Gina out of there. We loaded up the truck and tried to pack things low so it didn't look like we had anything to steal. We hadn't gone anywhere since filling the tank on the truck. There wasn't anywhere to go that was safe, anyway. We had another five-gallon can of lawnmower gas and a three gallon can of two cycle boat fuel. Draining the water heater gave us eight plastic milk jugs full, we had some cases of bottle water, and what food we hadn't eaten from Becky's store."

Becky and Chris both laugh a bit as Becky says, "For once, it was clean under the beds."

"Becky, Gina, and I, left our place just after midnight. I didn't use any lights and removed the lamps from the brake lights so they wouldn't give us away. We had a little slope to our driveway so I compression started the truck and we left. We drove in the dark and just idled along at twenty miles an hour. After bypassing Tahoka and Lamesa on ranch roads, we picked up speed a bit. Off one of the ranch roads we took to avoid Midland, we came across a house with a small barn. The sun was coming up so we drove into the barn, thinking the place was deserted."

"We were wrong." Becky says, "A man held us with a shotgun. I held onto Gina and was really scared. After Chris told him we had driven all night from Lubbock and didn't need or want anything except a place to rest, he looked over our truck and then asked us if we were hungry. They turned out to be real nice people. They had a little girl a year older than Gina and weren't much better off on water, than we were. We expected to find some creeks or streams to refill our jugs so we left them with all but a case of water and two gallon jugs."

Chris picks up the story from here. "Some stomach virus hit me that night but we left when it got dark again and made it to the airstrip where you found us. I was too sick to put the truck in the hangar and Becky didn't think to hide it. That's where your guys found us, and maybe just in time. The map showed plenty of streams and creeks but when we got there, they would always be dry."

Jackie explains, "The small creeks on those maps, only run in the spring or during rainy seasons. Even the Rio Grande slows to a trickle by late summer. You were lucky we found you. God was watching over you."

# Coffee:

Becky and Jackie grow close after their stay in isolation. At dinner in the community building, Chris and his family are introduced and welcomed to the camp. Jackie joins them and chats with Becky as Chris sits next to Gina and talks with Dad and me.

Gina is being shy and hasn't found a friend yet but when Greg comes back to camp, she saddles up to him right away. Greg is more than pleased with his new found friend.

"I've noticed," says Becky, "that most of the women have cut their hair. I'd like to join the ranks. This long hair is a lot to wash with just a bucket of water." Then in a playful tone, "Does the camp have a beauty salon and do they accept Visa?" Both women laugh as Jackie answers.

"Why yes, we do. My sister, Nicky, happens to have one of the few pair of scissors in camp but also does a pretty fair job. She's had a lot of practice with her sister's hair as they grew up. All us girls go to her. You might not recognize her shop though; it's the communication hut most of the time. Let me know when, and I'd be happy to introduce you. You'll need a mailbox anyway."

"Mailbox?" Becky looks confused.

"For camp mail." responds Jackie, "It's where you pick up messages or leave them for others. With all the different schedules, it's an efficient way to communicate."

The Spencer's join the small group of families still occupying the community building at night. Bob and Lisa Isham help them settle into camp routines and Gina becomes instant friends with their daughter Amber.

The next day, Chris leaves with Bob for a camp tour and to meet some of the others right after breakfast. Lisa offers to watch Gina as she plays with Amber and it gives Becky some free time to get her hair done.

Nicky Chambers is the envy of many women at camp. Her naturally wavy golden hair not only seems to look good with hardly any effort, but it is hers without the gift of peroxide. She is very intelligent and accomplished with an understanding of higher math. Her sister, Jackie, says men feel intimidated by how smart she is. Nicky also has a flair for composition, especially when it comes to hair. She sees a woman's facial shape, complexion, and hair color as a formula she can use to derive a perfect design. Ladies at camp appreciate her way with hair.

"Becky Spenser, this is my sister, Nicky Chambers. Nicky; Becky wants a new shorter look." Formal introductions are so stuffy for Jackie but her step-mom taught them to be proper. She said you can relax after you do the formal part.

Nicky smiles, shakes Becky's hand and says, "I'd be delighted to help. Did you have anything in mind?"

"Not really, Jackie said you were really good at knowing what would look best so I thought to let you do it. Long hair is fine when you have air-conditioning but without it, hair is difficult."

After some discussion and exchange of ideas, Nicky begins cutting hair. Becky doesn't want to look until it is done but when she does...

"That's me? It looks great! Wait 'til Chris gets a load of his new wife. He's never seen me like this. Nicky, thank you. You really do good work." Becky turns and gives Nicky a hug.

Then she says, "We ought to celebrate with a cup of coffee. Want some?"

Jackie thinks she is joking and replies, "Sure, know of a Starbucks anywhere near?"

Becky's answer surprises them both, "Well, no... but I have a five-pound sack of beans in our stuff. We can make some."

Nicky and Jackie just stand there a moment and look at each other, then to Becky. Jackie finally speaks. "The camp's been out of coffee for weeks. Most of us just finished caffeine withdrawal. You have coffee? I'm your friend for life, girl."

"There's one small problem," says Becky, "I only had an electric grinder and it got left. Do we have any way to grind the beans at the kitchen?"

Nicky says, "I'm sure Stephanie can come up with something; especially for a cup of real coffee."

Realizing the smell of coffee will never be contained, Becky hatches a plan with the girls. "Let's sneak the coffee to the kitchen and have them make enough to serve with lunch. It's all going to be gone sooner or later anyway; we might as well enjoy it together."

Nicky, Jackie, and Becky make their way to the community building where the Spencer's things are stored in boxes. Becky doesn't take long to find the large bag of roasted beans. She wraps it in a towel and the three head for the kitchen to find Stephanie.

"Five pounds!" Stephanie is excited. "That will last nearly ten special meals."

"Do you know how to roast coffee?" asks Becky, "Because I have another two pounds of green coffee. It was a new thing so I bought some to try. I didn't like it but never threw it away."

Stephanie stops and looks at Becky, eye to eye: "Are those green coffee beans whole? As in, not ground?"

Becky's big smile is attached to her nodding, 'yes.'

"Those are seeds, Becky, and this climate can grow coffee. At least it's going to grow a lot of interest," she says, "The beans they sell for making coffee aren't the best seed stock but they will germinate. Once they are roasted the bean is dead but those green beans are alive and should sprout. Coffee plants take a lot of care while they are young but we can recruit volunteers to become foster care to their very own plants. Once they get big enough, we'll plant them together and grow a mini plantation. "

"I thought coffee grew in a rain forest," says Jackie, "We're in a desert."

"It does," says Stephanie, "But we can duplicate a rain forest by building some trellis for shade. Especially when the plants are young, they need filtered sunlight and protection from diseases. If we start them in pots, they can be pampered into mature bushes. Besides, it will give the whole camp a little competition to see who can grow the best plants."

"Sounds like fun," says Nicky, "Just what we need."

Lunch is a surprise to everyone. In the institutional sized coffee server that normally holds wild herbal tea, is... COFFEE! To the caffeine deprived, it is a gift from heaven.

Dinner comes and the camp is still ablaze with the coffee news. Those who work "out-camp" as it is called, are consoled that coffee will return for Sunday Breakfast as long as it lasts.

Chris and Bob walk in together and while Bob is joined by his wife Lisa and their three children; Trevor, Hailey, and little Amber who is still playing with Gina; Becky is nowhere to be seen. Jackie tells Chris that Becky ran to get something and to go ahead and sit down. With his back to the door, Becky comes from behind him and kisses his cheek. Chris is used to Becky's long hair but when her short hair brushes his neck, he jumps, looking very startled. Turning to see who kissed him, he sees Becky posing with a big smile and her palms upturned by her face.

"Do you like it?" she asks.

Still stunned, Chris answers, "Is that you? Wow! It looks so different!" Then as disappointment begins to cloud Becky's face... "I love it!"

Stars shine in Becky's eyes again and she asks, "Do you really like it? The long hair was so much work. I can grow it out again later."

Chris takes Becky in his arms and gives her a kiss, "I really like it. It's a whole new you."

Almost forgetting they are in the community building with a dinner crowd all watching; they snap back to reality as applause fills the room.

Scott, now permanent party at the table where Roxanne sits, rises to make an announcement. Somehow the clacky sound of a spoon against a plastic cup fails to ring like crystal stemware but it does the trick.

"I understand that the Spencer's have also blessed us

with a supply of coffee beans.    It is with deepest gratitude that we salute you and wish you to know that were it within our power, the North Star, called Polaris, should be forever known as Spencer's Star."

Wild laughter mixed with "Hear Hear!" and hoisted glasses fill the room. If the Spencer's had any question of their welcome, it fades quickly.

Stephanie's announced request for volunteer coffee growers is met enthusiastically.    Every available container for planting a seed is scooped up.    As a school teacher, Melinda Wagoner has taught arts & crafts and has experience working with clay.    She is able to make slab style flower pots for the coffee plants and begins her first production line for pottery.    The finished pots are sent to the Pit for firing and though the first few pots don't survive the oven, they modify the temperature and begin successfully firing pots.

# Services:

Sunday breakfast is always special at camp. This Sunday is extra special with the addition of coffee, thanks to the Spencer's gift.

Pancakes delight the children. Made with a mix of milo flour and ground Mesquite beans. Mesquite seed pods have been harvested for a couple of weeks and none are let fall to the ground if the young men and women know about them. There is a small mountain of pods collected for the kitchen. Most of the pods are ground into sweet flour. It makes great pancakes, biscuits, cookies, and pastry. The seeds are too hard to eat but are returned to grow more Mesquite trees. Some of the pods are boiled for an hour to extract sweetness from the pods, when reduced; it makes a thin sweet syrup.

Several different religions are represented among those of us at camp but all agree that we want a service on Sunday. So it is that the 'Church of the Bend' forms. Unaffiliated and non-denominational, we have no formally trained pastor, but we have faith in a God who hears our prayers and who remains invested in our good.

Allen Duncan was a deacon and Sunday school teacher at his church before the collapse. He teaches many fine lessons from the Bible and brings a lot of encouraging messages. We share in the openness of our meetings. Prayer requests, Bible questions, and teaching new songs are common. We have no hymnals but it seems everyone has a favorite chorus, song, or hymn, and as we can, we teach others the tunes. We have informality but keep reverence in our service and it is a source of strength for our group. Travis and his three sons never miss coming to camp to join us on Sunday morning. We've lost the internet, telephone, television, and broadcast radio, but with that loss has come a change in values. In the past, church attendance was taken casually with only a percentage of people actually going. Here at camp the services are something we all look forward to with hardly an empty seat. I guess something good can come out of even the worst of situations.

Sunday is the camp's rest day. Children play, adults visit, and non-essential work ceases. Besides breakfast, the kitchen sets out what we call 'grazing food,' it consists of biscuits or bread in a large towel covered bowl, fruit (when available), and hard boiled eggs.

For Anna and me, it's time to spend together after church. A small shade tree is claimed by us and I love to relax with my head on Anna's lap while we talk. Anna muses about how our life has changed, yet hasn't. She smiles, which catches my eye.

"What's funny?" I ask.

"We are." Anna smiles, "Do you remember how busy we were in Houston and how we hardly had time to spend 'for us?' How has anything really changed, now that we're here? You have different work but it takes you away most of the day just like before. I have similar work but I'm doing 'it' most of the day. We still only manage to see each other for breakfast and dinner and we still live for Sundays."

Looking up at Anna, I say, "Allen Saunders first said: Life is what happens to us while we are making other plans. I guess he was right. We try to run away from the busy but it catches us just the same. On Intrepid we rested some but like you said, the destination was always ahead of us. Once we got here, we rested because each day was lived for itself and the future was unknown. But now we've settled into that same 'busy' we had before. Could it be life that keeps getting in the way?"

"Maybe," Anna replies, "but I'm not ready to trade it for what's next, just yet." We both smile as I sit up to plant a kiss on the wonderful woman I have found for my wife.

Scott and Roxanne wander over to the stream where the camp 'Pool Party' was held. It is much quieter without all the guests; there are no fancy woven grass hats but wonderful memories still remain. The fire pit is still there but long since cold. Water flow has shrunk some but a smaller stream still runs its course. They sit near a place where water bubbles over rocks.

"Roxanne, where do you call home?" Scott asks. "You hardly ever talk about it."

She clears her throat and begins to speak but it's obvious this is an important but private subject for her. "My parents live in California, east of the mountains in the high desert. I was born there. Most people think of big cities when they think of California but that's on the west side of the mountains. I'm a country girl that grew up in rural California. It's flat, windy, and dry."

"Do you think your family is OK?" Scott asks.

"There's a good chance they are. Daddy was interested in how the Indians grew food in the high desert without irrigation and started growing citrus, dates, and what he called 'dry footed crops.' Mom did a lot of canning too. They live in a small town with good neighbors. I would like to get back there someday to see them. With cell phones, we could talk several times a day. Living in Houston was like being across the street. Now it feels like they're on a different planet. I can't even write them a letter."

"You'll get back there again," says Scott. "It may take a while for things to settle down but radio still works. Maybe more radio hams will come out of the woodwork and you can get a message to your folks."

"Maybe," replies Roxanne. "Maybe."

The sound the water makes is soothing. Scott gathers some stones and tries to knock off the dangling end of an Agave leaf. Roxanne watches patiently as Scott misses every throw.

"Come on Scott, you aren't going to let a thing like that get past you, are you? Just hit the thing and be done with it." Roxanne enjoys taunting Scott.

With his final miss, Scott hands Roxanne a stone, "Well, if you think you can do better, have a fling."

Taking the challenge, she replies, "I was waiting for you to give up so I could show you how it's done." Roxanne calmly hurls the stone and clips off the dangling leaf as though it was nothing at all. Pleased there was only one dangling leaf, she will never confess it was a lucky toss.

Scott, in partial disbelief, proclaims in a loud voice: "And there you have it folks, Rocky Balboa wins by a knock-out in the first round!"

From this time forward, Scott takes to calling Roxanne by her new nickname, Rocky.

Back at camp, the name sticks, even for those who have no idea of the origin, they find it easy to call her Rocky. It fits her.

# Package:

Monday morning in the medical hut, Anna and Jackie take out the partially opened box of supplies that Jim recently sent. Medicine is stored, supplies are organized and put away, and bandages are packed into an air-tight box to keep them from becoming soiled.

Then, at the bottom of the box, Jackie notices another small wrapped package. She removes it and reads the tag, "For Anna, with love from Rita."

"This one's for you, Anna." Jackie hands it to her.

"Rita is so thoughtful; I wonder what it could be? I'm not expecting anything." Anna unties the string that Rita so often uses. Removing the paper exposes tissue paper wrapped around a small long box.

"What is it?" asks Jackie.

"It's a pregnancy tester. An E.P.T. Why would Rita send me an E.P.T.?"

Jackie suddenly gets very excited. "Anna. When was your last cycle?"

"No Jackie. Besides, how would Rita know this about me if I don't?"

Jackie asks again, "When? Since you came to camp?"

Anna's head is spinning inside. How could she have missed something like this? "I don't know. Everything has been so crazy since we left Hawaii. I thought it was just the stress from all the change. I don't even remember my last... NO, wait! It was just before we left for Hawaii." Anna grabs for the pocket calendar she keeps in her bag. "It was the first week of July."

Jackie has a huge smile, "And how many weeks ago was that?"

Anna quickly counts the weeks as a serious look comes over her. "I need to use this tester! Look, Jackie, not a word of this until it's confirmed and THEN not until I tell Jason. Promise?"

"I promise," says Jackie, "as long as I get to be a God-aunt."

Jackie throws a big hug on Anna's neck. "And you said you weren't expecting anything."

"We won't know for sure until morning, so don't go knitting any booties. Still, how did Rita know? If this tests positive; Rita is more than amazing."

Anna thinks Jackie might have trouble keeping the

secret but it is her own behavior that peaks my curiosity. At lunch and again at dinner, I ask her if everything is OK.

"Everything's fine. Why do you ask?"

"You appear preoccupied. Is there any problem at the medical hut? Are you and Jackie OK?"

"No, we're good. I just have some things on my mind that I need to sort through." Anna is acting nervous.

"Why don't you tell me about it? Maybe I can help." I am trying to understand Anna's strange behavior. Then in a more serious tone, I ask, "Does it involve you and me?"

Anna looks straight into my eyes and tells me, "No, Jason, we're very good. I'm very happy with you as my husband and wouldn't want my life any other way. I'll have this thing sorted out soon and I'll tell you all about it when I do, I promise."

I let it go with that and think it best to give Anna some space. I am concerned enough to pray for her and to wait.

Long before daylight, Anna follows the path to the outhouse as she has grown accustom to doing several times each night. On this trip she was thinking, *"Why didn't I recognize this earlier... I'm a nurse!"* She brings the E.P.T. and this will be the final answer.

Seven o'clock comes and I rise to find Anna already awake and dressed.

"What's with you?" I ask, "Is this the same woman I have to pry out of bed each morning?"

"We all have to accept changes. I thought this was a good first step for me." She is beaming and I am captivated by her. Anna is especially beautiful and radiant this morning.

"I think I'm going to like this new change." I say.

Anna hands me the E.P.T. with a plus sign showing in the window. "Good, because you're in for some changes too."

"What's this?" I ask, looking confused. Then Anna realizes I have never seen a pregnancy tester before.

"It means you're going to be a daddy! I'm pregnant!" Anna nearly knocks me over as she hugs my neck in excitement.

I don't know what to do, or even think.

"Well? Aren't you happy? You're a daddy! Jason? What's wrong?" Anna is growing concerned by my lack of response.

Taking Anna in my arms, I say, "Of course I'm happy. But I'm scared too. No doctors, no hospital. What if something goes wrong? I'm not ready to lose you."

"Jason," Anna replies, "women have been giving birth to babies for a lot longer than medical schools have been giving birth to doctors. I'm a nurse, remember? We'll do fine and our baby will look just like you!"

I scoop Anna up and kiss her passionately. "I can't believe it! I'm going to be a daddy!" We both laugh and cry and laugh some more.

We are a bit late getting to breakfast. Everyone is busy eating except for Jackie whose eyes are locked on Anna. Dad notices us coming in and says in a joking loud voice, "You have to get up earlier than that to win the race to breakfast."

Seeing my opportunity, I speak loud enough for all to hear, "Well, I thought to give you a head start... since you will be a GRANDPA soon!"

Breakfast is all but forgotten as pandemonium ensues. Mom is crying and hugging Anna, Jackie is saying she knew since yesterday and it was the hardest secret she ever kept. Dad is shaking my hand, and then hugging me. Even the kitchen crew comes out to applaud the new parents.

With all the reaction in camp; you would wonder if the Connors are having a baby, or the camp. Some will say it is a little of both. Perhaps it is the collective agony of hearts over lost loved ones and the lack of communication with family or maybe it is the uncertain future we face, but the camp begins acting more and more like a family. Vicarious bonds are forming and nearly everyone laughs or cries together.

# The Mission:

Camp has been our 'home' for nearly three months now and there are huts for all but a few of the families. Our water line is working and the laundry is somewhat mechanized on windy days. A small wind mill turns an eccentric shaft that operates agitators for the wash and rinse tubs. On days with little wind the laundry crew keeps fit by working the dashers by hand.

Between fresh air, hard work, and a natural diet, everyone appears to be healthy. Stephanie Sweeny is doing a good job locating and organizing the harvest of local food sources. The Connors' 'deep larder' is holding up. First calculations estimated our food would last only about seven months but with native foods added, new estimates carry us through winter and well into spring.

Having enough food doesn't solve all our problems however. Winter is coming and none of the huts have any means to provide heat. Already the daytime highs are dropping into the seventies with nighttime lows touching the sixties. This is comfortable weather but in another month the daytime highs will drop another ten degrees and nights will be in the forties. Huts with poor windows and floppy doors will be very uncomfortable.

It isn't that we don't have the tools or ability to make tight fitting doors and windows, it is that the wood we scavenge has been exposed to the elements long enough to be brittle. You can hardly cut it and driving a nail will nearly always split the wood. We have better luck tying boards together with the string we make from the Sotol bush. The huts are just not going to be weather tight.

Water collection is another problem. The spring pond that Fred and Harry built is holding plenty of water and is overflowing most days but in another month the winter drought will begin and water will grow scarce. A second catchment pond is under construction to contain more of the runoff but even that might not be enough.

We call a general camp meeting with Travis and his sons invited. We need input from all angles to best meet the winter challenges.

Dad thanks Stephanie and Christi for their report on food stores as he addresses the next subject.

"Well, it's good news that we aren't going to go hungry this winter, but we have two other issues and they aren't going to be easy to solve. First is our water. Harry, give us an update."

Harry Taylor stands and faces the group. "We've finished the second catchment pond and it's filling up but the spring is already slowing down some. We don't know how slow the spring will get but if it dries up completely, we'll only last about a month without a new water source."

Roxanne stands and is acknowledged. "Winter work at the pit should tame down quite a bit as well as the gardening. That's going to cut down on the water needs at the laundry since those are the sources of the most soiled clothes. We can also drop to taking showers every three days. Cold showers won't be missed much anyway as the water in the barrels isn't getting as warm as it did in the summer. If the spring temporarily dries up, could we stretch that month reserve into perhaps two?"

Harry and Fred both nod in agreement. Dad continues.

"OK, if the spring dries up, we'll implement water restriction and deal with that when it comes. That brings up to the hardest problem... heat. All summer long, we've battled too much heat but now we need to address the opposite. Winter's coming and it's going to get cold. None of the huts are tight enough to heat. Even if we make Chimineas for every hut, there isn't enough wood and coal to keep them fueled. We've already shut down the kilns at the pit and stockpiling what wood and coal we can. There still won't be near enough. We need to get our heads together on this one. If you have an idea, let's hear it. There are no bad ideas."

Hands go up all over the room. Many of the younger

men and women have ideas to share and this is encouraged. In most circles these teenage adults would be sidelined, but not here. They work like adults and are respected as adults.

Ideas are as varied as those that offer them. Direction is scattered at first but as thoughts are shared, responses become focused.

Two possible actions seem logical. We have to either locate a large source of fuel to heat leaky huts or we have to find better accommodations to winter at and move the entire camp population there. The first possibility is unlikely but the second is unthinkable. Leave camp? So much work has been spent making it livable. But like it or not, a plan is coming together.

A multipurpose scouting mission is commissioned. Travis McCann knows the area better than any. He will lead the team. Willie & Pete McCann will accompany him along with Bob Isham and Paul Sayer. For economy they will leave Travis' truck behind and take both Rangers, the one cargo trailer, and some extra fuel. They will be looking for heating fuel sources, possible buildings to winter in by the whole camp, water sources, and sign of survivors, perhaps friendly.

The team assembles before morning and leaves at first light. They plan to be gone for three days and will send PSK text messages over the portable two-meter radio every twelve hours on the tens. That will be ten o'clock in the morning and again at ten o'clock in the evening. They have no idea just how important this mission is.

By the first ten, the team has inspected two abandoned

shacks but find nothing of value. Each had heating stoves but they are rusted through. Terlingua is ahead. Long ago it was a bustling mercury mine but all that remains are ruins of a ghost town and a tourist-trap. Before the collapse it was visited by many of the Big Bend National Park tourists but it is likely deserted now. It does have some buildings that might be useful. Travis plans to check it thoroughly after returning to T-3. He will gain a lot of intel after visiting the air strip.

"Willie, here's our message for the ten." Travis is focused and alert, but conversational, he is not.

The message reads: **AR T3, NTR**.

Back at camp, Dennis Paterson has hiked up to the ridge with a portable two-meter radio and a converted PDA to read the encoded text message from the team. The message is right on-time but Dennis thinks the message is garbled. He waits for another message but after twenty minutes, he returns to the communication hut.

Dennis hands the radio and PDA to Pat. "This is all I got, Mr. Wagoner."

"Call me Pat. I appreciate the respect but we're working together on this. Pat is just fine." Pat Wagoner is easy to work with and prefers to have a relaxed work environment.

"OK, …Pat…, but what does the message mean? Did it get garbled? Was there more?"

"No, it's all here. AR means arrived and T3 is the

designation for the airstrip where they found the Spencer's. NTR is a military acronym for Nothing To Report. Arrived T-3, Nothing to report. I didn't expect more this early."

Dennis is impressed. "Man, it sure was short."

"Travis served in the military during Vietnam." Pat explains, "His specialty was commanding Force Recon units behind enemy lines. He was never detected and his unit was decorated several times. He knows what he's doing."

Travis doesn't care to stop where they will be exposed to logical observation posts. He passes the airstrip a ways and pulls to the side of the road for Bob and Paul to come alongside.

"We're going to go check out that hangar and the Spencer's truck. If any unfriendlies are around, there will be signs of looting. Willie, you and Pete follow this wash east to the tractor trail, then cut south to where you can cover us. Give us two clicks when you get in position. I'll respond with one click. We'll go in from the front after you're in position." Travis has a teasing grin as he turns to Bob and Paul. "We'll only need side-arms but don't let a stray cat make you shoot your buddy." Bob and Paul don't need to defend their safety practices. They are all good hunters and friends but this is a good natured reminder to be safe.

Willie sets down his preferred shotgun and picks up his Dad's 270 deer rifle. Pete is proudly carrying the 308 that I sent with him for this trip. They each grab binoculars and head down the wash toward the tractor trail. It doesn't take them long to get into position.

Willie turns on the HT radio and pushes the key twice. It is followed by one "click" sound from Travis doing the same.

"OK boys, let's keep fifty feet between us and go have a looky. Bob, you check out the truck and I'll check the hangar."

Nothing appears to have been touched. Bob and Paul come to the hangar after seeing the empty truck. Travis has already surveyed the Hangar. It appears exactly as it was when they were there last.

Paul tells Travis, "The truck's not been messed with. Even the glove-box was neat and tidy."

Travis asks, "Did you have to reach in and unlock the door? I locked the doors but left the window open about six inches."

Bob is impressed and says, "You are a sneaky man. Good thinking … and yes, we did have to unlock the door. I thought it was a bit strange to find the door locked but the window open."

Travis looks somewhat relieved, "Good. With the attention a plane must have caused, any looters would have surveyed the airstrip at least. This area must be clear of unfriendlies. Let's go check out Terlingua."

Travis keys the HT and says just the word "CLEAR." A single click responds and from about fifty yards behind the hangar come first Willie, then Pete. They all climb back into the Rangers and head for town.

# A Gift:

In the old cabin, Mom is beaming as she and Anna talk about the new baby. This will be her first grandchild and she feels overdue for the title.

"You have no idea how much I've prayed for this precious life. I do have a confession to make, however. I've known for some time now. I wasn't sure I could keep it a secret."

Anna's eyes are wide open. "You knew? How could you? I didn't even know until this morning." Then it dawns on her. "Rita?"

Mom takes Anna's hands. "I don't know how she knows these things but she told me the second night you were there. After the news reports, Jim and Pat, or Matt, get their business done, then I put the headphones on and Rita and I chat for a bit. She told me first thing. She said she knew by looking in your eyes and how you moved in the kitchen as you two fixed breakfast."

Anna looks dumbfounded. She sits down. "So that's why she sent me the E.P.T.?"

"Not actually." Mom replies. "She expected you would figure it out without it but when I told her how busy you've been; I guess she thought to prod you a bit."

Anna has a great big smile. "That scoundrel! Just wait 'till I see her again."

Both ladies laugh and are amazed at Rita's incredible inclinations.

"Oh, I almost forgot," Mom gets up and goes to her bedside. Under the bed she removes a package and comes back to where Anna is sitting.

Anna recognizes the package. "Rita's gift. That's the one I carried to you the day we got here. Why haven't you opened it?"

"Because the gift is for you. It's from Rita and she wanted you to give it to me for safe keeping until you knew." Mom's glowing smile can melt a heart at fifty paces. It projects a loving acceptance. She places the package into Anna's hands and says, "Open it."

The string is neatly woven to create a net over the brown paper. It unties easily and is kept, as string is useful for many other things. The brown paper will be folded and kept but not until after this package's contents are known. Inside is a baby blanket wrapped around cloth diapers, pins, and a beautiful sage green maternity dress. It is exactly her size; a detail so typical of Rita.

"This is so amazing! It's lovely." As Anna's tears stream down her freckled cheeks, "I can't believe how blessed I am to be here with you right now and to have Rita send me these things..." She can't speak anymore. Anna's heart is overflowing with joy and appreciation for God's goodness.

Over in Baja Sur, on the patio of a Tuscan style home, sit two deep souls holding hands. Both are smiling joyfully as a tear escapes the corner of the eye and rolls down Rita's cheek.

Anna hasn't begun to show yet but does notice her clothes fitting a bit snugger. She credited the kitchen's bounty of good food. So many of the flavors were new to her and she thought it was the fresh air that made her so hungry, but now she knows a miracle is growing inside her. She spends the rest of the morning with Mom and asks her to store Rita's gifts as our hut is so small and she doesn't need them yet.

Dad and I are at HQ, between the Communication and Medical huts. Dad is remembering when Mom first told him they were going to have a baby.

"Jason, I was panicked. You would have thought I was going to have the baby myself. The real fear I faced was if I was ready to be a father."

"Dad, I've been feeling those same fears, but you know what? I look to you as the example of what I hope to be. BUT this is not exactly the environment or state of the union that I hoped to raise him in... or her. I wonder what's going on out there, beyond this canyon."

Dad leans back on his chair. "It isn't pretty from what Pat is picking up from the radio. News is scattered but a huge number of people have died. There are some survivors but most are keeping quiet. The military is the big unknown. They had the resources and training to survive but no one knows where they are. There were some deployments but without world news, we don't know where."

"Is the grid coming back soon?" I ask.

"There's no word, but without workers, restoration would be spotty at best. I think we've seen the last of a national grid system. The same goes for fuel. It takes electricity to refine oil and refined oil to run the service trucks to keep the electric going. Once it stops, I guess it's not easy to get back."

"What about news from overseas?"

Dad thinks a moment then says, "With the U.S. out of the picture, you can bet the Middle East is a war zone. China is probably taking over Taiwan and Japan is in the cross-hairs. Russia may be spreading its skirt too. If Mexico weren't so weakened by the loss of US foreign aid, I'd expect them to try to take back Texas. It would be a foolish attempt but they might try it if they thought they could get away with it. I guess it depends on how many Texans survive this thing."

I agree, "Texas has always had the desire to stand

alone. Maybe they'll come out of this as a new nation after all. They have the resources to pull it off, provided they still have a population. It would be good for Texas but maybe not for the world. With everything so screwed up, I wonder what kind of world my children will inherit?"

# Terlingua:

Travis slows and stops. Ahead is a turn from the highway that leads to a cluster of buildings defining what is called 'town.'

"Willie, Pete, same plan. It's about seventy-five yards over this rise. Get some distance between you to cover multiple angles and buildings. Don't shoot unless you have to."

Travis has raised his boys well and never has to tell them not to shoot unless necessary but it has become a habit and slips out easily.

"Bob, Paul, we'll do the same as we did before but let's search together this time. If there's anyone here, they may spook if we're scattered but just the same, let's keep about five paces between us. "

Travis gets the double click on the radio and replies with one click. The Rangers pull up to the largest building and the men cautiously begin looking through dirty windows.

"It looks deserted but hasn't been looted." Says Paul, "Might be big enough for a main building."

"There's a big stove in the center," adds Bob. "Looks serviceable too."

Travis tries the door but it is locked. "Let's check the back door."

The men find the back door closed but unlocked. Inside is uncharacteristically swept and clean. Travis speaks softly, "Buildings left to themselves accumulate dust quickly, this place is a bit too clean."

A voice from behind them accompanies the unmistakable slide of a pump shotgun. "That might be cuz these buildin's ain't abandoned. Now set yer guns on the floor, turn around real slow with yer hands where I kin see 'em, an state yer business."

All three men do exactly as they are told but before Travis turns, he catches the glint of a rifle scope through the window he is facing. One of his sons has their abductor clean in his sights.

"My name is Travis McCann, this is Bob Isham, and Paul Sayer. We're on a scouting trip to find a place to winter an honorable group of survivors. We have provisions and skilled people but not enough firewood to stay warm in our drafty huts. We are not here to steal or cause harm. Can I ask who I'm speaking to from the rude end of that scatter gun?"

"My name's Lucas Maxwell, I run this place, or at least I did when there was a country to come visit. You the folks what met that airplane a couple weeks back?"

"That was us." Travis answers. "We found a sick man and his wife and baby up in one of the hangars, took 'em back with us and got 'em better. They're with the rest now."

"Saw ya take 'em wit ya. Didn't know they was there 'til after ya left. Mighty kind o' ya." Lucas takes a deep breath and says, "I guess you aren't here to do no harm or you wouldn't have took that family wit ya." He lowers his shotgun. Lucas is an older man in his late sixties, a bit overweight with somewhat of a pot belly. The balding top of his head is encircled with curly white hair and a full beard to match. I'm sure tourists took him for a left-over miner from the ghost town.

"Lucas, I have two sons watching our backs from outside. Mind if I call them off and let them come in?"

Lucas lays the shotgun on the counter, "I guess ya best. I ain't much of a commando anyways. Not sure what I was gonna do with ya if'n ya WAS bad news. The wife an me has been pretty lonesome but we been hearin' of folks doin' real bad things. Lootin' and killin' just over water. We git news over shortwave 'bout three times a week. There's folks out here on the ranches but I guess we're too far out to attract trouble. I was real fearful you was the first."

Travis radios a single word "CLEAR," Pete stands up from his hide, just fifty feet beyond the window and directly in line with Lucas. There was only a bush to give him cover but it is dense enough that Lucas never saw him. The look on Lucas' face as he sees Pete stand with a scoped rifle in his hands is memorable to say the least. Willie comes from a different direction and both men come to the front door with weapons lowered. Bob asks Lucas if it'd be OK to unlock the door. It strikes Paul a bit funny how polite the atmosphere becomes with so many firearms in the room.

Lucas asks, "What sort o' place are ya scoutin'? I know this area an most o' the ranchers. We talk on commercial band; just call 'em ranch radios."

Travis responds, "We have fifty-three, with the Spencer's. Fifty-six if ya count me and my boys. The springs will be drying up soon and cold weather is coming. We have food enough, some medical, even a nurse. What we need is a place to stay warm 'till spring."

Lucas appears a bit uncomfortable with the news of so many people. "Just what sort o' folks are we talkin' about?"

Travis explains, "We're like a small town. Most are one way or another, connected with a corporation out of Houston. They're families with children, single men and women, grandparents, and friends. All God fearing and decent living folks."

"Looks like ya stumbled on a right place," says Lucas, "This here's a resort. Don't look it from the road but behind us is a ghost town and DE-LUX accommodations for sixty at most, if'n some don't mind a couch or cot. To tell the truth, me and the missus could appreciate the company and added security. Let me show you around, but watch for snakes."

Lucas' warning and the "VIPER CROSSING" signs have Willie's undivided attention. Willie hates snakes. He claims he and snakes don't agree; the snakes are long dead before he is done killin'.

Travis asks if it'd be best to pick up and holster their side arms and Lucas agrees.

Out the back door are other smaller buildings, one is a residence.

Lucas calls to the house. "Adelaide! You can come on out. These are some good people."

The house door slowly opens and a kind looking grandma steps out. She appears nervous at seeing the five armed men with her husband but she relaxes after introductions and Travis' softer and kinder nature comes through.

"Adelaide does all the guest registration. She knows the room layouts and can put folks where they'll best fit." That announcement takes Adelaide by surprise as Lucas hadn't told her about guests. "Oh, I'm sorry dear, these men are looking for a place to winter a group of folks that need shelter. This is about the only place and they have their own food. I figure we can use the company and the help."

"Just like a man!" Adelaide rolls her eyes and addresses Travis. "How many rooms will you need? It will help if I know more about your people. Are there women in your group?"

Travis always removes his hat when speaking to a lady. It is a habit of showing respect. "Ma'am, we're a mix of men and women, some young families with children and some older, we have some single men and women as well. All in good health thanks to a good kitchen staff and our nurse. We're fifty-six people and all hard workers."

You can tell that Adelaide is a bit overwhelmed at the number but also relieved that they aren't booking a company of soldiers.

"It's going to be full rooms but we'll make it work." Adelaide looks more hopeful. "When will they be here?"

Travis is trying to work out the logistics of transporting people, belongings, and supplies for that many people.

"We have the ATV's and a trailer that can carry five plus some cargo. I have a truck and trailer that can haul about seven with cargo. We'll have to make several trips because the two other trucks we have are gas. Both their tanks are dry and all we have is diesel."

Lucas speaks up. "We might could help there. In back is a 300-gallon tank of gasoline. We could go get that truck at the airport and bring ya gas to drive your other rigs here. Might git the job done in two trips."

They talk more at dinner for which Adelaide insists they stay. She says it's a pleasure to fix a meal for more than just the two of them and that between the store and restaurant stock, they have plenty.

Somehow, when people sit down to eat together; you get to know what they're made of. Willie asks to say the blessing and does so with ease that comes only from regular practice. Adelaide and Lucas lose any fears they may have retained.

Adelaide takes special interest in making sure Willie and Pete have seconds and dessert.

Lucas explains, "Water is no problem at Terlingua. The town is named after three creeks that combine right here and flow all year long."

After dinner they retire to the living room where a single oil lamp provides enough light to fill the room softly.

Paul comments, "I can't remember the last time I sat in a soft chair."

"Me neither," says Bob, "or to have carpet under my feet again."

"Your camp must be rather primitive." Adelaide says, "Is it up in the canyons?"

It is understood that Travis is the only one to share facts or resources of the group. Nothing was said but an understanding is known and all think it best this way.

"It started as a deer camp, ma'am." Always polite, Travis explains. "One cabin for six at most, and a small cook shack. When folks began showing up, mostly friends and folks from work, they made a large addition to the cook shack and turned it into the community building. Huts were built with adobe over stacked stone and a home-brew cement floor, but the doors and windows aren't tight. It's not a bad place, they even have running water and a laundry but it won't be comfortable when it gets cold."

Adelaide has a look of contentment as she thinks about the families. "I can imagine the ladies will appreciate a warm shower and a soft bed to sleep in."

"Ma'am, you have no idea." Travis realizes this will be the selling point for moving the camp.

Pete asks, "Ma'am, pardon my asking but how do you run a hot shower without power for a well pump and water heater?"

Lucas answers. "Ingenuity. Being so far out, we lose power pretty regular. Long ago, we laid a water line from way up stream. It runs ta somethin' called a surge pump. That's a pump that uses water flow ta pump a little water into our tower tank on each cycle. Pressure ain't high but she flows. Add ta that a gas water heater an a thousand gallon underground propane tank, and we have what ya might call, a rather fortunate situation."

That night is hard to beat. An actual mattress and sheets are almost as refreshing as taking a warm shower. They all know the precious nature of water and none use much of it. They use enough water to get wet then turned it off. After soaping up they use enough to rinse away the soap. Conservation has become ingrained by life at camp.

Willie sends the ten o'clock text message that night:

**"CON FR RTB MA"**

Morning comes and the men can hardly believe how well they slept in a real bed. Adelaide fixes a good breakfast and they head to the airport to fetch the Spencer's truck. Lucas finds an empty aviation fuel barrel at the air strip and a barrel pump to go with it. They even find a bung wrench. What they can't find are the keys to the Spencer's truck so it will have to make the trip to camp for the second load, if we find the keys.

# Caravan:

The team's message spreads fast at camp.

"Contacted Friendlies, Returning to Base, Mission Accomplished."

What can it all mean? Did they find fuel? Who are the friendlies? There are many questions but no answers until the team returns.

Nearly all the camp is standing along the roadway up to the community building when the two Rangers roll in. They are two days early and carry good news.... at least we all hope it is good news. Some hope the team has located enough fuel to allow us to remain at our home in this canyon. Others realize the camp's limitations and are looking for a better home. How can the prayers of both be met?

Travis, Bob, and Paul, first meet at the HQ hut with Dad, Fred, Harry, and Sam. After a quick briefing they all proceed to the community building to share the news.

Dad speaks first. "First, I want to express my thanks for the safety and good fortune that the scouting team was shown. But since you didn't come here to listen to me..." low laughter spreads across the room "I'll ask Travis to share what they found."

Travis stands and the room gets deathly silent. "Well, it was a short trip. First place we went was back to the last landing strip for evidence of unfriendlies that would have been alerted by the plane. Good news is that nothing was touched. It looks like the bands of roving looters we've heard about, either never made it this far, have quit," Travis pauses a moment. "or have died. We went back to the small tourist stop of Terlingua to look at buildings that might suit our needs or had resources we could use. What we found was a couple still living there with secluded resources that can comfortably house our entire camp for the winter."

A mix of emotion covers the room. Some applaud, some sit emotionless, and some are clearly disappointed. Travis signals for quiet as he continues.

"Now, I know this camp means a lot for all the hard work invested making things nice, and it is a great improvement to sleeping on the ground or in a tent, but what has been offered to us are real beds with sheets and rugs on the floor." He sees the attention shift and with it, the possible conversion of at least half of those who previously wished to remain. "And for the last of you hold-outs..." Travis enjoys holding the best for last. "They have flush toilets and warm showers!"

Well, that does it. Not a single person wants to stay. Our camp is moving!

All hands begin packing and arranging passenger loads and cargo for the trip to our new winter home. No dishes or cooking pots and pans are needed. A fully functional kitchen is attached to the small restaurant.

The first caravan carries many of the women and children with a complement of armed protection. We don't expect trouble along the way but Travis is a man of caution and hasn't survived this long by being careless. Four men take lead in the four-place Ranger. Seven people squeeze into the Wagoner's extended cab truck with goats and chickens in the trailer. The Ramos family of six, plus four younger riders, fit into their truck and camper. Ramone had almost given up hope that his truck would ever move again. The gas cans that Lucas sent are a real joy. Following them is Travis' truck and trailer with five in the truck and two more riding on top of cargo. Lastly, the two-place Ranger follows with a full trailer. It is about half the camp when you consider the drivers have to return for the second load. Lucas is right; they are going to make this in two trips.

They begin at dawn. Progress is slow and methodical. Each curve, bridge, and narrowing of the road is first glassed with binoculars then negotiated by the lead Ranger while being covered by those in the convoy. Once they are well past, they provide cover as the next vehicles pass through. When the last of the group is past the choke point, they proceed to the next. Many have never seen this procedure and some think the men are 'playing army,' but all the convoy arrives safely and without incident.

"That's how it's done," comments Travis, and he doesn't care what anyone thinks about it.

The keys to the Spencer's truck are found in Chris Spencer's jean pants pocket. Chris' truck will replace the Ramos' camper that remains at Terlingua.

When Lucas and Adelaide see the children and how well-mannered they are; they are overjoyed to play like grandparents. The children's behavior is a tribute to their parents training, hard work, and the way they are valued at camp. You would have thought the camp had come to bless the Maxwell's instead of the reverse. Maybe, blessings will pass both ways. At least, that's the way things should work.

They unload quickly and retrieve Chris' truck from the airstrip. Each gas truck gets a little more fuel for the next round trip and returns to camp for a final load. By tomorrow the camp will be buttoned up and empty.

Mom and Dad stay behind with Fred and Irene Livingston, Harry and Rachel Taylor, Bob and Lisa Isham, Pat and Marge Wagoner, Anna and me, and a few others.

Tonight is a regular contact night with Jim and Rita so the radio will go on the last load. There is a joyful sadness around camp. We have seen God protect and feed more than fifty at a camp designed for ten. Every obstacle was met with cooperation and hope. We can't think of a single major quarrel that has erupted. Our peace and success can be attributed to the central hut in camp, called HQ. It is where our camp's leadership met after dark to pray for the needs of each precious soul entrusted to us. There is a holiness about the camp and a protective presence that circles our small canyon like a hedge.

Tomorrow, camp will be vacant; closed up for winter and void of need for further prayer. We will have to find a new prayer closet in Terlingua.

# Last Night:

Dinner is more of a sack lunch with the kitchen packed away. Christi Duncan made sure there was both dinner and breakfast for those of us staying for the second caravan but it's not the same with half the camp gone. Each empty seat cries for one who's no longer there. This place has brought the greatest sense of fellowship but now is a testimony to emptiness.

At least the communication hut is small and with all remaining ears listening to the news and then sharing the updates, it is a bit more alive.

Jim's voice is comforting. Though it is technically an FCC violation to broadcast over amateur radio, this is a whole new world. I'm sure if the FCC becomes re-established, Jim will follow their rules again. Until then:

"Welcome to the first of November and about fifteen weeks past the crash. We're getting a bit more chatter from hams across the country due to noticeable reduction in looting and violence. We've learned of more remote towns across the country bringing up localized power. One that we reported earlier, has an electric locomotive running power for the whole town, others in Alaska have operated this way for decades and never skipped a beat. Fuel is still a problem and roads are generally impassible because of abandoned vehicles. Still, pockets of survivors are beginning to move about. For those living near metropolitan areas, it is strongly recommended you avoid traveling into the city. Nothing in there is worth contracting a disease. Reports are rising, especially from warmer climates in the south, of cholera, typhoid fever, and typhus. With little medical help available, these can be very bad news. Please stay away. On the good side, some farmers are beginning to talk of spring planting. Without fertilizer or machinery, the crops won't be large but there will be crops again. Finally, I'd like to leave you with a word of hope from the Bible. This is found in Nahum, chapter one and verse seven, The Lord is good, a stronghold in the day of trouble, and he knoweth them that trust in Him. For all you who are listening, God bless."

"Thanks Jim, this is Pat, we'll be breaking down after tonight but will be up again by next contact. " Pat and Jim continue passing text data with details of the move as the rest of us slowly filter back to our huts for the night.

"Anna, you know what I want to do tomorrow?" I ask.

"Hard tellin'... what?" Anna's answer is cautious.

"I want to burn our sleeping mat. Sort of a ceremonial

fire, signaling the end of the hard and return to the soft."

In a sentimental tone, Anna replies. "Let's don't. I know they are no foam mattress but the Palmer girls worked hard to make them and I know they won't be any good after the field rats and rodents have a hay day... but they're a tribute to what was here. They're a message that we beat the odds and survived. Maybe the world fell apart but we didn't. Let's leave them where they are."

I hold Anna close and look into her green eyes, "With you on our side, what can we do but survive? Our kid will be blessed with a fantastic mom." As I kiss Anna, there is quietness throughout the camp, a foreboding quietness that perhaps even the canyon and huts are going to miss us. This is the final night of a great chapter in the history of this place.

Ten people meet quietly in the HQ hut; perhaps for the last time though the idea is raised that we could make an annual pilgrimage if the world stabilizes again... but it probably will not.

Later that night, Mom and Dad talk in their bedroom.

"Cynthia, when we bought this place, I never dreamed it would become so important for so many. I knew a few could come here but look at what it has become. It's beyond my wildest imagination. I wonder if we'll ever make it back. I wonder if it's over."

Mom's wistful look reflects her amazement at what was accomplished and sadness that such greatness is now concluded. These are opposite emotions and her heart is somewhere in the middle. Mom is outgoing in her interactions, quick to befriend or meet a need, but she is introverted in her thinking. Her judgments and opinions come after a lot of contemplation and prayer. When she speaks, you can be sure that she believes and stands behind each word. She is a rock for Dad and he respects the wisdom that his wife and soul mate provides him. More than her careful examination of facts, Dad has learned to value her intuitions. There were times when facts strongly leaned toward one decision yet Mom's spirit moved her differently. Following that intuition saved the family business on two occasions and has prevented many destructive associations. She is a remarkable woman with a deeply spiritual walk. She also has a well-developed sense of humor and is fun to be with. All these things are what Dad loves about Mom. He is truly blessed that they can share life together. From the window, they can see much of the nearly vacant village that has grown over the past few months. With Dad expecting profoundness, Mom takes a deep breath and speaks.

"Well, we shouldn't let all this sit vacant. You going to list it for rent?"

Dad is instantly jolted from his melancholy and bursts into laughter. He wraps Mom in a big hug and they both laugh and cry at the same time. A wave of both joy and relief sweep through the room and soon, they are gathering belongings into boxes for the morning trip to Terlingua. Certainly, they have 'more hills to climb and bears to shoot,' as Mom's grandmother used to say. She feels a little understanding of what

Grandma meant by that; and wonders what is ahead.

Anna and I find our way to the small shade tree we have shared on so many Sunday afternoons. "You know, Jason, I'm actually going to miss this place."

I'm somewhat surprised. "We still have time to get our grass mat to sleep on. How about a water-can to continue taking splash baths?"

Half laughing, Anna continues. "Not that. I'm not even sure I remember the feel of clean sheets on a real mattress or a 'for real' hot shower, but this place has quickly become 'home' for whatever it's worth. I know we'll become comfortable at Terlingua but I've grown attached to this place. It's where I've felt safe and protected from all the chaos that's engulfed the world around us. Terlingua is nearer that world and we'll be that much closer to having to face the destruction and sorrow. I'm not sure I'm ready for that. I may never be."

Taking Anna's hand, I answer. "I know what you mean. I can hardly wait to transition from camping to living again, but a piece of my heart has taken root up here. As for the rest of the world, we're not going to explore that for some time. It won't be safe for many more months and some places won't be safe in our lifetime. We have to be really careful."

Anna's eyes turn to mine. "What do you mean?"

I explain. "Nuclear plants; the reactors shut down automatically but there hasn't been power to the pumps that keep water in the spent fuel rod tanks and the water that was there has certainly boiled off. Depending on prevailing wind, there's a lot of radioactive poisoned territory to contend with. It will be hard to find a safe place anywhere east of the Mississippi but I wouldn't go within 200 miles north of either Houston or Dallas. Jim helped us draw some maps that we printed and laminated. They show every U.S. nuke plant with prevailing wind notations. We should be able to locate safe places to live.

Anna has a concerned look. "I think I remember you telling me about this before. What about people who don't know about the radiation? What if their homes are there or they move back?"

"Radiation poisoning is slow," I say. "There are people, mostly elderly, who never obeyed the evacuation plan around Chernobyl. They're probably still living there without any side effects. They are already old enough that by the time cancer develops; they will have died of other causes anyway. It's the young and future generations that get hit by radiation. We have a precious package to care for and for his sake, we're going to be very careful."

Anna quickly responds. "Or for her sake. We could have a girl, you know."

First light finds the trucks loaded and all are ready to start the drive. One last walk to check every hut and every building for neglected things; there are none. As we gather for prayer before leaving, Rachel Taylor makes an observation.

"Did you notice the huts were all cleaned? The dust is

sure to pour in as soon as we leave but every hut was swept and straightened like we were coming back in a day or two. It says a lot for our people, I think."

Rachel's husband Harry offers an answer. "It's respect, I think. What we had here was crude but it was built on the sacrifice and hard work of many. Leaving it clean is a way of expressing thanks. It speaks more than words for me, at least."

We all join hands and pray for safe travel then take our assigned spaces among all the packages of food and belongings.

Travis ties three small scrubby trees to the back of the cargo trailer behind the last Ranger. It raises some dust but also erases the tire tracks left by our caravan. It will be difficult to locate this canyon home by tracking, and with the entrance so secluded, a person will have to know where it is or be guided by God himself. Either will be OK with us.

This chapter of our life is closed but a new one is just beginning.

# Settling In:

The ride to Terlingua is slow but enjoyable. We're in no hurry and there are many memories to sift through as we pass landmarks that trigger them. Anticipation mounts as new vistas come into view. We finally get word that we are about there.

Turning into a cluster of buildings that defines Terlingua, it's not evident that it could accommodate our needs but half the camp is already here and settled. There's obviously more to Terlingua than meets the eye.

Scott is first to meet the trucks. "Glad you made it! We sure missed you guys. It feels like reunion time."

Grinning, I reply. "After only one night? I didn't think we were that close, Scott."

Leaving the truck, I reach to shake Scott's hand and we start unloading bundles. "This is the last of it. We left a small cache of food and water but not much.  How are things here?  Is everyone finding a spot to call home?"

"This place is pretty nice." Says Scott. "It's a big step up from Camp.  Nicky teamed up with the innkeeper's wife, Adelaide, you'll like her, and they put people and rooms together pretty well.  They even have rooms all picked out for the rest of you.  I think they have you bunked in the goat shed."

"Thanks Scotty." Anna says.  "It's always good to know you have my back."

Scott helps carry our bags to a wagon-like cart.  "It's a bit of a walk to your room but you'll like it."  Scott leads the way.

Anna replies, "Good, I can use a walk."

We follow a path with signs pointing to a ghost town.  Other signs are marked 'Viper Crossing' and Anna speaks up again.

"Scotty, I think I might prefer the goat shed.  Where are you taking us?"

With a big grin, Scott explains.  "You're going to love this.  The guest rooms are actually IN the ghost town.  In fact, some of the rooms are restored ghost town buildings.  Don't judge this book by the cover, you gotta see this place."

At least I see some of the others from camp and none of them appear unhappy.  Everyone's relaxing and appear to be taking a day off. Nobody seems to know what to do, apart from exploring new surroundings.

We pass ruins of derelict buildings and arrive at a beautifully restored cottage. Anna comments, "This is nice. How many are bunked here?"

Scott stops pulling the cart and answers, "That depends on how many you invite to sleep over. This is all yours and Jason's. Welcome sorta home."

"You're kidding." I reply, "You mean there are enough lodgings for everyone to have their own place?"

"Not exactly," he says, "There were enough lodgings for all the families to have their own place but we single scum still have to bunk up." Scott is smiling at his self-deprecating humor. "Actually, we chose it that way. All the single guys are on fold-a-beds and staying in a place they used for conferences. We still have soft mattresses, clean sheets, and private showers so there's no love lost. We've kinda grown on each other so the company is good. The single girls all took one of the bigger family cabins and everybody is happy. I can tell you this; I slept really good last night. Wait 'til you re-explore the wonders of modern living."

Entering the cottage, Anna is delighted. "This is beautiful. Jason, I can't believe it."

I am impressed but add, "Five months ago, we would have just said this was 'nice.' It's amazing how the end of the world can change your perspective. It does look good after such a long time."

Scott has hardly gone and I hear water running. Anna has found the shower. She doesn't run the water for long and I hear her excitedly call to me. "Jason, they have soaps and shampoo here! I think I've died and gone to Heaven! You have to see this shower! It's made like a stone wall."

The water runs and stops a few times more before Anna asks me, "Are the windows closed? ...I mean the curtains."

With a quick pull on the cord to close the blinds, I answer. "All secure on the western front."

Anna emerges from the shower area, wrapped in a big bath towel. She is radiantly smiling as if she had ridden her first horse. "I feel WONDERFUL!!!!" Then she wraps her wet arms around my neck and plants a soggy kiss on me. Pulling her head back, she shakes her head and sprays me with water from her wet hair.

I kiss her back and say, "Hold on beautiful, there's water enough for me to take my own shower."

Anna goes to our bags to find some clean clothes to put on and when she bends over, I pop her on the backside as I head for a quick shower myself. I am going to like this place.

It's amazing how good you feel after a real shower. It's not that the 'splash baths' we had at camp didn't get the job done, but there was always a line waiting for you to get done so they could clean up. Having our own shower is a luxury.

We find most of our leadership team, along with Travis, in the large building near the road. They are meeting with Lucas and Adelaide Maxwell.

Mom is speaking with Adelaide. "Adelaide, I want to thank you again for your kindness in offering us refuge for the winter. Whatever we can do to help is yours for the asking."

Adelaide replies, "Cynthia, I have to confess, I wasn't too sure what was coming on us when Lucas told me y'all were going to stay. But when your precious families arrived, I was sure it was the Lord's doing. These children have slain my heart and I'm glad you're here."

Lucas interrupts, "To tell ya the truth, we was gettin' pretty lonely and thought about leavin'. There's a few ranchers left and we kin reach 'em on the ranch radios but some of them are thinkin' we's all that's left. Don't look like we'll be spendin' a lonely winter this year." Lucas' smile was a mile wide.

Fred speaks up, "We don't mean to be an inconvenience to you folks. We have a lot of talented people and everyone is a hard worker. Even the children have learned to pull their weight. We can cook, clean, wash, mend, and build. At camp we had daily routines and projects that kept everyone busy all day. It would be a big help to us if you could provide us with a list of things you need done. I'm not sure this group knows how to act if they're idle."

Crews are formed as food and supplies are loaded into store rooms. Adelaide shows Stephanie and Christi the restaurant kitchen as Roxy and her crew locates the laundry area. There's still no electricity but the stoves run on propane and the ladies quickly assign work teams to begin setting up clothes line.

I'm amazed again at how well our people rise to a challenge. I just hope Lucas and Adelaide don't become overwhelmed by our invasion.

Lunch is served in the restaurant with Lucas and Adelaide joining most of the leadership team at their table. The restaurant is also the theater and saloon but hasn't had much business since the crash. Anna and I sit across the table from Mom and Dad.

Lucas comments, "We haven't eaten in here in months. Since the country went south, Adelaide and me has been all there was. No sense firing up that big stove just for the two of us. This is a grand room; I've always liked it here."

Mom notices Anna's hair. "Anna, your hair looks very pretty today."

Anna is anxious to tell, "Mom, they have REAL shampoo and soaps here. I couldn't wait to use a real shower. It was HEAVEN and it smells SO good."

"I'll be looking forward to that!" Mom replies, "Tell me about your room. Where did they find for you?"

"They call it "Clem's Room" for some reason but it's elegant and I love it. The shower is made of stone and it's beautiful. Have you been to your place yet?"

Mom answers, "We're sharing the Cinnabar Suite with Fred and Irene. We have two separate bedrooms just like at camp." With a twinkle in Mom's eye, she leans toward Anna and says, "We must have you over after the maid cleans up."

Both ladies laugh as Harry stands and gets everyone's attention.

Harry speaks, "Can I have everyone's attention?" The room grows quiet. "Thanks. I believe I share a common feeling that God has been caring for us and providing for our needs during these difficult times. Camp was a blessing for its protected location and also for its needs. The work we accomplished kept us occupied and our minds from worries beyond our abilities. Now we have found another temporary place that affords us protection from the cold of winter. On behalf of us all, I offer thanks to Lucas and Adelaide Maxwell for being our gracious host." The room erupts in applause. "I would also like to offer a prayer of gratitude for God's care and have asked Allen Duncan to lead us in that prayer."

Allen stands as hands fold and heads bow.

"Gracious Father, we offer thanks for your protective hand and the provision you have made for our many needs. May your blessings fall on this place and your angels protect it from harm. Thank you for your grace shown to us through the Maxwell's and may your blessings also fill their lives. We rest our future, our health, and our path in your care. In the blessed name of Jesus, amen."

A unified 'amen' rises from the room as Dad stands and announces, "We'll meet tonight, after dinner here, to discuss plans for the future of our group. I find it hard to call you a group because I feel more like we are a family than anything else. God bless each of you and thank you for getting us here. We couldn't have done this without each of you making it happen."

Adelaide sees everyone buss their own dishes and as each table is cleaned and chairs set in order, she says, "I think I'm growing to like this bunch more and more. They sure are house broken."

A hearty chuckle rises from the group at the table they are with. We all head back to our rooms or continue exploring the old mining camp.

Travis and his sons head back to their cabin but plan to visit when they can. Pat and Travis meet before they leave and Travis tells Pat how he can be contacted.

"We listen to Jim's reports without a miss. If you need us for something, tell Jim that he's more than welcome to drop on by. If you're having a social event and want to send us an invite, just tell him that he's welcome to drop on by. We'll come up for Sunday services every other week and all the regular holidays."

"Sounds like a good plan." Pat says. "We'll miss seeing you more often but understand the fuel shortage. Be careful on the roads."

Travis, Willie, Greg, and Pete all shake hands with Pat and several others that come by to say farewell. As they get into their truck for the drive home, Christi and

Stephanie hand each of the men a box of fresh made chocolate chip cookies to tide them over until they can make it back.

Willie says, "Ladies, you're going to spoil us rotten but it's the best rotten I've ever felt. Thank you."

"Us too," say Pete and Greg. "Thanks."

The engine starts and Travis slowly pulls out. We're waving as though we'll never see them again but even two weeks seems like a long time to be away from friends.

# Organizing:

Terlingua is not without its challenges. Finding a corral for the goats is not a problem but making it so that the goats can't walk right out.... is. These are horse corrals but we can make them work. The goats will just have to stay in their trailer until we get it adapted for them.

There is a secluded cottage that will serve well if we need an infirmary. For now, the medical center is at what used to be the store. There are counters here and for most needs, it is a centralized location. Anna and Jackie are setting things up. It's also where the new communications center is. Pat Wagoner is busy setting up his ham radio gear and catches interest from Lucas.

Lucas makes small talk as he helps Pat set up. "Yer antenna is better than what we been usin'. All we got is a shortwave set so we don't git ta talk, just listen. Still, we hear a guy three times a week and he tells the news. It helps."

Pat is intrigued. "That wouldn't happen to be XF1-FNF and a guy named Jim, would it?"

"That's the guy! You listen to him too?" Lucas asks.

Pat stops to give Lucas his full attention. "Jim is our contact in Mexico. He's actually a remote part of our group. We'll be able to talk with him tomorrow evening, I'm sure he'll be glad to know there are others who listen for him."

"I'm not the only one." Lucas says, "Most the ranchers out here tune him in. It's a big help ta know at least somethin' o' what's goin' on in other places."

As Pat and Lucas work on running the antenna wire outside, Lucas has an idea. "Ya know, a while back, we had a three legged metal pole that hung a light for the store. It was handy but took away from the looks o' things. Didn't belong in a ghost town. Well, that don't matter now and I bet it'd suit hangin' your wire on. Let me see if'n I can lay hands on it."

Lucas comes back with good news. "I found it. A couple o' your men are bringin' it around. It was in the back o' one o' the buildings next ta the horse shed. It bolts on a cement pad ta the right o' this window."

Pat goes out to look at what is obviously a forty foot communications tower. "Lucas, I think you just found a gold mine. This is exactly what we need to set up a really good antenna."

Bolted down to the concrete pad, the tower needs no other support. Pat rigs a carbineer to act as a pulley and a rope to pull up the antenna, once the tower is in place. Pat turns to Lucas and says, "Care to spend a sleepless night listening to ham radio?"

"I bet we can snoop the world for news. When ya wanna start?" asks Lucas

Pat replies, "How about nine? We should be able to work Europe by then."

"Good by me," says Lucas

Pat asks, "It's none of my business but I'm interested in how you and Adelaide found your way out here to this place. Terlingua is unique and you meet a lot of interesting people but yours is hardly an occupation you would find in a jobs listing. Is it a good story?"

"Some think so," he says. "I come home from serving in Korea. All da news was on Vietnam but I ends up in Korea just da same. I was young an' a bit disheartened by how we was treated by da government. Folks back home never knew what we had did an' then we was just dumped out an sent packin' by the Army. Heroes one day an' extra bags da next. Discharged, they call it. More like tossed out. I bought me a motorbike an' went drivin'. No place special, just seein' places. I come by dis place an here was Adelaide, workin' tables an' anythin' else dat needed doin'. Her folks started da place so she come along as free help. Our eyes met an' I was done. I stayed, an' worked fer room an' board 'til Adelaide got convinced ta marry me. We ran off, intendin' ta make a life away from here but it didn't take. This place called us back. No place else ever fit. We couldn't git comfortable anywheres else so we come back.  When Adelaide's folks passed, we took over.  Bin here ever since."

Pat's smiling.  "That's a great love story.  I don't know that I've ever heard a better one.  You and Adelaide are both blessed to have found each other.  Thanks for sharing it."

Nicky is setting up the 'mailboxes' from camp and has found a place over the counter for the community information board.  Marge Wagoner helps her as they chat about the biggest news to hit since they all arrived.... Anna and Jason's baby.

Marge mentions first.  "Have you heard when the baby is due?"

Nicky replies so quickly that it has obviously been on her mind too.  "No, does Anna even know for sure?  I heard from Jackie that it was a surprise to both of them."

Just as Marge was about to answer, Melinda Wagoner walks in and joins her mother in law and Nicky.  Marge greets her.  "Hello dear, we were just talking about when Anna's baby will come."

Melinda jumps right into the conversation.  "How exciting.  Being a nurse, at least she can give herself good care."

All the ladies laugh as several more women walk into the building and join the conversation.  Questions, comments, and predictions fill the room until they spot Jackie and Anna about to enter the room.  Everything goes from full cackle to a graveyard hush in a quarter second.

Anna looks over at the silent group and says. "Half a dozen ladies gathered in one place and nobody has anything to say? Now I wonder who you could have been talking about before I walked up?"

Nicky speaks up. "YOU were, silly. Get over here and tell us about the baby. We're dying for news like a bunch of gossiping old hens!"

All the women laugh again as Pat turns to Lucas and says, "Let's get out of here. This place is going to be busy for a while."

As Lucas goes out the door with Pat, he turns and asks with a high pitched voice, "So Pat, when ya s'pose the baby'll be born?"

Pat and Lucas just laugh and keep walking.

The meeting after dinner is more of a jam session for speculation but it does provide focus for the group.

Dad starts it off. "Thanks again to everyone for helping out and making things work. Lucas and Adelaide... on good advisement; I am assured that every shower in Terlingua has been tested." The room erupts into raucous laughter.

Dad continues, "As nice as Terlingua will be to winter in, we must remember that spring will come and that we are in the midst of a desert. Without extensive supply of outside resource, it cannot support our numbers and we must make plans for migration to sustainable land. Some may choose to remain with the group but some may have plans more fitting to their individual needs and circumstance. What we each need to do is actively think of what our desires and plans will be and to voice them so that others may act accordingly. Would it be appropriate to ask that we each state our intentions in two weeks?"

Sam Elliott stands and is recognized. "Matt, before I say anything, I want to personally thank you for your care of this motley crew that we now call a family."

Applause and some cheers fill the room and subside as Sam continues.

"I am not the least in doubt that many of us would not be here today but for your generosity and kindness. Personally, the thought of leaving has not crossed my mind, though eventually we all need to cross that bridge. One thought I do wish to share is that spring comes early in these parts and two weeks is a long time. I recommend we shorten that to one week. If we all take the time to work on it, I think we can know what we will do in that time-frame."

Paul Sayer says, "I second that."

Dad responds, "Well, we've never been sticklers for Robert's Rules of Order but we do have a motion on the floor and a second. Are there any questions or further discussion regarding this subject? "

Nicky stands and is recognized. "Some decisions may change based on the decisions of others. I have family that may still be alive in Montana but I have no way to get there. If I could ride with a family going that way, I might decide to join them but won't know of that possibility until decisions are due. How can we address this potential situation?"

Dad replies, "Good point, Nicky. And I pray your family is well as we do for all our extended families. I believe the first wave of decisions will be the most difficult with contingent plans a bit easier. Let's not hold the one week plans as final and allow the second week for alterations to those plans. Is that acceptable by all?"

After a loud response, Dad continues. "It appears unanimous but any opposed, same sign. "No response is heard. "Well, that carries it.

That evening in their room, Mom eases herself into a soaking tub of hot water and bath salts. She is taken with how luxurious it feels and how romantic the room looks in candle light. As she relaxes and lets herself unwind she feels just a twinge of guilt that she has perhaps the only tub in Terlingua. Maybe she should tell, but not right away. After nearly four months of splash baths, a bath tub is simply amazing. Mom will sleep well tonight.

# Lists:

The community information board is rearranged and clipboards are hang on nails at the bottom edge. The list with the most names is under the heading "STAYING WITH THE GROUP" but another is marked "GOING TO MEXICO" and begins with Ramón and Imelda Ramos and their three children Thomas, Lupe, and Zach. A third list begins under "TEXAS HILL COUNTRY." On it are Bob and Lisa Isham with their three children, Trevor, Hailey, and Amber. Under their names is Paul Sayer.

No other lists appear for now but there are asterisks by three names on the list to stay with the group. They are Nicky and Jackie Chambers, who are considering passage to Montana, and Stephanie Sweeny, who is looking for contact and perhaps travel to north Colorado.

Some have not decided on a list yet, some are still thinking it over but others such as Travis, Willie, Greg, and Pete will remain in the Big Bend area.

Deciding where to go as a group is not an easy decision. It took us two trips to drive here from camp and that was with trucks and trailers belonging to Travis, the Isham's, and Paul Sayer. We need to find serviceable vehicles that can transport everyone and all cargo in one trip. Before that, we need to decide where that place will be.

Our leadership team gathers in the dining area to discuss options. Harry speaks first.

"I think we'll agree that north is about the only direction we can head. Mexico won't let us in." Smiles and chuckles come from several. "We also have to avoid metropolitan areas." Harry lays out a map of the southwestern U.S. with oblong circles reaching north of Houston and Dallas/Ft. Worth. "These circles are the radiation hot zones emanating from nuclear power plants. Prevailing winds are estimated to establish the zones. We're lucky in this part of the country. There isn't much of the eastern U.S. that isn't hot. You can see that in the west, we have a good pathway between the zones. Next we need an area that can support dry-land farming because irrigation systems won't be running. I've rated farming communities that look favorable from one to five according to the attributes of, consistent weather, prime agricultural farm land, will support dry-land farming, isolated from metropolitan areas, and within a thousand miles of here."

We all look over the map as Fred Livingston comments. "Good job, Harry. Why don't you rate the Lubbock area very high? Never mind, I know already. Except for the new cotton, everything needs irrigation."

"Not that everywhere can't have drought," says Dad, "but we're certainly more prone to it down here. I agree that things look a lot better up in Kansas but that's nearly a thousand miles. Getting us all there with our equipment is going to be a challenge. Currently we don't have vehicles to make the trip. We'll need a scouting trip too."

Sam Elliott has been pondering the road trip requirements. Sam is a logistician and gifted at working out details, which no doubt lent to his success as a project manager at O.S.I.

"I figure a scout trip in late February will be about the earliest the weather will let us travel that far north. By then I doubt many hostiles will have survived and those who prepared should start coming out again. We could send a work truck with two extra barrels of diesel and a ranger on a trailer for backup. That should be enough fuel for the round trip. As long as the roads are passable and bridges still standing, a team could make the trip up and back in a week. They'd have three days to scout the area."

"OK," says Harry, "do we have a rough plan to put before the group?"

"It's still rough but it's a plan." Says Fred, and we all agree to offer it to the group at the next meeting.

I find Anna and we take some time for a walk together. Anna's pregnancy is showing and I think she looks beautiful.

"How are you feeling?" I ask.

Anna is simply glowing and replies. "Well, I didn't think I was having any morning sickness but now the 'off feeling' I was having has gone away, maybe that was morning sickness. At any rate, it's gone and I'm feeling better." Anna stops walking and puts my hand on her tummy. "Can you feel that? I just felt the baby move."

I wait a moment and there it is. "I feel that! There really IS a baby in there; and I thought you were just eating too many cookies."

Anna's mood suddenly changes as she turns to me and asks. "Jason, do you think I'm fat? Do I look ugly to you?"

I've not seen Anna like this before. She isn't playing with me or angry, she's genuinely unsure and vulnerable. I've hit a soft spot in her Viking armor as I realize how much she needs my protection during this time. In my most sincere voice, I take her into my arms.

"Anna, you have never been more attractive to me than right now. The sight of you carrying our baby is the most beautiful image that I will cherish forever. Your skin glows, your hair glistens, your eyes sparkle, and you are doing all that while growing our baby inside you. I couldn't love you more and I'm excited to be your husband and lover."

Her arms squeeze a hug around my chest and I can detect some wet spots on my shirt. Anna sheds tears as she says "I love you." Nothing more needs saying.

We slowly continue our walk and end up on a rise that affords a vista of the surrounding landscape.

She says, "This place has its own kind of beauty but I'm glad we're not going to live here. I could get real tired of all this, especially after it gets hot. Have you guys come up with any ideas where we can go?"

I reply, "Harry has the map identifying areas to stay clear of and areas with prime farmland. It will help narrow the field and make an ultimate decision easier for the group but it's looking pretty good for rural Kansas."

"Kansas!" Anna has her smile back, "Isn't that where Dorothy and Toto got into trouble?"

I pull Anna to me again for another hug. "You are my amazing wife and I love you."

Thanksgiving arrives and we purpose to keep our thoughts on what we have to be thankful for and not on the failings of our government or the acts of an unbridled society. We hold services in the restored ghost town chapel and Allen Duncan delivers a really challenging message. I think Allen may have found his calling. It feels good to be in a real church again even though the pew benches have no backs to them. Our group nearly fills the space and our singing never sounded better reverberating off the high stone walls. The chapel is restored to host special events and weddings but to have it serve as a church again somehow feels so right. After all the work to restore the building, it looks as though now the spirit of this place is restored however I'm not sure how long we will continue to use the chapel as it's not heated. Anna and I sit together with her wearing the beautiful green maternity dress that Rita sent and a blanket for us to both sit on and wrap over our shoulders for warmth. I'm thankful for the two weeks we spent in Hawaii before sailing Intrepid. I had packed some nice clothes for dinners out and I'm wearing them again for the first time since we left Hawaii. They aren't designed for this cold but at least they look nice. I'm also thankful for a warm blooded pregnant wife to sit with on a chilly Sunday morning.

Thanksgiving must also have come for the many feral hogs around Terlingua. Neither Bob Isham nor Brent Palmer manage to bag one for our feast. Adelaide Maxwell saves the day. From the back of their pantry, she pulls out three Country Hams and two canned hams. Stephanie Sweeny and Christi Duncan join with Adelaide to put together a magnificent feast with mashed potatoes and gravy, ham, deviled eggs, sweet potatoes topped with marshmallows, biscuits, and even pumpkin pie served with real coffee.

Lucas had never seen or tasted milo flour but everyone understood his comment.

"I don't know what da women done wit da biscuits an pie crust but it were plum fit."

It's late afternoon and the sun is already starting down. We eat late and some food is still out, if anyone could possibly be hungry. We don't need another meal today.

Sitting with Anna in the dining area, where everyone seems to congregate, she starts the conversation. "I've noticed a conspicuous 'not noticing' of Scott and Roxy. Have you?"

"Now that you mention it, they've been real quiet and to themselves lately. What do you think is up?"

"I'm not sure," says Anna. "Scott is spending all his time with her and she doesn't seem to mind. In fact, she's got that 'twitter-pated' look about her. This might be getting more serious."

"George and Jackie seem to be falling more 'in-like' with each other too." I add. "We could be having ourselves a situation. Might even have to ordain us a minister."

Anna's look is priceless. It's a cross between shock and realization of natural occurrences. Her response says volumes.

"Maybe this is the start of a new beginning. Maybe it's the hope we all need."

# Winter:

There's not a lot to do during winter in Terlingua. The hunting teams seem busy and are bringing in some fresh game but we aren't pressed to build or solve as many problems like we were at camp. Mostly we're waiting for spring. To pass the time, we do chores for the Maxwell's and listen to short wave radio for news.

The news isn't good. Canada is holding on but not thriving and Mexico is struggling to maintain. It appears a lot of countries depended more on the U.S. economy than they care to admit. Europe is in shambles. England, France, Spain, Ireland, Italy, and Portugal are consumed with domestic troubles with Islam. Greece and Turkey have fallen. Open fighting by insurgents against the European police and regular army is hampered by borders that they won't cross but the terrorists do. The Middle East is erupting in continued battles. Each Arab country is taking shots at Israel only to find retaliation with force. Without U.S. aid, a battle of attrition will favor the Arabs. The only thing slowing the attacks is that without the U.S. economy and its thirst for Arab oil, they lack capital to buy advanced weaponry and even Russia is strapped to produce enough for their own campaigns, much less sell any to Islamic states. Most former eastern bloc nations have been recovered by Russia, and China has taken Taiwan and its surrounding islands in an expanded new empire. America is seen as a wasteland that no one wishes to visit. What's left of the American military is suspected to be harboring near the west coast as the eastern half of the country is unsafe from radiation. There is still concern that an invasion of American soil could bring a response from missile silos deep in hardened sites with their own power source. For now, foreign invasion seems remote.

America's population loss is considered by most credible sources to be at or perhaps more than eighty percent. To think all this change has happened in four short months. I'm deeply saddened as I grieve for a once great nation that started with God as her head.

Here in the southern tip of America, it seems so far away. Technology had made the world a smaller place. I could board a jet and in a day, be solving oil field problems for some remote country half way around the world. Today the world is large again and our greatest problems are right here in a little town called Terlingua.

Without a lot of chores, morning comes on its own. There's little reason to rise early. Stephanie and Christi have more than enough volunteers to help in the kitchen and the Palmer girls have taken to washing all the dishes just to have something to do. Winter is a slow time.

The extra sleep and reduced work load is good for Anna though. She seems to need more sleep as the baby grows. She needs more time to eat too but it's all going to the baby.

Christmas is coming but there is no shopping center or money to buy with. Anna and I are sharing notes from what we observe.

She says, "It seems everyone is being sneaky about something. There are signs of craft projects in process but nothing to see. A lot more sewing is going on. The ladies have gone to time sharing for the treadle sewing machine. Irene Livingston has found a sudden interest in her teaching a knitting class. Several women and young ladies all seem to have something important to do but when you ask them what they're doing, they say nothing."

"The guys aren't much better." I say, "I see shavings of wood carving everywhere but no object of their efforts. A whole pile of stretched and tanned rabbit fur suddenly went missing but the owner of said furs wasn't complaining. There were even some extended absences that were unaccounted for but when concern is made to leadership, they say it is OK and not to worry. Allen Duncan is even up to something with Scott and George. Figure THAT one out. There's some Christmas hustle afoot and I think it's maintaining sanity for an otherwise stir-crazy group."

Winter weather is bringing lower temperatures and

many in our group didn't pack for it. The July 'bug out' wasn't expected to last this long and a lot of people thought they would be returning home. Most of our former homes are now in the Houston hot zone so we have all we're going to get from there. Jim and Rita send a few things but Baja Mexico is no place to shop for winter clothing. I locate Harry to talk this over.

"Harry, I have a concern with the spring trip up north."

Harry is good natured and easy to talk with. He keeps an open mind. "Just one? I like that. It ought to be easier to solve than all the 'ones' I have. What's on your mind?"

"The weather is getting colder and I've noticed a lot of our group doesn't have much in the way of warm clothing," I say. "If we're cold down here, how do we plan to stay warm through a Midwest winter?"

"Good call but you're not the first to come up with it," he says, "We expect to pass through some towns and suburbs of cities that are uninhabitable now but should have a lot of clothing that held little value during the collapse. We'll be doing some careful scavenging as we go but only by select teams. What they'll have to sift through to find what we need, won't be a sight for children's eyes. I don't think any of us will like what we see."

"Aren't we avoiding populated areas?" I ask.

"We are," he says, "but the trip will be eight months after collapse, there won't be airborne pathogens to worry about. We'll bring our own water, keep to the road, the scavenging teams will use gloves, and everything will be washed before use. The real threat will be contaminated ground water. I wouldn't even trust a sealed well within fifty miles of a heavily populated area. We're already working a list of high priority items to look for."

"Sounds like you're working out the bugs." I say, "Thanks for the insight. When it comes time, count me in for the team."

"Thanks, Jason. I'll do that. It's appreciated," he says.

Our Christmas dinner and celebration lasts nearly the whole day. We hold services in the theater/dining hall since both day and night temperatures have dropped nearly ten more degrees. It's comical to see members of our group wearing socks for mittens and towels for scarves. Each person seems to have at least one secret bundle with them.

Bob and Brent snare a feral hog that dresses out at a hundred pounds. It is too cold for anyone to volunteer watching an outdoor pit barbeque, or maybe it's that they don't want to be away from all the people inside. Either way, the pig is quartered and roasted in the gas oven.

Gift exchanges are a private event but they occur all over the dining room. Lucas and Adelaide seem to have withdrawn from the group and sit to one side but several children and some adults seek them out to give them gifts from the heart. The look of unexpected joy on their face is truly what Christmas is about. I do believe I see some tears in Lucas' eyes. Adelaide can't speak much but she sure passes out the hugs.

There are knitted scarves, mittens, socks, and two sweaters. Several hand sewn shirts and a well-made pair of work pants are gifted. Carved toys and decorations for a wall explain the mounds of shavings I saw. Bob Isham steals the heart of every younger lady in the room when he gives rabbit fur mufflers to all seven girls under the age of sixteen. Then he gives his wife Lisa a beautiful rabbit fur jacket. The gifts go on and not a single person goes without at least one. Then from the corner of the room, Roxanne lets out a scream.

All eyes shift to find Roxanne sitting on a bench seat and Scott kneeling in front of her. She has just opened a small box and in it is a hand crafted ring. Though no one but Roxanne has heard what Scott said, everyone hears her excited scream and instant answer.

"YES!!! I will marry you!"

With the whole room breaking into a mix of applause, clamor, congratulations, and a rush to greet the newly engaged couple, Anna's expression is joyful but not surprised. Her words say it all.

"Saw THAT coming didn't we?"

There is little hope of getting anywhere near Scott and Rocky for a while so Anna and I sit by ourselves as she expresses some concern.

"I've been thinking this over. How do we make marriages without any license or documentation? I mean, will it be legal?"

I take a moment to compose a good answer. "Well, there have been marriages made long before the government poked their nose into things; I guess we can do without them again. One marriage from the Bible has always peaked my interest. When Isaac married Rebecca; all that's recorded is that she got off the camel, Isaac took her into his mother's tent, and they became husband and wife."

Anna has a provocative smile as she says, "What? Not even a rabbi, no ceremony, no tax deductions?"

Joining her humor, I add. "And not even a wedding cake or reception. THAT's not right. You gotta have a reception. If there's a marriage, you gotta have dancing and cake."

After a pause I continue. "For generations, the record of marriages in a family was the front page of the family Bible. The government only got into it for tax purposes. Taxes were the only claim for licensing or regulation. After that, they took the ball and ran with it until today; most think the State is the authority."

Anna's smile drops to a more serious look. "And they made sacrilege of it with divorce rulings, consensual polygamy, and gay marriage. Marriage belongs to the church. The government should never have been allowed use of the term. We should have limited them to civil unions. It would have stopped a lot of problems.... So, how are we going to facilitate this Biblical marriage? I don't think Scott should just take Rocky to his tent."

I'm chuckling. "No, I doubt Scott, Rocky, or anyone

else would feel comfortable with that. Like I mentioned, Allen may have found a new calling. We began 'Church of the Bend' without a pastor but we seem we have one by default. Allen has done a great job and everyone enjoys his spiritual attention. If he's willing, maybe we need to make it official. A church answers to God and is granted authority to approve and call leaders. We don't need outside approval."

No sooner does the commotion settle down over Scott and Rocky's engagement then another announcement is made. This time it's George Hardin standing on a chair calling for everyone's attention.

"First, I want to congratulate Scott for catching Rocky at a moment of indiscretion and her acceptance of his proposal." Low laughter is heard among most of us there but smiles are everywhere. "However, with stunning forethought and anticipation of stealing half their wedding cake, I have asked Jackie Chambers to marry me and she has said YES!!!"

Jackie is beaming, Nicky is hugging her neck, and pandemonium again engulfs the room.

I stand, applaud, turn to Anna and say, "We better make Allen official, he's getting behind."

# Church:

I guess it's fortunate that Christmas came late in the week this year because 'Church of the Bend' is in need of a business meeting. Mittens and fur mufflers have replaced most of the socks that used to keep fingers warm. Lisa Isham is the 'belle of the ball' with her new fur jacket. Allen is already prepped with advanced notice of my intentions and will accept the will of the group. As everyone sits, waiting for the service to begin, I stand to speak.

Having church services in the dining area has its advantages. We don't have to go far for dinner. The bad side is having to smell the food during the message.

"Good morning everyone. Before we begin our service, I have an item of church business that I would like to offer before you. I've enjoyed Allen's ministry and look forward his message each week but when we began, we didn't see a need for a pastor in an official capacity. Though we saw no need, we apparently had the need and Allen has filled it well. Today, we have not one but two freshly engaged couples who would like to marry." All eyes turn to Scott, Rocky, George, and Jackie who are seated together on the second row of chairs. "I propose that we, as an independent church, officially call and ordain Allen Duncan as our pastor, so that he might perform these weddings as a duly appointed and called minister of the gospel."

Fred Livingston stands. "I second the motion. Let's make official, what God has made obvious."

Without even a call for vote the unified voice of the congregation says, "AYE!!!"

Bob Isham speaks loudly from his seat on the third row. "We may have butchered Roberts Rule but it looks like we have a pastor, if he'll accept us."

Allen Duncan stands and all grow quiet as he speaks. "Thank you for your confidence and calling, I will accept the position as long as you don't make me wear a robe or funny collar."

Among joyous Amen's, church begins with a secure feeling that we are not just passing time with shared devotions, we are now a real church with a mission.... and soon, a double wedding. Singing is powerful, giving rise to a unified group with hope amidst a country in despair.

Dad and I are left stranded as Mom and Anna get some time with Rocky and Jackie to make wedding plans. Dad is truly a great leader and it shows not only through our companies but in the quiet way he supports people with what they need to succeed.

"Jason, this double wedding couldn't have come at a better time. When we first got here, I was concerned that idleness would get people down but the newness of getting organized carried us quite some ways. Then we caught new wind with all the guessing over your baby coming. We got busy with Thanksgiving and followed it with Christmas gift making."

I interrupt Dad for just a moment. "I heard from several that you brought up the subject of Christmas gifts and when they lamented not having stores, it was your suggestion that they make their gifts like in pioneer days. I think you secretly orchestrated this Christmas bash from behind the scenes."

Dad smiles knowingly and says, "Wasn't it Ronald Reagan who said that it's amazing how much can be done when you don't care who gets credit for the ideas? All I did was feed imagination that was already there. That's my point though. Right after New Years, people often make decisions that are not well considered because they are empty inside and have lost hope. Christmas and New Years are such epic events that the sudden stop, coupled with a cold gray winter, makes for rash decisions founded on despair. It's going to be a long wait from New Years to mid march when the team goes on recon. This wedding needs to be big and involve the whole camp. It's what will provide purpose and hope until we find the next chapter. Every exit plan needs to be the beginning of the next action."

I finally see where Dad has done this with our family all along. Generally, we had a lot of events coming naturally but there were a few times when he would come up with a party, road trip, or vacation that fit right into a schedule void and require a lot of organizing. I see now that it was all according to plan. It was the expectation and anticipation that sustained us. He's rightfully still my hero.

Anna and Mom are talking with Jackie and Rocky about their plans but are especially interested in their rings.

Anna asks Jackie. "Your rings are beautiful and I hear the boys made them. How did they do it? Did they tell you?"

Holding out her silver colored ring proudly, Jackie answers. "They may not be gold but I wouldn't trade mine for a pound of gold. Allen... maybe I should say Pastor Allen now... Anyway, he helped the guys with the metal pouring but George and Scott each designed our rings first, out of candle wax. Then they put them into plaster molds and heated them up so the wax would melt out. This is where Allen helped. They gathered aluminum and melted it so they could pour it into the mold. Once it hardened they washed away the plaster and smoothed and polished the rings. George told me they had to do it three times before mine came out right. Aren't they beautiful?"

Roxanne shows off her ring with a triple rose pattern while Jackie's has an eagle with outstretched wings along the band. Roxanne says, "They say they'll replace these with gold ones when they can but I'll never let this one out of my sight. I found out the guys got Christi to teach them cake decorating tricks so they could apply that to wax carving. She never caught on to what they were planning."

"I guess we know where to get a cake decorated." Mom says. "Have you girls decided when you want the wedding? The whole camp seems to want to help."

"The four of us were talking it over," said Roxanne. "The boys don't care so it's up to us. We thought about a small intimate wedding but with everyone so excited, I'd hate to disappoint them. Even the Palmer girls said they'd weave a grass runner."

All four ladies laugh, but Mom says, "You know... that might be a nice touch. It could add a link to the camp where you all met. Maybe not a full runner, but maybe a mat to stand on. It could add some symbolism."

Jackie says, "It will have to be two mats, but I like the idea. I guess it will depend on when the Johnson grass grows down here. Flowers too, for that matter, I wonder when they start blooming in this desert?"

Anna comments. "One thing will be easy. No need for invitations or a guest list."

The ladies continue with regular bursts of laughter. They are having a great time and Anna is grateful that her pregnancy is no longer the center of attention for the camp.

# New Year's:

With only seven days between Christmas and New Years it seems like the celebrating just continues. A party is held in the theater/dining area and for entertainment we have a talent night. Most of the talent is comic but some of the Wagoner children are very accomplished at the piano. Everyone is impressed.

George Hardin, John Stubbs, and Scott Iverson perform the first skit called "Watch Your Hat & Coat." On the stage is a table, covered with a floor length table cloth. A coat rack stands behind them next to a sign that reads, "Not Responsible For Stolen Items." George and Scott walk on stage as George explains that even though this restaurant is in a really bad part of town, it serves great food. He does admit that he has only eaten lunch here and that dinner time clientele look creepy. They both appear nervous as they constantly look back at their coats. John enters as the server while nerves seem to get the best of Scott and George. They order just a cup of soup for dinner and eat it hurriedly. Feeling good that no one has touched their hats or coats, they stand to leave with only their long underwear showing as someone apparently has stolen their pants.

The entire audience laughs hysterically and the mood is set for the night.

Our night ends with a more serious tone. Allen brings a short message of hope and we join in prayer as each person names friends and family we are concerned for. Every year is different but this begins one like no other. Most of the world we knew is gone and we have no idea what this new world will be like.

George Hardin and I talk of the changes and anticipation of what's expected. George says, "I don't think we can ever be prepared for what's left of things. When I was in Junior High, the principal came to our class and called me to the hall. Everyone thought I was in trouble but I had the feeling that it was something else. Even knowing that wasn't enough to prepare me for what Mr. Arboghast had to say. Our school secretary, Mrs. Anders, was with him. I could tell she had been crying and Mr. Arboghast was upset too. Then he put his hand on my shoulder and told me there was an accident and both my parents were killed instantly. Jason, there's no way to be prepared for your world to change that much; that fast."

"George, I never knew that about your life. What happened after that?"

"You'd think that was enough for any kid but it was

only the beginning," he says. "I had no brothers or sisters and with no parents, I was at the mercy of the state. It was a circus between both sides of the family. Everybody wanted 'me' but I think it was more of wanting the house my folks left and I was the extra baggage. Aunt Dee and Uncle Ed were who I was sent to after a judge said the estate would be put in trust for my care and education. Most relatives dropped interest when they learned they wouldn't have control of the money but Dee and Ed still wanted me. I had to move to their farm in Iowa and attend a rural school; what a change for a city kid. I'm tellin' ya, my life changed... big time."

"How did you adjust?" I ask.

"Well," he says, "My first fight happened on the first day of school. Some big kid made a crack about my folks and I lit into him hard."

"Did you win?" I'm surprised and curious.

"No," he says with a smile. "He beat the crap outa me but afterward, when he found out about the accident and my folks dying, he apologized and became my best friend. Dan and I stayed in contact right up to the collapse. If he's still alive, he's on the family farm in Iowa. Their farm isn't huge but they grow much of their own food. There's a good chance they'll come out of this."

I ask, "How long did you stay with your Aunt Dee and Uncle Ed?"

George stands and turns the chair around that he was

sitting on then sits backwards on it again. "I graduated high school and went on to Iowa State. Working on Dee and Ed's farm built me up pretty good but I still couldn't make the cut to play football, so I opted for civil engineering. I got my bachelor degree and ended up leaving Iowa for Houston. Three years ago, I was hired at O.S.I.:"

"What attracted you to O.S.I.?" I ask.

With a big grin, he says, "I heard you had a really cute girl working in accounting."

Laughing with George, I say, "That's as good a reason as any."

At camp and now here in Terlingua, we live in a controlled environment. Our faith is unified and we exist as a family. Concern for one another is what binds us together and we are still isolated from the destruction that has torn our country apart. This is about to change. In ten short weeks, we send out a survey team and upon their return, we will be baptized into the ugly reality of what has become of our homeland.

Our prayer tonight is sincere and in earnest. God's grace and favor has sustained us but we will need that grace abundantly in the following days.

Anna is into her third trimester and her tummy is weighing on her more noticeably. Walking has become a means of finding another place to sit down with no pleasure in the journey.

We're in our cottage talking. Anna's sitting on the bed and I'm a little concerned about near events.

"Have you thought out how we're going to deliver our baby? I mean, you're the most highly trained medical person we have but it's you that's having the baby? Who's going to attend the birth?"

Anna generally has things like this under control and this is no exception. "I've been talking this up with the ladies and found that Marge Wagoner is quite the pioneer woman. She makes soap, raises chickens, and grows a garden."

I interrupt. "That's great if you believe babies are found under a cabbage leaf but can she help with delivery?"

"You silly." Anna replies. "I was getting to that. Marge has been interested in pioneer life for a long time and has read most of all four Foxfire books. She has also attended the home births of each of her four grandchildren and assisted with two of them. She will be my midwife and Jackie can assist her. I've been teaching Jackie a lot about emergency medical procedures and she learns quickly. I think I'm in good hands. Besides, you'll be there too."

"I will?" I ask as I move behind Anna and cuddle her in my arms, "What's my job?"

"You, my dear husband, are there for me. You are my labor coach and comforter."

"Who's going to comfort me?" I ask, with a smile.

Anna smiles back. "Your comfort will be knowing that you are doing what God put you here for. It was in the vows.... Remember?"

"Oh, yeah" I say. "I almost forgot that part. I'm glad you were listening."

Anna pokes me in the ribs with her elbow but she's smiling and I give her a squeeze hug back.

# Showers:

With the activity surrounding a double wedding it's hard to believe that February will be here in another week. Adelaide finds a bolt of beautiful white fabric and though it isn't enough to make two full wedding dresses, it is enough to make two full skirts with trains that look like the bottom half of a wedding dress. With the brides wearing a white blouse and veil, they will look beautiful. Of course, I haven't seen the dresses but Anna tells me all about them. There's some superstition of bad luck if the groom sees the dress and since I'm male, the women decide the rule must apply to all men. I think they are using this to justify their hen parties.

After dinner, everyone stays put. Something is up. The door opens and Bob Isham comes in with something large under a sheet. We all think it's for the wedding couples but he stops in front of Anna and sets it down.

"Anna and Jason, this is for you," says Bob.

We are both surprised as Anna takes off the sheet to reveal a beautifully handmade baby cradle. Anna is in tears.

"It's beautiful!" she says. "Thank you, it's perfect."

"We haven't forgotten about you two," says Mom, as many stand in line to place handmade gifts into the cradle. There are toys for the baby, knitted baby blankets, and Jackie brings a gift that evokes a hug from Anna. Jackie has learned to knit from Irene's class and made some booties for the baby. It is a throwback to the day Anna opened and found the Early Pregnancy Tester that Rita had sent.

Anna said, "Well, now I guess IS the time to knit booties. Thanks Jackie. This means so much."

The kitchen doors open as Stephanie, Christie, and Kathy Palmer each parade in with cakes in their hands. The first says 'Happy Baby'; the second says 'George and Jackie'; and the third says 'Scott and Rocky.'

Mom says again, "We didn't forget about the wedding couples either."

As the cakes reach the tables where the couples are seated, gifts are placed on the tables next to the cakes.

Some gifts are funny messages, like a medicine bottle with 'Patience' written on the label. Another is more serious and sincere. It's an envelope with coupons to the new wife from the new husband for: chores to be done, dates out, back and foot rubs, and other acts of kindness that are always appreciated. The other envelope contains coupons of similar nature from the wife to the husband.

Eating the cakes becomes a group effort and in short order, there are few pieces left.

Nicky, Jackie, and Roxanne walk back to their cottage after the shower. With the wedding in just a few days, they talk of future plans.

Nicky begins, "Do Scott or George have plans set for after you're married?"

Jackie and Roxanne look toward each other but Jackie answers first. "George and I talked it out. He knows we want to find out about our folks in Montana and he has family in Iowa. For the short term, we plan to stick with the group. Things are still pretty unstable but when it's safe, we'd like to make the trip."

Roxanne appears to relax as Jackie shares their plans. "Scott and I have about the same idea. My folks are in rural east California and Scott's family is up in Alberta. We know his family is OK but we still don't know about mine. When travel is safe again, we'd like to go see them but for now, we're also staying with the group. There's safety in numbers."

Nicky shares. "It looks like we all want to find out about family but I'm glad you're waiting 'til it's safe. I'd be willing to bet our parents are as worried for us as we are for them. I'm going to talk with Pat to see if they have any answers from the ham radio."

Pat and Lucas are setting up the radio after the

bridal/baby shower so Nicky goes to listen in and talk with Pat.

"Hello Nicky," says Pat.   "What brings you out tonight?"

"Hi Pat... Lucas."  Lucas doesn't like to be called Mr. Maxwell.  "I wanted to ask you about what ham radio is doing since the collapse."

"Ask away," Pat replies. "The chatter won't start for a few more minutes. Things start to wake up about ten."

Nicky gathers her thoughts.  "Well, since phone service is gone and the internet is dead, radio is all that's left. Are there ham operators in every state?"

"That's not easy to say," Pat says.  "There are a lot more listeners than are willing to transmit.   Violence has come way down and operators are starting to come back on the air. What did you have in mind?  Are you trying to reach somewhere in particular?"

Nicky continues.  "My parents don't have a radio but I'm pretty sure someone in their town does.  I was thinking that if we could organize all these radios to work together, we could sorta build a message system. I know there are a lot of people who are separated from family. It would be nice to get word to them."

"Nicky, amateur radio is way ahead of you.  Amateur operators have been working with the military to assist passing emergency and other messaging since 1925. The system is called MARS, Military Auxiliary Radio Service. Since then, two other emergency message services have been formed under FEMA. RACES stands for Radio Amateur Civil Emergency Service and ARES is the Amateur Radio Emergency Service. All three practice message passing over designated frequencies and times. Right now, we're seeing the system start to rebuild as operators get back online. One problem we're finding is that the old system depended on home address, email, and telephone number. None of those work anymore so we're developing work around methods. Another is that everyone is on battery power and that limits each station's transmit time. We're working to establish a digital text network to save power and increase up time for the stations but it's all just coming together at this point."

Nicky pulls up a chair as she asks, "How do you find a ham operator that's near the person you want to get a message to?"

Pat pulls out a rolled poster size map of the US/Canada/Alaska. Unrolled, Nicky can see that it's marked into grids with longitude, latitude, and numbers assigned to squares. "This map is called a Grid Square Map and it gives us a quick general location for any place in the US or Canada. Officially, we go by longitude and latitude plus the grid square number but many just tell us the state they're in and add the grid square number to localize it. We use a form to pass messages we call 'traffic.' It starts with the 'local operator,' me, and a 'distant operator,' who I pass the message to. The message has name and location information of the person originating the message, the message, and the name and location information of the person we're trying to reach. I search for a contact with an operator who is closer to the destination and pass the message to them. They do the same and eventually, the message gets to who we're sending it to. With the huge reduction in population since the crash, if we get a message to the local area, people there should know something about them."

Nicky is impressed. "When do you think it will be up and running? Could we send a message now?"

"We can always try," says Pat. "Who are you trying to reach?"

"Northwest Montana," Nicky says as she looks at the map. "My folks would be in square thirty-six or thirty-seven."

Pat begins to write. "From N5OSI; to... we'll fill that in later. Originator, Nicky..."

"Nicky and Jackie," Nicky adds.

"Nicky and Jackie Chambers," Pat continues. "To,..." Pat looks up at Nicky

"Ron and Jennifer Chambers, Rock Creek Road, Philipsburg Montana" replies Nicky

"Ron and Jennifer Chambers; Location, Rock Creek Road, Philipsburg Montana, grid square 36/37; Message,... OK, what do you want to tell them?"

Nicky ponders a moment and then replies. "We are safe and well with good company. Jackie is getting married to George Hardin. He is a good man. I approve. Miss you greatly. Please reply. Love, Nicky."

Pat laughs and says, "It sounds like a letter from camp but it will work. If it gets through, I bet you get a response right back. I'll send it off tonight. This may take several days to get there and the same to get a reply. On the other end, they may need to ask around to locate your folks and that could take another few days. This system isn't perfect or fast but it does work. Let's hope for the best."

"I just want to know they are alive and well," Nicky responds. Not much else matters."

Nicky returns to her cottage while Pat and Lucas begin working the radio bands for news and message traffic.

316    Showers:

# Wedding Plans:

"Adelaide," says Mom, "where are we going to put these two new couples for their wedding night? Can I help?"

Adelaide pulls out her room booking chart and looks it over. "Hmmm, good question. With our two grooms moving out of the Rock House, we can move in some of the older boys from the Perry rooms. That gives us one more room there. Next, we can move Nicky in with Stephanie Sweeny and that gives us the second room for the newlyweds."

"Adelaide, you are amazing," Mom says. "I can't tell you what a blessing you and Lucas have been to us. There aren't words to describe it. We are surely going to miss you when we give you back your space."

"Cynthia," says Adelaide. "I'm not sure who's going to miss more at the end. We've grown kinda sweet on this big family. It's going to be real lonesome without you and especially the children."

"Adelaide, you can be sure the children will miss you and Lucas both, but we'll all stand in line for that. I'm not sure what's ahead but you'd be welcome to join us. The Midwest won't be as hot as south Texas and you would have the support of a big family. We'd love to take you with us."

"Cynthia, the offer is tempting but I'm pretty sure our place is right here. We've spent most of our lives here. I suspect we'll finish it out here too. We have enjoyed having regular church and your ladies cook some fine meals. I've enjoyed the vacation, let me tell you. But I expect some of our help will make it back, now that things are slowed down, and we'll start the place back up. We might trade rooms for supplies rather than money but trade will resume in one way or another. We'll get buy."

The wedding day has come and with it a realization that flowers do not grow here until April. Not wishing to delay the double wedding another eight weeks, both couples concede to forgo the blooms. The Palmer girls also found the Johnson grass isn't plentiful enough to weave the grass mats they intended for this blessed day but Willie comes to the rescue. He and Pete go back to the camp and find two woven mats that are still in fair shape. When Travis and the boys get to Terlingua, Willie finds the Palmer girls and tells them the story.

"I got to camp and started going through the cabins. Not a single mat was useable. I guess the winter was tough on the mice. There wasn't a single mat that wasn't chewed to bits." The girls' faces look sad as they had hoped Willie would have found some good mats. He continues. "Then I went to the community building and looked through the stacked ones there." The girls started to brighten up. "You know, those mice got to every one of those too. There were even some bugs that had taken up nesting in between some of the mats." Almost ready to give up hope, the girls waited patiently as Willie finished. "Then I looked up and you know what I saw?"

"MY MATS!!!" Exclaims Kristen. "I tossed two mats up on one of the long boards in the ceiling. Were they all right?"

Willie has a beaming smile. "They were! Not a mouse bite on either one, and no bugs! I have them in the truck."

All three girls throw hugs on Willie's neck, nearly knocking him down. They tug his arms toward the truck. With their prize in hand, Kristen, Kelly, and Kory march triumphantly to the chapel with their mats. There will be two wedding mats for the couples to stand on as they take their vows.

The wedding is beautiful. Both brides wear white blouses and simple skirts but they are wrapped with an outer layer of fabric, much like an apron worn in reverse, that flows like a wedding gown behind them. Each with a veil, the ensemble has all the appearance of a full wedding dress. The grooms wear dark pants with a white shirt and look equally handsome. Allen officiates perfectly. Both Roxanne and Jackie stop and tear up as they see the grass mats the girls made. They too had given up hope of this tie to camp days, only to have a miracle save the day. Dad and Fred stand-in to give away the brides; Nicky stands as Jackie's maid of honor while Stephanie stands for Roxanne. John Stubbs is George's best man and I am Scott's best man. Adelaide finds some silk flowers to make two bouquets so the brides have something to throw and Christi Duncan passes out milo for everyone to toss instead of rice.

As we witness the union of these four of our friends, tears fill the eyes of many. One pair of soggy eyes are Willie's as he sits amidst three young ladies who are ever grateful for his help in making this day extra special.

We adjourn to the dining hall for cake and dinner. As the single ladies line up to catch the bouquets, both brides toss them over their backs. Stephanie catches one and Lupe Ramos catches the other. Dinner is wonderful and the wedding party sits at the head table while many make toasts and well wishes.

Standing, I raise my glass to the couples. "Rocky and Scott, may God bless you together, better than you could ever know apart. Scott, you have been, and are, my best friend. I've noticed your distraction and I've watched your distraction. Now I know her name. Roxanne, I salute you for capturing a fine husband, and Scott; for winning the heart of a beautiful wife. Congratulations to you both. Now to George and Jackie; I pray God's blessing upon you as well. Jackie, you are also a beautiful bride as well as a talented worker. George, you have found gold. May God bless you both as you continue to discover the depths of love and the character you each bring to making this marriage a lasting success."

"Here, here!" is echoed across the room.

The ladies have outdone themselves in making the wedding cake. A large sheet cake makes the base but there are two upper tiers, side by side, and two bride and groom statues atop those tiers. Over the years there have been several weddings held at the Terlingua Ghost Town and left behind are ample wedding cake fixtures to accommodate the women in fashioning a wonderful cake. Another link to the camp is concealed under the frosting of the top tier cake layers. These small tiers are two layer cakes but the lower layer is somewhat heavier due to the milo flour it is made from. Both couples choose to share a piece of that cake in the traditional cake cutting ceremony. It's a solemn event. Links to the past with hope for the future is not marred with foolishness. These couples are accepting a huge challenge that is still unwritten. They are taking their vows seriously and with devotion. Probably mixed with a bit of fear also.

The couples are showered with milo as they make their way to each newly decorated wedding suite. Much like a shivaree, most of the group parades the couples to their roosts and cheers as each groom carries his bride across the threshold.

Scott closes the door and looks deeply into Roxanne's brown eyes. "I can't believe I found you and that you have blessed my life with yours. I love you, Rocky." Scott gives Roxanne a lingering kiss and their arms wrap each other into a single embrace. As he lowers

Roxanne to the bed and sits beside her, the unmistakable rattle of a cow bell clangs out. Almost immediately an uproar of laughs is heard outside their door mixed with 'congratulations, you two!' Someone has tied a cow bell to the bottom of the box spring and they have been waiting outside to hear it.

"Very FUNNY!!!!" shouts Scott as Roxanne covers her face in her hands and laughs. The crowd moves on as Roxanne questions, "I wonder what they did to George and Jackie?"

# Recon:

## [Chris' account of the expedition.]

At daybreak, the recon team forms up, making ready last details to vehicles and provisions. As much as Jason wants to join us, Anna is too close to having their baby for him to be away. Our team consists of Sam Elliott, Randy Fowler, John Stubbs, and me, Chris Spencer. Randy leads our team with me as second in command. It suits us all and Randy has a good head. Jason gives me the .308 and M79 he brought from Intrepid. They're good to have and I believe it provides him a sense of being part of the team even though he can't be with us.

Fred Livingston gives some final instructions. "You guys are as prepared for this trip as you can be but there's a lot we don't know. Be careful and stick to the plan. Keep the artillery out of sight but always ready. We don't expect any remaining hostility but be alert for the unexpected anyway. You have the list of priority items to bring back with you and things to note on the map for collection later. Again, be careful and may God bless this trip. We'll be praying for you until you return."

Pat Wagoner offers some communication updates. "We were able to mount a multi band HF radio to the truck. Keep the whip tied down like it is because it will transmit better that way. Stick to the time tables and frequencies we trained on and be prompt with your check-ins as we'll all be nervous wrecks waiting for each one. We'll probably only have reliable NVIS reception for three quarters of the trip. When that fails, loose the whip and try regular HF. I'll repeat Fred's advice, be careful and may God bless."

Allen Duncan offers a prayer and all heads bow. "Heavenly Father, please bless this trip and may your angels protect our men as they seek your will and our future home. Guide them by your providence and shield them with your grace. Amen."

All the group is there to wish the team well but Stephanie Sweeny gives Sam incentive to be safe and return home soon by planting a big kiss on him for all to see. Sam expression is startled but it's instantly replaced by a huge grin and I think I detect his chest sticking out a bit more.

Becky and Gina, likewise give me hugs and kisses. I tell Becky, "This won't be dangerous. We're being careful and we'll be back on schedule." I tell Gina, "Be good for mommy and I'll see you soon."

We have the O.S.I. truck that Allen originally drove

from Houston and they have Travis' trailer on loan. The two seat Ranger is loaded in the trailer along with three barrels of diesel that Jim has been bringing over the past few months. All our food, clothing, and supplies are in the bed of the truck behind two barrels of drinking water. We look ready to go but none of us are ready to say goodbye.

As the team nearly pulls out, Travis and his sons drive up.

Travis gets out and walks up to us. After handshakes, Travis gives some advice.

"I'm glad we made it in time. You boys be careful. Don't let yourself get lazy. Practice safe crossing at every overpass, bridge, and choke point. It's boring, tedious, and slow but it will get you home. Remember, avoidance is twice better than engagement."

As Randy starts the truck and pulls out, every eye is on them and some of them filled with tears. Nicky steps close to Stephanie while Christi draws close to Becky and Gina.

Christi says to Becky, "They'll be back in only a week but that week will be very long for some, won't it?"

Becky looks up, and with Gina in her arms, her eyes are wet with tears.

"Becky, why not help us in the kitchen this week? Gina can play in the dining area and she'll be easy to watch there. She could also play with Amber and Hailey Isham on some days. Keeping busy with Stephanie and me will help the time go by."

"I think I'd like that," says Becky. "This feels the same as when Chris deployed. It's never a good feeling."

We plan to take 385-N to 90-W, then cross over to 67N. It avoids most population centers and offers few choke points. Our speed climbs to forty miles an hour and stays there as we remember Travis' training:

*"Faster will cause you to miss something and it's what you miss that may not miss you."*

Travel is with windows open and every eye scanning the road ahead. Mile after mile passes without so much as an overpass until Marathon. Every few miles are abandoned vehicles. Stopping takes time to glass the area with binoculars and to pay special attention to the presence or lack of footprints. Footprints indicate fresh activity and perhaps trouble. Though no sign is found, each site has to be checked. Outside town, the truck comes to a stop.

"Let's unload the Ranger and take a stretch break," says Randy. "Marathon isn't on our scavenge list. We'll have to work the ranch roads to get around it. No telling what we'll find. Chris, would you take lead with Sam driving? I'll take rear guard with John at the wheel. Is everybody good with that?"

All nod agreement and the Ranger is unloaded. The ranch roads are vacant and uneventful but worse is the ten to fifteen mile an hour speed. More care must be given to dirt roads and then there's the dust that's raised.

Reaching highway 90 was supposed to be a relief but it is choked with abandoned vehicles.

I put my fist in the air, signaling all stop. I get out and walk back to the truck.

"This is a no go. How far does the map say this service road goes?"

Randy checks the trucker's atlas that Lucas had at the Terlingua store. "It looks better. Several points of access to 90 and it follows the rail tracks all the way past 67N. It could be choked and it could be set up for ambush but it doesn't look like we have much choice."

"Slow and careful rules the day," I say. "This is getting way too interesting. I hate interesting."

Weaving through abandoned cars and trucks on the service road is challenging but the highway is a death zone. Cars and trucks are everywhere and some have been burned out. Windows are broken and then... bodies. Or what's left of them.

John sees them first. "Do you see that! There's half a man over there." The top skeletal trunk of a man's body is half pulled from an open door of a car. The seatbelt is still attached from his neck to his waist but there are no legs. "What happened?"

"Scavengers," Randy answers. "Coyotes, most likely. He could have died by most anything from heat stroke to heart attack. From the looks of things, some of these people may have turned on each other."

It looks like a scene from a Halloween set. Few recognizable bodies are left but plenty of skeletal pieces torn by animals. The service road isn't vacant but it's passable.

I give the 'all stop' signal again and inch up on a truck to the side of the road. After looking inside, all I can do is kick the door and walk back to the truck.

"That truck could have been me and Becky! There's a man, a woman, and a baby inside with the doors locked. It looks like they ran out of fuel, pulled off the road and just died there. "

I'm pretty shaken up by what I saw in the truck so we sit there a bit and drink some water. Nothing prepares you for this. Nothing.

It's been slow going but we make it just short of a small town with a population barely under ten thousand. It's just inside New Mexico. This town meets our requirements for scavenging. The population size is high enough to employ a city water and sewer system and it has less than a two percent rural population. Being in the rocky desert, there are no suburbs or rural homes. Basically, this town is not habitable without power but it is small enough to have avoided the riots that destroy larger towns quickly. Those with means have left for better ground and those who remained didn't last long enough to ransack the city. We'll spend some time scavenging in the morning.

No nighttime fire is the rule. Any warm food will have to be heated tomorrow. The Ranger and truck are parked to block the wind and shifts are taken so each man gets at least a six-hour sleep. Sitting in the near dark after sunset, the others want to hear about my deployments with the Army.

"What we saw today brought back a lot of bad memories. Afghan civilians who waited too long to evacuate would have to pass right through incoming Taliban soldiers. Those animals would rape and plunder whatever caught their eye and kill anyone who resisted. They weren't soldiers; soldiers fight for a cause. Taliban are just filth and it doesn't take a soldier long to get over killing them. "

"It must have been really bad," says Sam.

"It leaves a mark," I say. "Most Afghans don't know what they believe. They're just told they are Muslim because they live in a Muslim country and that's their culture. Underneath, they are just plain people. Then there's the hater; brainwashed from the cradle to think the world is out to get them and they will be rewarded for killing and hating back. Those are the filth. You won't get into their head because they've bought into the lies. I used to think it was a Muslim thing but the same ideology has grown among inner city blacks. Then I thought it was just the Muslims and the blacks but it has been growing in the Hispanics too. So I thought it was a minority problem but the same attitude is among the gays, white supremacist groups, and liberal politics. It isn't the 'who,'... it's the 'what'... and the 'what' is hate. Hate knows no skin color or ethnic boundary. My fight is that I hate the hate so much that it blurs the difference between the person and the hate that drives them. It's easy to become what you're fighting against."

"That's what Allen was saying a few weeks back," says Randy.  "He made the point that when God said *vengeance is mine*, it was because we aren't capable of dishing it out without it getting all over us.  God said *I will repay* because evil can't spoil perfect holiness."

"I've seen it.  Good kids, raised right, then their soul is destroyed in war," I say.  "They call it post-traumatic stress disorder but I see it as just a conflicted soul.  I think it's the vengeance that does it.  Until I got a grip on the purpose of God's wrath and God's personal forgiveness of the hate that started growing in me; I was headed for death by combat.  Some of those kids couldn't go back home so they'd stay another tour.  They got bolder, took unnecessary risks, and in time, they went home in a box with a medal awarded to their family.  There's no time during a deployment to think about why you fight.  Everybody fights for the guy next to them and you do what you have to do to stay alive.  It's after you get home that the ghosts come out.  You aren't sleeping in the cot next to the guy you fight for or who fights for you.  At home, you're all alone with your soul and continually in review of every single thing you did.  It's a trial by one, and it never ends.  If you can't make it to God's judgment seat and find complete forgiveness, Satan doesn't have to come for you; you'll deliver yourself to his will.  I quit my personal quest for justice.  I couldn't kill every Taliban or even make enough of a mark to matter.  What I look for today are the ones who can be delivered from the hate.  If I can reach someone before the hate starts working, they can be sealed from its effects.  I'm still a soldier who can send a round where it needs to go but it's not personal anymore."

Sam, Randy, and John have a lot to ponder while standing guard or trying to sleep. Morning comes too soon. Sam digs a Dakota Hole for the small fire that heats a pot of cowboy coffee. It is a reserved gift from the last of Becky's stash.

We've made good time but avoiding Odessa took most of our evening. Today, we should make our way out of Texas.

# Picking:

[Chris' account of the expedition.]

Randy gives the morning briefing. "We're going into what Travis describes as a 'death-zone.' We'll probably see some disgusting things but data on this isolated town says there should be no survivors. Rural population is less than two percent with no surface water and no dry farming. Those who lived here depended exclusively on grid power for water and sewer. Being a small town, they probably didn't riot when the economy failed but when the power died, they only had a short time to get out. It's been over six months since then and we don't expect bad smells but don't open any walk-in boxes or refrigeration units. We're skipping food stores, liquor stores, gun stores, and Jewelry stores. Those will have been cleaned out first. You have the list of priority items but keep an eye out for quality warm clothing, undergarments, and work boots. The collapse started in July so it's not likely they were thinking about winter temperatures back then. If you see a pool and spa supply, look for alum based water-clarifier without algaecide, and 'Super Shock' with chlorine being the only active ingredient. Another high value item is salt. We stick together and don't plan on being here more than a few hours. Any questions?...... Good, let's go."

On the way to the shopping district Sam spots a pool supply store. It's small but yields a hundred-pound bucket of Trichloro-S-Triazinetrione.

Randy says, "This counts for a win if we don't find anything else. A quarter teaspoon will treat a barrel of water."

It appears most people did leave town early, but older cars are abandoned next to lines of all sorts of vehicles piled up at fuel stations.

"I wouldn't count on any fuel in those tanks," says Chris. "The station's tanks must have been pumped dry or these wouldn't be here."

Convenience stores at these stations are cleaned out. Not even a can of beans is left on the shelves. The town is eerie quiet with storefront doors wide open. Some windows are broken but for the most part, the town is intact with only certain stores stripped bare. It isn't like highway ninety; we aren't finding bodies. They must be here but there are no bodies on the street and there is no sign of scavengers having carted them away. No blood stains either. Looting obviously happened but there is no sign of chaos and violence.

Pulling into the shopping district provides a different

story. There are some bodies, or what's left of them, and a few broken windows next to locked doors. As expected the shells of jewelry stores, gun shops, and sporting goods stores, stand as a testament to greed and foolish priorities. Most of the scattered bones and bloodied clothing are next to those stores. In a western boot store, shoes and boots are piled highest in the athletic shoe and dress boot aisles but much less in the work boot area. Good work boots replace old shoes on each team member and about a dozen pair come with us for individuals with worn out shoes back in Terlingua. Most of the clothing is on the floor but a few Carhartt jackets make our cache.

A big hardware store is just too messed up to spend time sifting through its aisles. A smaller hardware and garden store yields a few good shovels, hoes, and tools. Their quality is better than what come in the 'big box' store anyway.

After a few hours of targeted scrounging, the trailer now holds several pair of good work boots, dry chorine powder, a fifty-pound bag of salt, and an assortment of light jackets, some underclothing, and tools. Winter clothing wasn't on the racks when these stores closed but work gloves will do.

"OK guys," announces Randy. "Daylight is burning and we need to put some miles under us. I think we've done all right for this trip. Is the map marked with this place? We might make a return shopping trip in the future."

"Got it," says Sam. "I have to say the stores are a bit messy but the self-serve aisles are great."

A mile out of town, the Ranger is put back on the trailer and Kansas looms ahead.

After seeing the chaos on the highway outside of Marathon, Sam suggests taking extra measure to avoid anything larger than a small village.

Several hours go by without incident or town that can't be bypassed.  In this country, the highways bypass the towns and unless you take an access road, you can keep on your way.  Approaching a place where two roads cross, John points forward and says, "Full stop!"  Ahead is what appears to be a roadblock made of two rows of vehicles stationed across the roadway at a dry creek crossing.

Glassing the situation carefully, I hand the binoculars to Randy and say, "Have a look.  I don't see activity but that was built on purpose.  Someone intends to stop traffic.  Can we get around it?"

Sam is already surveying the map.  "Not without a huge delay.  That dry creek bed runs a long way.  The Ranger might make it through but not the truck and certainly not with the trailer."

"It looks old," says Randy.  "Maybe it can be pushed out of the way."

"There's not much choice but to recon this thing and safe it if we can," I suggest.  "John, you want to go for a drive?"

"Ready!" John and Sam are dismounting the Ranger as I turn to Randy.

"Randy, who's the better shot, you or Sam?"

"I'm not bad but Sam hunts more and I think he's a better shot."

Tactical command is my job and fully supported by Randy, Sam, and John.

"Randy, you and Sam drive to about a hundred yards and glass the hel... heck out of it. Look for any footprints in the dirt or dust wiped off fenders or door frames where someone may have put their hand. If you see ANYTHING out of place, wave me off. I'll do the same from the far side. If it still looks old, I'll get closer after dragging the other side for wire. Sam, you keep the .308 on those car windows. If you see any activity, have Randy wave us off but keep your cross-hairs on target."

Randy comments, "Chris, I'm glad you're along. You've already covered things I would have missed. Experience is a big help right now. Thanks."

"It's OK," I say. "Just keep your eyes open. John and I will have side arms with the M79 as backup but let's hope we don't need it.   These leave such awful potholes."

John drives the Ranger off-road and toward the dry creek bed, looking for a spot to cross.   About two hundred feet east of the road, he begins his traverse. Randy is already creeping toward the roadblock while Sam glasses each car and the ground around them. The Ranger makes it over the creek bed easily and begins weaving slowly toward the cars.  I look over to Randy several times, not wanting to miss a wave-off. Randy and Sam are in position, Sam is now glassing the cars with the .308 and Randy has the binoculars. Still, nothing. John stops the Ranger as I take out a newly acquired garden hoe from the back. I begin dragging the hoe on its edge, making a narrow but deep furrow in an arc shape around the cars.

"What's he doing?" asks Sam.

"Trolling for wire," answers Randy. "He's checking for an I.E.D. I think."

Completing my furrow to the edge of the road, I cross and begin again on the far side. At Randy's eleven o'clock position, I stop cold. Slowly, I lift the hoe and there is field wire caught on the back of the blade. Signaling both Randy and John to back up as I begin unearthing the wire and following it west. Pistol drawn, in about another hundred feet, I stop again at a large growth of brush. I signal Randy and Sam to walk west and provide cover from the creek bed and for John to do the same from the roadway just north of my position. As each get in position to provide covering fire, I slowly drop to the ground and begin creeping on my belly around the brush. The wire runs to the end of a pipe sticking out of a short concrete wall.

# The Bunker:

[Chris' account of the expedition.]

"Randy, do you see that?   Behind the brush," says Sam. "You'd never see it from the road. What is it?"

"It looks like a transformer bunker," Randy answers, "like in housing areas that have underground service. What is something like that doing out here in the middle of nowhere?"

The low structure only rises a foot to eighteen inches off the ground but the dirt gradually mounds to this place, making it a vantage point that looks natural.... but it isn't natural. I move to the northwest corner and slowly move my hoe toward what appears to be a latch on the lid. With the latch released, I again use the hoe to raise the hatch while keeping my belly to the ground. Slowly, peering inside; shading my eyes with my hands I can only see the top of a ladder and blackness beyond. I return to the Ranger.

"I can't see anything but the top of a ladder and what looks like a small window facing the road. I need a light. Let's get back to the truck."

At the truck, Sam locates a small flashlight as I form a fresh plan. "It looks like the cars are rigged but it doesn't look like there's anyone to blow it or they would have by now. There's a hide behind that brush but no footprints and no sign that any have been brushed out. Randy, you return to where you and Sam were. Sam, you cover the hatch from about twenty yards back and off to the side. John, you cover the same from the north. I'll look inside."

With everyone in position, I move close to where I was and toss a rock into the hatch. The sound of the echo seems to indicate a larger room with a hard floor but there is no response from inside. Attaching the light to the blade of the garden hoe by its pocket clip, I slowly move the light over the hole and barely look inside a dimly lit room below. With more confidence, I lower the light and turn it to survey the small room.

"Come closer," Chris says. "He's dead."

With the flashlight in hand I climb down the hole. At the bottom of a seven-foot ladder is a room with a small window facing the roadblock. The remains of a man are piled up on the floor. Lying next to the bones and clothing is a rusted automatic pistol with the hammer still cocked. I release the magazine and force the slide back to remove a round from the chamber before setting the pistol back down.

"Looks like suicide," I comment. "There's a hole the

size of a baseball in the top of his skull and old blood splatter on the ceiling. Don't come down 'til I find where that wire goes."

The pipe stops just inside the room with about six feet of wire hanging loosely from it. On the floor sits a gel cell battery like would be used for a small motorcycle. I move the battery to the other side of the room.

The back of the room is covered with a dark pleated curtain and as my body disturbs the air by moving the battery, the center of the curtain moves back further than the sides do. Keeping to the side, and using the hoe to examine behind the curtain I discover a doorway directly behind the ladder. Almost missing it in the dim light, there is an AR-15 leaning against the corner at the far side. Protected by the curtain, it looks in fair shape and is definitely loaded. Removing its full magazine and checking that the chamber is empty, I lean it against the front wall and pull the curtain fully back, exposing a doorway.

"You guys gotta see this. Come on down but one of you stay up there and cover."

Randy and John come slowly down the ladder and wait at the bottom for their eyes to adjust to the dim light. Shining light through the doorway behind the ladder exposes a nearly eight-foot-wide passage leading backward approximately twenty feet into the dirt mound behind the hatch.

"Looks like a bunker," says Randy.

"Be real careful," I caution. "If this guy had the road

rigged, there's no telling what he's done down here. Don't touch without looking from all angles."

Inside the doorway and to the right, there is a light switch. Following the wires down from the switch box, they end at a bank of batteries on the lowest level of the row of shelves on this side of the corridor. The other side of the switch runs up to what looks like RV light fixtures on the ceiling. Making sure they go nowhere else, I break the plastic switch cover and examine the switch wiring. Satisfied that there are no hidden wires, I close the switch and the room lights up. Shelves line each wall along the short corridor. On the shelves are cases of military MRE meals, cases of military ammunition, several loaded rifle magazines, dozens of sealed five gallon pales labeled with food descriptions, ham radio equipment, two expedition size water filtration systems, and two backpack pump water filters. Some of the equipment has been damaged by rodents but there are enough supplies to last someone a very long time.

"Can you believe all this stuff?" asks John.

"Yup," Randy comments. "This was a prepper's lair."

"Looks like it's just for one," I comment. "I think we've found a Lone Wolf's cave."

"What's a 'Lone Wolf'?" John asks.

"A Lone Wolf is a prepper who thinks he can hide out and fight off any who may attempt to take what he has," I say. "Most of their stuff is military and they have a combat mentality. Every problem has a tactical answer and obstacles are generally met with force. This poor guy probably spent years making and provisioning this hide. I'm guessing he came here at the first hint of trouble and eventually lost his mind waiting for a fight that never came. I doubt anyone ever knew he was here."

"All dressed up, and nowhere to go," added Randy.

The end of the passage meets the middle of what appears to be another CONEX box. A flashlight sits on the end of the right hand shelf. Handing it to Randy offers them better lighting. Against the wall to the left of the second CONEX box is a single cot with a large backpack hanging on the wall, loaded and ready to go.

"Looks like he was getting ready to go somewhere," says John.

"Probably his Bug-Out bag," I reply. "It's typical to keep a fully loaded backpack in the event there are only seconds to escape an overwhelming force. Not a bad idea but where could he run, out here?"

On a small table next to the cot sits a multi powered shortwave radio with a wire twisted around the antenna and running up through a small hole in the wall, near the ceiling. Using the butt end of the hoe to strike the metal wall of the CONEX box, the resulting noise is a dull thud.

"This guy really put some work into this. I think the outside of this bunker is shelled in concrete to keep the walls from caving in. They aren't meant to be buried like this without support."

Over the bed is a small shelf of books that says a lot about the man who hid here. Every book relates to survival technique and combat tactics. Everything is about how not to die but nothing about making a life worth living. I check the book shelf from below and behind before removing a military training manual. The cover reads, RECONDO, 1970 Recon Team Manual.

"I studied this in the Army,"

As I open the book, a pin with a ring attached falls out on the bed.

Smirking, I add, "Humph, Rambo even used a grenade pin for a bookmark. I bet he felt macho."

I announce, "I'm going to check out the roadblock and see what this guy planted at the other end. Once we get the truck to this side, we can start loading all this in the trailer. I'll bet Sam is wondering what's become of us by now. You can start moving things topside but before you move anything, look for wires or anything suspicious. Look good and from several angles."

I climb out and call to Sam. "It's a bunker! There are supplies down here! I'm going to check out the roadblock and see if we can pull these cars out of the way!"

Sam acknowledges and heads to the truck to move it closer.

Following the wire back to the road, I find it surfaces where the tire of the first car almost perfectly conceals it. Wire is tucked up under the cars and passes through a small drain hole in the trunk of the middle car of the first row. The cars are situated so that the engine of one car is parallel to the trunk of another. This roadblock was well designed and an explosion from the trunk of a car in the first row would be directed by the mass of the car behind it. Thinking to myself, "*This guy was shrewd. He knew what he was doing.*"

The trunk with the wire is locked but the car has a mechanical release that's activated by a lever on the floor next to the driver's door. Getting a pair of wire cutters from the truck, I talk with Sam.

"Sam, it'd be best to pull the truck back a few hundred feet until I get this trunk open and defused. There's no telling what this guy did but he was pretty smart."

Cutting the two strands of field wire, one wire at a time to avoid making contact between the pairs and pulling the wire from the bunker, I make a loop at the end and put it over the trunk release handle, then out the driver's window and back to the side of the road as far away as the wire will let me be. From on the ground, I pull the wire, almost expecting detonation.... there is none. The trunk lid pops up about six inches and stops.

The flashlight allows me to see the wire come through the drain hole in the trunk where it connects to one lead of a blasting cap that's stuck into the end of a single stick of dynamite. The other lead of the blasting cap is not connected and the second field wire end is also hanging in the air. Raising the trunk lid exposes a twenty-pound propane cylinder sitting next to the already defused dynamite. Carefully, I inspect and remove the propane cylinder, cut the single connected lead to the blasting cap, and use the wire cutters to very slowly slide the cap out of the dynamite. After placing the cap in the culvert beneath the road, I signal Sam to bring up the truck.

Sam sees the whole thing through binoculars and says, "That could have worked out badly."

"You're telling me," I say. "The guy must have prepared for everything except wire connections. One lead came loose from the detonator cap. It never would have blown had he tried it. He's dead in his bunker and never got to live out what he made ready for. Blew his brains right out of the top of his head. I need a break."

Exhausted from the tension I exclaim, "I'm getting too old for this."

Sam looks up to see Randy and John coming from the bunker and says, "We'll start making a hole in this barricade. You take a rest."

John arrives first and looks shaken. "Chris, we found something that isn't right. If it's what we think it is, it's REALLY not right."

Randy has now caught up. "You gave some good advice, Chris. We didn't find any wires but when I started to move one of the pails, something was behind it. From the side, I could barely see what looks like a hand grenade between the pails. We didn't move anything else."

"Ohhhh...crap," I say. "I should have known. The guy has a loose pin in his book and I missed it. I'm really sorry guys. My carelessness might have gotten you killed."

"Chris, you gave us good warning and THAT's what saved our butts," replies Randy. "Don't' be hard on yourself."

"It's not worth getting blown up for ANY of that stuff but we can't leave it for someone else to find and get blown up either, I say. "Let's move these cars first and then see what we have down there."

# Perspiration:

### [Chris' account of the expedition.]

As each car is sequentially moved out of the way, I make an observation. "This guy appears to be book smart but inexperienced. He set up a good roadblock but didn't flatten the tires. NOT that I'm complaining right now. He employs a textbook force enhancer with the car bomb but let a wiring detail make it useless. His bunker is perfectly built but the location is awful. It's like he was consumed with survival but never prepared for what comes after that."

"I guess you don't have to be a survivalist to fall into that trap," Sam says. "I've seen people do this their whole life, spending fortunes and effort to extend their life only to die without a thought to what comes next."

"Speaking of what comes next," as we push the last car off to the side, I turn to Randy and announce, "I need to go back down that hole and see what you found. Tell me exactly which pails you looked at and where you saw a grenade."

"From the bunk area, facing the ladder, it is in the pocket behind and between the first and second pails on the bottom row on the left." Randy is drawing in the dirt on the hood of the car they just pushed off to the side of the road.

"OK," I say. "Give me that flashlight. I'll be a while cuz I'm going to clear the whole bunker. Unless you hear a big boom, I'll be back in a bit."

I break off a rear view mirror from one of the cars as Randy hands me the flashlight. "I might need one of these."

"Be careful. I don't want to hear any booms," says Randy.

Descending the ladder, alternative options flash through my mind along with images of Becky and Gina. Taking a moment on the floor of the bunker, I shut out those thoughts and enter a singular focus on the mission at hand. Someday, perhaps years later, a child may find this place and make it their play fort. Because I found it first, they will live to tell about it.

Ripping the cover from one of the training manuals over the bed, I look around the room and find some duct tape. It's the cure to most things broken and a staple item for any prepper. I roll the cover into a long tube and kneel down beside the pails on the left shelf unit. Carefully and slowly examining the grenade from every available angle, I can see the pin that keeps the safety lever in place has been removed. The safety lever is spring loaded but now is held in place by the side of the five-gallon pail. This booby-trap is designed to injure or kill an unsuspecting looter when one of the pails are moved and the lever released.

Finding four pails that are not rigged, I arrange them exactly as the ones holding the grenade and form the book cover into a cylinder just small enough to slide into the pocket between the four pails. Securing it with duct tape keeps the sleeve from expanding.

Back at the grenade, I tape the flashlight to the shelf unit to give me use of both hands. There is just enough room between the top of the pails and the next shelf, to work the sleeve down the space and around the grenade. The intent is to keep that safety lever in place after the pails are moved. The next few seconds will tell... if I got it right.

Gently, I slide the second bucket forward and work my hand into the gap to keep the grenade from falling over. With my hand holding the sleeve, I can feel the grenade inside as I remove it from its hiding place. Taking the roll of duct tape in my left hand and using my teeth to peel back the end of the roll, I start wrapping the cylinder with tape.

*"That's one," I say. "Let's hope this was his last hope."*

Realizing I'm talking to myself, I remember something my weapons trainer once told me.

*"Talking to yourself is normal, arguing with yourself is questionable, but losing those arguments is certifiable."*

It seems funny now.

Beginning at the bunk, I systematically and thoroughly inspect every crevice. Working around the room takes time when you're trying to get a cockroach view of the world. Discovering nothing more, I climb the ladder with my duct tapped prize.

Sam asks, "What can we do to help?"

"Do we have any scissors? "I ask.

"We have some bandage scissors in the first aid kit." Randy says. "I'll get 'em."

With scissors in Sam's hand, I hold the bundled grenade tightly with both hands and direct Sam to begin cutting the cover away from the top.

"Sam, we only want to expose the top inch of the fuse. I have the pin in my shirt pocket. Once the hole is exposed, get the pin from my pocket and put it back where it should never have left."

"Got it," says Sam as he slowly begins cutting away at the sleeve.

As the fuse and the pin hole come into view I tell Sam, "There it is, that's enough. Now get the pin from my pocket and work it back into the hole at the top of the lever. Make sure it comes out the hole on the other side."

With the pin in place I can release my grip and slide the grenade out of the paper sleeve.

As soon as the grenade clears the sleeve, I see it. "I DON'T believe it! The idiot never released the Jungle Clip! This thing wouldn't have gone off."

"What's a Jungle Clip?" asks Randy.

"This little wire thing over the lever," explains Chris. "It was added in Vietnam because jungle brush would sometimes catch on the ring and snag out the pin while the grenade is still on your pocket. That could create a lot of extra stress; to put it lightly. To fix it, a secondary safety clip was added. To arm a grenade, you have to release the Jungle Clip, THEN pull the pin, and release the lever. Our lone wolf just made two strikes. He didn't secure his wires when he rigged the roadblock and he didn't know how to arm a grenade. I bet he learned to shoot from watching movies too."

John added, "I guess suicide was strike three."

No one spoke for a moment, pausing to consider John's comment. Then I conclude, "Looks like he lived for a fantasy that never played. Let's load up what we can use and get going. We've burned a lot of time here."

Without further interruption, the Oklahoma border yields to Kansas but not much beyond as nightfall claims the day. Making a cold camp is routine but the four extra blankets from the bunker are already appreciated in this Kansas Spring night. Dinner tonight is MRE's and thanks to heating pouches that warm food packs by adding water to start a chemical reaction, it's a warm meal.

"Don't tell anyone I said this but MRE's aren't too bad

when you don't have a kitchen handy." I proclaim.

Randy unpacks the tablet computer and modem that Pat set up for texting over radio and connects it to the microphone jack of the radio. He sends a recorded text message on a preset frequency and awaits a reply.

[Text Message]  CQ CQ CQ   KF5OSI, RT1 CQ CQ CQ

After several attempts a reply is received.

[Text Reply]  RT1, KF5OSI... copy.

[Text Message]  KF5OSI, RT1... START: Delayed by abandoned  roadblock.    Recovered  new  supplies. Crossed TX/OK, arrived KS.    Should  reach  target tomorrow mid day. All safe, missing you all. OUT

[Text Reply]    RT1, KF5OSI...  START: Message received.  Praying for safe and successful return. OUT

# Full stop:

[Chris' account of the expedition.]

Sam digs another Dakota hole and heats water for coffee. After a chilly night on the ground, even instant coffee is a treat.

Randy comments. "The MRE's will be a big help on this trip. We won't have to stop and prepare meals."

Laughing, I add, "Or stop for nature breaks. MRE's are known to stop you up when you're just sitting."

With a more serious look, Randy adds, "I guess a morning walk would be good medicine. Maybe I'll start soaking a pot of beans for tonight."

"I like beans," says John. "But do we want to give away our position like that?"

"We won't need a fire," Randy says, "I can use the solar cooker as we drive...."

Then it dawns on him what John meant by giving away their position and everybody laughs.

As the miles continue to pass, Sam observes. "I haven't seen a circle field in hours. For that matter, I don't see any irrigation pipe or sprinkler systems. Let's pick a small town and look around."

"There's a fair size river up ahead with small rural towns all along it," says Randy. "No telling if anyone is there or what we'll find but we have to start somewhere."

Turning off the highway toward the next farm town, Randy's question is soon answered.

Sam stops the truck at a large clump of brush and announces, "This looks like a fire hydrant to me. Any of you dogs that need to, this is your tree."

John walks around to the front of the truck toward a small tree when the dirt explodes about six feet in front of him with a CRACK!, followed a moment later by a soft boom!"

"What was THAT!" John yells.

"That is a universal, DON'T take another step command," I explain, "I'd suggest you obey it. Everybody, stay where you are!"

John is really scared. "I'm supposed to just stand here and let someone shoot me?"

"These people have been shooting deer at twice that

range," I explain. "If they wanted you dead, you wouldn't be standin' now. Just stay put. I'll bet they're glassing us right now. I'm going to make nice."

In one hand, I take the AR-15 we got from the bunker and in the other hand the .308 from camp. Holding them over my head and walking about fifty feet in front of the truck, I lay them on the road and walk back to the truck.

In a low calm voice, I give instruction. "Now slowly, walk to the front of the truck and kneel with your hands folded behind your head. No fast movement."

Randy asks, "You think it's smart to just give up?"

"Sam's right," I say, "Did you notice the delay between the crack and the boom? The crack was from the bullet breaking the sound barrier. The boom was the rifle going off. That short delay says our shooter is between three to six hundred yards away and we already know he's a good shot. I'm willing to gamble that whoever's behind that bolt, doesn't want to shoot us down...yet."

Quietly, the faint sound of a motor grows louder and closer. A Gator ATV makes its way toward us with a driver and two armed men with shotguns.

The armed men get out and separate by about twenty feet as the driver says, "You men are fortunate to be alive right now. Two months ago, you would have been shot where you stand. We've suffered a lot of would-be looters and buried most of 'em. I want answers to three questions and you had better convince me you're tellin' the truth, or... well... we've already discussed the fate of previous liars. First, what's your names?"

"My name's Chris Spencer and to my right is Randy Fowler, Sam Elliott, and John Stubbs."

"That's a good start," says the driver. "Now, where are you from?"

Chris responds, "We came from south Texas near Big Bend, we've been on the road two days."

"Now what are you doing here?" the driver continues.

"We're scouts," I reply, "trying to recon a suitable place for a group of about fifty civilians who can't go back to their homes and need a place to begin a new life. We're not looters and mean no harm."

"We'll see about that," he says. "I'll be having to take you into town for further questioning. You'll be bound and one of these two men will be driving your truck."

"We've nothing to hide. You'll want to disarm us further," says Chris. "Each of us has a sidearm either on us or in the truck. I set out the long guns as a show of good faith... and recognition that your shooter, who's still has his crosshairs on us, is a fair shot. We're not bad men."

"Son, you're rather perceptive," says the driver, "only the shooter isn't a him but a her. She's my daughter and I've seen her drop a running deer at eight hundred yards. Uncanny how she does it."

One of the men holding shotguns moves to retrieve some rope from the back of the Gator as the driver gives further instruction. "One at a time, you boys step forward with your hands behind your back. We'll load you up in your truck for the ride into town.

Watching someone collect all your defenses and empty your guns as they tie up both you and your friends is a new level of humility. Making a run for it may had been successful but at what cost? Somehow, as bad as this appears, it seems the right thing to do.

Attempting to talk with either of the two guards proves futile. They make no sound and clearly don't wish to talk with us. One drives the truck and the other holds guard over us.

True to my guess, the Gator stops about five hundred yards up the road and picks up a young girl who can't be out of high school yet. She carries a bolt action rifle and shooter's bag. The way she carries herself and her equipment reaffirms we made the right choice not to run. I've seen plenty of US military snipers and there is a tendency for them to be a quiet sort who rarely talk shop. This girl appears no different except that she's so young. Her dark brown hair is straight, pulled back, and braided to keep out of her way. She appears athletic and has haunting gray eyes that are difficult to forget. I only get a glimpse of her eyes as she hardly pays us a glance. This girl is all business.

About a quarter mile further we come to a stop in front of a gas station/convenience store, a small post office, an old church, and a grange hall. In the distance is what looks like a small rural medical building but that's all there is to downtown wherever-we-are.

Two more men mount the truck and remove us as our guards stand ready.  The only words we hear from anyone but the driver, come from one of the two other men who simply says, "This way."

In the Grange Hall we are seated in four chairs, each in a different corner of the Hall.  It appears we are to be questioned apart from each other.

A rope is tied over our lap and under the chair, then again around our chest and behind the chair back. Now our hands are untied and questioning begins.

"What's your name?" comes a surprisingly pleasant tone from one of the previously silent guards.

"I'm Chris Spencer, recently separated US Army."

"I suspected as much," replied my interrogator. "Where are you from?"

I begin telling my story, "I grew up on a farm in Iowa, joined the Army and my wife and I and our daughter lived just south of Lubbock until the world fell apart. Things got ugly so we headed south, only to have me get sick and I nearly died in an abandoned airport hangar.  Some folks found us and took us with them to their camp up in Big Bend.  We've stuck with them since, that's where my wife and daughter are.  Those are who we're scouting a home for.  They're good people."

Prompting me to continue, the guard asks, "Is that

where your people are now?"

"Not exactly," I say. "We couldn't winter there. Buildings are too loose and hard to heat. We found a small town that took us in for the winter but it's not a place to grow food."

"Where is this town?" asks the guard.

"I'm not ready to give that up just yet," I answer, "not until I know they'll be safe."

"Understood," says the guard. "What sort of people are they?"

I continue, "Good people, God fearing. They even formed their own church and called a pastor. Most are from the same oil company in Houston. The owner took preparedness seriously and offered a lot of training. He owns the ranch where we stayed in Big Bend."

Prompting further, the guard asks, "Can these people take care of themselves?"

"The group has gardeners, engineers, hunters, fishing guides, cooks, builders, welders, soap makers... you name it. We even have a registered nurse," I explain.

At mention of an RN, the guard's attention noticeably intensifies. Taking note of the change I gather there may be a need for medical help among these people. The guard steps away and confers with the other interrogators.

Another interrogator steps up and asks similar questions, then a third, finally the fourth. After what seems like a long time of discussion between the interrogators, our ropes are removed. The driver of the Gator enters the hall and says, "Your stories match so we've decided to cut you loose. You're not free to go yet but we'll give you liberty to walk around a bit while we consider things further. Please understand that if you try to run, you'll be shot before you get to the road. We have shooters watching every way in and out. Now this is my son Josh. He'll show you where you can wash up before dinner."

Well now, I know the name of my first interrogator. Josh is still very quiet and won't give up any information about the town or what is to become of us. A pail of water is waiting on a bench outside the Grange hall and a hand towel. We each take turns washing the road dust off as I notice activity across the street in a small park area under the trees. I hadn't noticed picnic tables in the park before but a woman and two girls are setting up what looks like lunch.

Josh says just two more words, "Over there," and we walk to the park table.

As we cross the street, I see that our truck and trailer are gone, "What have you done with our truck? We have supplies in there that are needed by a lot of innocent people."

Josh only says, "It's safe. Don't worry about it."

I can see Randy, Sam, and John are real uncomfortable with how things have turned but it's not like we had any choice in the flow of things.

Lunch is simple but an improvement over MRE's. Egg-salad on a bread roll and tea taste remarkably good. Complementing the ladies, "Ma'am, we've been on the road a few days and this egg salad sandwich is really good. Thank you."

Randy, Sam, and John each nod in agreement but seem reluctant to speak.

The ladies simply say, "Your welcome," and walk away. They are polite but don't care to engage in conversation.

# Hazel Creek:

### [Chris' account of the expedition.]

After lunch we are instructed to rest here at the park table until called.  I get the feeling there is a meeting going on and our fate is being decided.

About a half hour passes and the driver of the Gator returns and tells Josh, "They're ready."

Josh and the other guard motion us to follow our Gator driver.

I mention, "It would be a lot easier if I knew more of your names than Josh, here."

No response is given.

Walking past the convenience store, I notice several of the windows are broken out and what appear to be gunfire damage to the siding.  We are directed into the church and upon entering, see a table with five men seated behind it.  Standing before them has the feel of an inquisition.

The man on the far left speaks first.  "My name is Vince Parker; I'm the acting mayor of Hazel Creek.  That's the name of this farming community that you've stumbled into.    My apologies for what you might consider inhospitable treatment but I assure you these are kind and God fearing people.   Your stories all seem to measure up but I have some further questions after examining the contents of your truck."

Vince then removes a cloth that has been covering the M79 Grenade launcher and several rounds of its ammunition.  Next to them is the hand-grenade.

Vince continues, "Would you mind explaining where you got such hardware and what 'God fearing, peaceful minded souls,' such as your selves, are doing with it?"

Skepticism is evident on each of the five men's faces.  But doom and gloom paints the faces of Randy, Sam, and John.  Strangely, though I should be frightened, I am not.

I clear my throat and begin speaking.   "I am prior military and have used grenade launchers such as this during my Army service; however, these are not mine.  It was provided to us for protection by Jason Connors who retrieved it from his father-in-law's ocean going sailboat.  Though it is considered illegal in nearly every port and country, it is one of the finer deterrents to piracy and was kept for that purpose.  Our scouting mission included the possibility of crossing paths with similarly unpleasant persons and we carried it for that purpose. I hope you understand."

Standing before these men, I remember a line my father used to tell me.

*"Truth unlocks doors a thousand lies can't open."*

I hope he's right today.

Vince covers the M79 with the cloth again and asks a few more questions.

"Pardon my skepticism but what kind of scouting mission requires thirty-seven hundred rounds of ammunition and a grenade launcher?"

I'm sure Vince was caught a bit off guard when I smiled before answering his serious question.

"I bet that does look just a bit suspicious. Yesterday, about mid-morning, we came to a roadblock protecting a bunker. The bunker wasn't active but the roadblock was wired with explosives and we had to get through. On entering the bunker, we found the single occupant had ended his life and most of the ammunition, the rusty .45, hand grenade, and the AR-15 belonged to him. That's where we got the MRE's and other survival gear. Additionally, we scavenged some essentials from an abandoned small town in New Mexico. We intend on taking that back to our group."

Vince continues his questions. "You have ham radio gear in your truck. Can you reach your group in Terlingua with it?"

Instantly, I look toward Randy, Sam, and John. It's John who lower's his head.

Vince continues, "Don't think poorly of your friends. Each person protects different information and these are minor details. Besides, we have no intention of attending the next chili cook-off. Can you reach your group from here?"

Randy answers, "We can. To save power, we use a small tablet computer with a modem to send text messages. We check in every night at ten o'clock."

"Can you talk with them, by voice?" Vince seems to be driving at something.

"We could ask them to go voice and then switch over but at first they'll be set up for data and won't recognize a voice signal." Randy explains.

Vince says, "I would like you to do that tonight while we are there and I want to speak with your leaders there."

"I'll do that," replies Randy.

Vince is the only person to have spoken more than a few words since we arrived. The others seem cold and distant.

"Your truck will be brought to the Grange Hall tonight," Vince says. "All your gear has been removed for now but it is safely stored. We aren't thieves. Tonight at ten o'clock, you will contact your group and establish a voice connection. You will only tell them that you require a voice connection, nothing more. Is that understood?"

"Understood." Randy replies. "Next to the radio in the truck is a radio log book. It contains alternate frequencies and information that I might need if the propagation changes."

Before he can say more, Vince replies, "It will be there with the radio."

We are ushered out to wait in the Grange Hall under guard. The guards don't seem as tense but they still aren't willing to answer questions. The hours pass very slowly.

John says his first words since we were apprehended and his emotions are running high. "Chris, if these people kill us, I may NEVER speak to you again. What the hell is going on?"

Randy adds, "I can't figure these people out either. They all act like they stepped out of a horror movie."

"This looks bad on the surface but I trust my gut on this one," I say. "If they wanted to kill us; we'd already be dead. If they intend to loot our supplies; why haven't they done it? Something happened here but this is Kansas and these people are farmers of America's heartland. I think they're scared and cautious but exactly the kind of people we're looking for. Their questions are honest and as long as our answers don't hide anything, we'll be OK.... and John, I truly value your conversation and wouldn't dream of jeopardizing it."

For the first time in Hazel Creek, we have something to smile about.

Sam speaks his first since arriving.  "I've been watching.  Vince is the spokesman but the others seem to have a say.  They're like a board or something.  Their concerns seem to be answered but they're not sold yet.  This is like a contractor bid meeting.  We're still in the game but the decision is pending."

"What do we do if this turns ugly?" asks John.

"Let's wait and see." I suggest.  "It's too early to implement an exit plan but I've been noting all the routes out."

# Town Meeting:

## [Chris' account of the expedition.]

Supper is a far cry from bread and water. We're certainly not being fed like prisoners. A large basket is delivered to the guards with plates and cups for us to eat from the same food the guards are fed. Chicken and rice with biscuits, gravy, and fresh milk makes for a good meal. The only difference is that we are only allowed spoons while the guards get forks. We still can't get the guards to talk, not even over supper.

Evening turns to night as the sound of our truck's engine stops at the door. Vince enters and motions for only Randy to follow him.

[Text Message]  CQ CQ CQ   KF5OSI, RECON TEAM 1 CQ CQ CQ

[Text Reply]  RECON TEAM 1, KF5OSI... copy.

[Text Message]  KF5OSI, RECON TEAM 1... START:

arrived KS  Request voice link OUT

[Text Reply]    RECON TEAM 1, KF5OSI... copy
Request voice link OUT

Randy is escorted back to us and fills us in.  "I requested a voice link and as soon as Pat came on, Vince took the mic and they brought me back here. The only warning I could give was spelling out RECON TEAM. Pat came up with that as an alert but I had no way to tell him what the alert was for."

"Who all was out there?" I ask.

"Larry, Moe, Curly, Shemp, and Vince," Randy replies.

"Funny," I say, "but save the names until you know what motivates them, still... in the absence of real names, you can get stuck with what pops up."

After nearly twenty minutes, Vince returns with the four others.  They're not frowning and the reduced tension is obvious.

"I think it's time we introduce ourselves.  You know my name's Vince Parker, this is Daemon Eckerd, Elmer Tousley, Dwight Woodard, and Louis Roth.  I guess you could say we're the clearing board for Hazel Creek. I just spoke with Pat Wagoner and a Matt Connors. They corroborate your stories and seem like good folks. I don't want to get your hopes up but our report will have to be accepted by a community vote and if they approve, there may be room in this town for your group.  We've certainly lost many more than that this year.  I can't say which way the decision will go.  These people have been through an awful time and may want to just be left alone.  You do have resources we could use and that may help.  Tonight was the first friendly contact we've had from outside town since the lights went off.  We have a retired doctor among us but he is stretched thin and says he could really use a nurse.  Hazel Creek is a fine town with good people who have been stretched beyond the limits of most.  I hope you'll understand our need to check you out.  I'd like to offer you my hand."

Vince steps forward and offers his hand to me.  It's not an imposing handshake that he expects to be received, but rather a humble offering.  I accept it and when our hands join, the room suddenly loses its hostility and handshakes follow between each of us, the board, and the guards.  Voices flow, guards suddenly have names and voices, and best of all... the shotguns are set aside.

"I'm Josh Bennett and this is Keith Reed," Our former guards shake our hands.  "I'm real glad we didn't have to shoot you guys.  You're different than the others."

Sam and I make eye contact and both of our eyes are raised.  "I'm real glad you didn't have reason to." Sam replies.

Elmer explains, "We'll give our report at the meeting tomorrow mid-day.  There'll be a time for discussion after which, you'll all be brought in.  Each of you will introduce and tell something about yourselves, then you'll leave and a vote will be taken.  The vote is final and has to be two thirds in favor for approval."

"What if the vote isn't enough?" asks John.

Daemon continues, "You've already been cleared of being a threat. No harm will come to you. If the vote to accept you is declined, you'll be free to go but not to return. If you are found after that... well... don't be."

Randy asks, "What of our truck and supplies?"

Louis answers, "Nothing you have is of concern to us. Our defenses are effective and disciplined. You will be allowed to take what you brought but we may barter a bit if you have a mind to trade."

I sleep some but not soundly, anticipating the fateful meeting and perhaps a possible answer to our mission. We're allowed access to our personal bags which lets us clean up and shave in the Hall washroom before the town gets a first impression.

Sam comments as he rinses his face after shaving, "I feel half human again."

"Now if you could do something about that smell." Randy's quick wit reflects a hopeful attitude.

"You know," I say. "I've been noticing the truck doesn't smell fresh anymore. It'd do us all well to be friendlier with the soap."

Half laughs fill the washroom as the four of us share two small sinks.

Most farms keep large fuel reserves to run tractors and farm equipment but when that is gone, there is no tanker truck coming for a refill. Fuel is precious and many come to the town meeting by bicycle or on foot.

One truck pulls up with a hay wagon full of people. I guess that's the new mass transit. We watch through the Grange Hall window and wait to be called.

Josh steps in and motions us to follow him. "Everybody's seated in the church for the meeting. I'm going to let you sit in the foyer on the bench but don't make no sound."

The double outside doors open to a small foyer with a pew bench against the right wall. Inside, another set of double doors apparently leads to the auditorium. We quietly sit and can hear the meeting.

Dwight opens the meeting, "As we begin, for the sake of order, I'm asking you all to refrain from making any comment until discussion is opened. I realize this is a tough subject, especially for some, but please hear all of what we present before making judgment or comments that might hinder someone from making their own informed decision. For the first time, we have apprehended some visitors that appear peaceful. They have been thoroughly examined and each of them confirms the exact same story. They fully confess that they are a scouting party for a group of about fifty men, women, and children whose homes have been destroyed or rendered such that they cannot return to them. Last night, we allowed them to contact their group by radio and without notice we took charge of the radio and spoke with their leaders who verified both their needs and the mission of this team. These people are much like us except they have been driven from their homes by various causes. They are engineers, homemakers, builders, and have among their numbers a registered nurse whom I have learned as of last night is very close to birthing their first child. Now before we open this to discussion, I must entertain a motion from the board."

Vince Parker stands and addresses the room. "Thank you, Mr. Chairman. After thorough examination of these four men, and after speaking to their leaders, and with unanimous support of the board, I motion to accept this group of about fifty persons into our community as neighbors."

Dwight continues, "Thank you for that motion, do we have a second?"

"Second," says Daemon Eckerd

Dwight resumes, "The motion is moved and seconded to accept this group of about fifty persons as represented by the four men we have found, into our community as neighbors. We will now open the floor to discussion. Please speak clearly and in turn, we will allow for everyone who wishes, ample time to express their feelings on this matter."

Fred Elkhart stands and is recognized. "Where are these people from and how far away are they now?"

Vince stands, "Currently they are wintering in Terlingua, Texas, and having visited there on two occasions, I can tell you they can't last there long. Prior to that, they fled from the Houston area mostly but a few are from surrounding towns in south Texas. It would take them at least two days to get here, if approved."

Dick Reed stands and is recognized. "I'm tryin' real hard to believe there are good men left in this world but after those bastards killed my wife and little girl last summer, I'm real slow to warm up to the idea. I think one of the best things we did was to put an outhouse over the pit where we buried the sons-a-bitches.

Dwight has to regain order as I begin to realize some of the evil this town has faced.

Emily Bennett stands and is recognized. "Lisa Reed was my best friend and Dick, there's not a day I don't grieve her loss and for Emma too. We lost a lot of neighbors and friends in the battles. Some of those losses are deeper than flesh as I see the change that came over my own daughter Karin after she learned to kill a man as quick as she could a deer. We've all paid a huge price and I just want it to be over. If these people are like you say, maybe accepting them can be a first step forward to building a better place for our children."

From the foyer we listen as others speak of horrible acts committed by despicable people. Our safe harbor of 'Camp' insulated us from the spilling out of horror that ensued as desperate, violent, and unprepared masses, spiraled out of cities to the surrounding communities. These honest, God fearing people learned from losses to fight back, but the soldier's curse was there to consume them. Now they are being asked to exercise compassion over hate. Can they bury their anger as they have their enemies? This vote will tell.

Dwight addresses the room once more. "If everyone

has spoken their peace, before we take the vote, I want you to meet these four men and hear from them yourselves. Josh Bennett, please bring them in."

# The Vote:

[Chris' account of the expedition.]

"My name is Chris Spencer. I'm recently separated honorably from the United States Army. I have a wife, Becky, and we have a three-year-old daughter, Gina. We lived near Lubbock and after the power failed; our neighborhoods began to be looted by gangs from town. It wasn't safe so Becky, Gina, and I loaded what food and water we had and headed south. I got dehydrated and took sick. We were hiding in an abandoned airport hangar when people from this group found us. They took us to their camp and saved my life. We've stayed with them since and I can tell you, they have been angels of mercy for my family. If you accept us, they will be an asset to your families."

"I'm Randy Fowler. I grew up with the son of the owner of the property referred to as 'Camp.' It's where we hid while the world came apart. Watching the leadership team pray for us and organize a group of fifty to live in a space designed for ten; not only allowed us to survive, it allowed my faith to grow. We saw God provide for our needs on a daily basis. These people are good people and if you vote no, God will provide for them in some other place, but if you vote yes, you will bring that blessing right here."

"I'm John. I've worked with Randy and seen him supervise what we call 'the Pit.' It's where we burned limestone to make our own cement and crushed dried clay for other building needs. It was hot, dry, dirty... and one of the best jobs I've ever worked. We all got along like brothers and I've seen that same attitude in the others. There's something special about this group and I hope you accept us as neighbors."

"Sam Elliott is my name. I was a project manager for the company that Matt Connors owns. He and his son Jason are not like wealthy business owners who get wrapped up in their money. They each take personal interest and care for every person they come in contact with. The business reached beyond the employees and included families. Now I've been listening to what these other guys have been telling you and it does sound a bit much to believe that people 'that good' are out there. If I wasn't part of it, I'd probably have trouble swallowing it too. What I can tell you is that no matter where they end up, I want to be there with them."

Dwight again takes the podium. "As our guests return to their place outside, we'll call for the vote.

Returning to the foyer, we hear the vote being called. "All those in favor of accepting this group of fifty, or so, people into our community, please signify by saying aye."

A large group of voices can be heard. "AYE!"

Dwight continues, "Opposed, same sign."

A lesser but still significant group of voices can be heard. "NAY!"

Dwight proceeds, "All those in favor of accepting this group of fifty, or so, people into our community, please signify by raising your hand for a hand count."

There is silence as the count is made.

Dwight continues, "Opposed, same sign for a hand count."

With the count completed, Louis Roth presents the count to the chairman.

Dwight reads the count. "Of eighty-two perspective votes we have by hand count; fifty-nine votes in favor; twenty-two opposed; with three abstaining, the ayes have it. Josh, please bring in our new neighbors."

Vince Parker steps to the podium as we enter. "Friends and neighbors, this can be the beginning of our return from the ashes IF our new friends decide to accept US as neighbors. It is ultimately their choice now. Chris, Randy, Sam, and John, this valley has rich soil and enough precipitation to farm without irrigation. Furthermore, we are blessed with good amounts of game and fair fishing in the river that flows through town. Sadly, there are many vacant homes and good farms that need occupants. Will you consider moving here and becoming our neighbors?"

Their offer seems sincere but we haven't seen much of the area. I try to make my answer friendly but with explanation. "First, I want to thank you for the offer. We've not seen much of the land yet but I do personally know of some of what you've had to endure these past few months. War changes a person and that change doesn't wash off. You have treated us with respect and in light of how you have been treated by others, it speaks well of the kind of people you still are. If we can be allowed to complete our mission and see the area, I can assure you of a favorable report to our leadership board."

"I know this to be one of the sweetest places God created," Vince replies. "At least it was before the world fell apart. I'd be glad to arrange a guided tour, if you'd like. There's a lot more to this place than these few buildings."

Many of the townspeople come and shake hands but most of the smiles are only complimentary. A tall man without any smile approaches Sam and shakes his hand before speaking.

"My name's Dick Reed. I'm one of the votes against the measure but I don't want you to take it personal. You folks sound like good people but there's a lot of hurt in Hazel Creek. Folks need some time to heal and I think they'd do it best with just their neighbors and friends. I'm outvoted and it's the way of things but I'm not your enemy and I'll help you folks settle in once you get here."

Sam looks him in the eye and says, "Thanks Dick. I hope we can change your mind and help the recovery. I think your town paid an awful price and we're grateful for a place to settle."

Sam does not smile when talking with Dick. There are times when a smile cheapens your words and this is one of those times.

Randy, Sam, John, and I go in different directions, spending the day exploring Hazel Creek. It is much as described and there are plenty of available homes. Randy and our former guard, Josh, take the Ranger while Sam and Byron Bennett take the Gator he was driving the day we came to town. John is enjoying his literal ride through the country as he and Elmer Tousley are on horseback. I'm spending the day with Vince Parker in his mid-size pickup truck. I apologize for taking up their gas but he has a good answer.

"We might as well drive it while we can. Most the farms have fuel tanks but gas doesn't last past six to eight months and we're close to that already. Stabilizer can help but we only ever kept enough to winterize small equipment. We're trying to drive the gassers now. The diesel lasts longer but even that won't last us more than another six months if we ration our use. I've been meaning to ask you... how are you getting your people up here? Do you have it worked out?"

"Partly," I confess. "We have some diesel saved up but we're short a few vehicles. It's not an easy drive and I'd hate to make two trips."

"Let me work on that," says Vince. "We may have an option."

Touring the many farms and properties around Hazel Creek sheds light to how bad their struggle has been. Several homes are burned out with unmistakable sign of massive weapons fire. Even charred wood is riddled with bullet holes and the fresh graves I assume are former residents. As explained at the meeting, bad guys receive no honor or grave marking.

At the edge of town, a small park stands vacant. Nearly the entire front grass area appears to have been tilled but not furrowed for planting. In the center of what looks like a sixteen by twenty-four-foot plot, stands a solitary outhouse. The only marker for this town's 'boot hill.'

Randy, Sam, John and I, regroup after our sightseeing and follow directions to where we are to eat tonight. Supper, as they call the evening meal here, is served for us at the home and farm of Bryon and Emily Bennett. Their long driveway serves two houses but the second house has been burned to the foundation. Only the barn, pump house, and feed shed still stand.

"Welcome to our home," says Byron as he comes to greet us. "I see you found us, I hope the directions were easy enough. Please come in and meet the family. The girls would come out but they're busy in the kitchen."

We follow Byron through a side door entering into a rec-room of what appears to be an addition to the traditional two story farmhouse. Mrs. Bennett comes down two steps from the kitchen area, wiping her hands on her apron before shaking our hands.

"I'm so glad you could come.  Would you like some tea?  Please, have a seat."

Byron begins introductions.   "Emily, this is Chris, Randy, Sam, and John.  Gentlemen, this is my wife Emily and up in the kitchen there," Byron points up to where a young girl is stirring something on the stove, "is my daughter, Karin."

Karin turns and waves but doesn't appear too apt to join any conversation.  It is then that I recognize the young sniper we picked up on the way into town.

"Now, for that tea; would you like yours without sugar or unsweetened?"   Emily's smile is the first genuine smile we've seen in Hazel Creek except for Josh when he said he was glad he didn't have to shoot us.

Randy, Sam, and John take the hint and all request 'unsweetened.'  Testing the water for levity, I request, "I believe I'll be different and have mine 'without sugar' if that's all right."

With another genuine smile, Mrs. Bennett says, "That will be just fine," and she disappears to the kitchen.

Small talk with Byron fills the short time until Karin comes with a serving tray and five glasses of tea.  Karin is a beautiful sixteen-year-old girl who stood ready to drop us in our tracks when we first approached town. In most ways, Karin looks sixteen but deep in her eyes she is much older.  Youth and the silliness of girlhood has been denied her.  She sets the tray on the coffee table and departs with an emotionless look that I recognize from my deployments.  It's called a "combat stare" and soldiers develop it after the shock of war wares off and killing becomes just another part of a day.

Reaching for a glass of tea, I notice the glass is sweating.  First touch confirms my guess.

"It's cold!  I haven't had anything really cold since winter when I wished it was hot.  How do you do it?"

Byron's grin reveals his proud secret.  "We have a camper trailer on the north side of the house and the refrigerator runs on propane.  It's not big but we can keep a few things cool.  We have a big underground tank because when it gets real cold in winter an above ground tank can freeze up.  Since the power went off, the furnace won't run so the propane only runs the stove and that little refrigerator out there."

All of us savor every cold drop of our tea.

Supper is roasted rooster, canned corn, biscuits and country gravy.  We give compliments to the ladies for the meal and though each says thank you, only Mrs. Bennett smiles.

Evening brings reception again and we contact camp.

# Returning Home:

[Chris' account of the expedition.]

[Text Message]  CQ CQ CQ   KF5OSI, RT1 CQ CQ CQ

[Text Reply]  RT 1, KF5OSI... copy.

[Text Message]  KF5OSI, RT 1... START: All is well. Request voice link OUT

[Text Reply]  RT 1, KF5OSI... copy Request voice link OUT

Randy keys the mic, "KF5OSI, RT1, do you copy?"

"RT1, KF5OSI, read you readable but with static, over."

"Roger that. Is this Pat?"

"Roger, this is Pat. Is that you Randy?"

"Yes. I wanted voice link to explain that we are all well and have made contact with survivors."

"Copy that. We spoke with them last night. I take it the vote was approved."

"That is affirmative. We have surveyed the area and all looks well. Returning home tomorrow; will continue text each night."

"Copy. Looking forward to having you back. Travel safe. KF5OSI clear."

"RT1 clear."

Turning to Sam, Randy comments, "You know? I like this radio stuff. If the FCC ever gets restarted, I'm going to get a license."

Our trailer and equipment are in a nearby barn where at first light we are loading it for the trip back. We decide to leave the water treatment chemicals and most of the ammunition here, along with the garden tools and pails of food from the bunker. Anything not essential to our round trip does not merit us having to bring it back. One extra item catches our attention and is going to slow our departure. Randy and I come to the same conclusion as we find the multi band ham radio we got from the bunker.

Randy says, "You know we can't just leave this without setting it up."

"Yeah, I was thinking the same thing." I respond. "How long will it take us to set it up?"

Randy looks the equipment over. "It looks all here and even has some instructions for setting up the antenna. I think, with help, we can have it up in a couple hours."

"Let's do it." I say. "Vince! Got a minute?"

It's a good thing our "Bunker Rambo" had some instructions with this radio gear because none of us really knows what we're doing. Pat set up our truck radio and we need a crib sheet to operate that. As best we can, the radio is set up in the church foyer. Using two sets of jumper cables from the battery of a truck for power and running the antenna cable up the steeple and then across the street by a rope to the maple tree, we are as set as we know how to be. Pat can laugh at us when he gets here but we really won't know how well we've done until tonight after ten o'clock. Randy powers on the radio and pre-sets some frequencies and modes to be the same as our truck radio. If all goes well, we should all be able to talk to each other.

With the truck and trailer loaded we say our goodbyes and just start to pull out when a horn honking gets our attention. From behind us, a big yellow school bus pulls around the corner and rumbles up alongside us. In the driver seat is the other guard, Keith Reed. He opens the door and announces:

"Pop said you'd need this and I can come along to help if you'll let me. This is our team bus for football. Dad and I went and got it after things turned bad. We knew it always had full fuel tanks and a reserve but didn't think 'til last night that it would be useful as a bus. It'll hold sixty so we removed some back seats for cargo. We added two barrels of diesel in back so we won't have to look for a gas station either way.  Can you use it?... us?"

Looking at Sam, Randy, and John; the look on their face says enough.  "I think we can use it... AND you, if you're willing.  Thanks.  And Vince, be sure to give our thanks to Dick.  We'll try the radio on voice by ten – fifteen.  Let's hope we did things right.  If not, we should see you in two weeks, regardless."

"Safe travels!" says Vince.  "Do you have my cell phone number, just in case?"

Hearing the tone in Vince's voice tells me a grin is all I need reply.

"Wait a minute guys," I say, "with the bus AND the truck, we can leave the Ranger here and have more room coming back.  Let's unload it."

It only takes a few minutes to unload the Ranger and I hand the keys to Vince with the remark, "only drive it to church on Sundays.  See you in a couple weeks."

I take the M79 and 'Bunker Rambo's' AR-15 to the bus with me and Keith while Sam, Randy, and John keep the .308 and shotgun.  Each of us has a side arm.

I ask Keith, "Are you good with a pistol?"

Keith answers, "I can hit what I'm aiming at and keep heads down while reaching for my long gun."

"Great answer," I say.  "Here's a .45 we found on the way here.  It had surface rust when we picked it up but

I've cleaned it up and it's serviceable. Here's two extra mags to go with it."

"Thanks!" Keith says. "Let's hope we don't need it."

"I like you more already," Keith seems to hold a healthy attitude about the use of force. "We're going to backtrack the way we came. It's not a direct route but it gets us around major towns."

"Good," says Keith. "Dad and I went to Wichita a month after the power went out. He thought maybe it was just our area that was down and we might find stores open in a big city. Were we ever wrong. We could see the smoke from fifty miles out. Even staying off the main roads, we couldn't get very close for all the wrecked and abandoned cars. People were shot in the street and some right in their cars. A wounded man came staggering out of where storm-water meets the river. He was bad hurt. We gave him water and sat with him."

"Did you get him some help?" I ask.

"There wasn't any place to take him," Keith continues. "Even the hospitals were burned. He said the trouble began when the money failed but really got bad when sections of town started celebrating the fall of the U.S.A. When the power failed and the police pulled back, he said an army of civilians started a massacre of that whole area. They never had a chance, but I guess they lit their own fuse."

"You're lucky to have gotten out of there," I answer. "We heard from ham operators that what you found was a copy in nearly every metro area in the country. Not even the military had enough manpower to control it.  The government has been walking all over the Constitution and letting foreign interests insult America.  I guess thirty million armed citizens decided they'd had enough.  Did your friend make it?"

"No," Keith answers.  "He died just as it got dark and we snuck back to the truck and got back home.  This is the first time anyone has been outside our town since."

The remainder of the trip back to Terlingua is without incident.  The bunker is as we left it and we don't go back into the town we scavenged on the way up. Nightly radio contact is successful, including contact with Hazel Creek.  I guess we didn't goof things up too bad.

Both Keith and the bus will be a surprise for the folks at home.  As a game between the five of us, we never let on about either until we all rumbled up to the main building.  We almost blew it on one radio contact but we managed to keep the surprise.

Becky jumps me with hugs and kisses as Gina grabs my legs.  It sure is good to be home.

# Packing and waiting:

[Back to Jason's perspective.]

"What a trip!" says Anna. "I'm SO glad you weren't along. I'd have worried sick."

Trying to comfort Anna, I say, "Well Becky sure was a wreck when we got the coded distress message. She would have been better off not knowing."

"She knew before the message," Anna quipped. "In her heart, she knew the whole day that something was wrong. She told me so."

"Did she tell you when the baby will come?" I'm trying to change the subject from Anna worrying over me, even though I didn't end up going.

Anna just shoots me that universal message every woman seems to know how to do from birth. I get 'the look.' "Nothing more than everyone knows. This baby is coming anytime soon and I'm VERY ready."

Trying to console Anna, "At least it's not the dead of summer. Winter is a better time to snuggle a baby on board."

"Jason, you're not helping. There IS no good time to have a baby on board. She puts both feet on my bladder and stretches, then plays soccer with my stomach, then stretches again so that I can hardly breathe, then kicks my bladder again. Now to top things off, my breasts are getting so big I can hardly fit into my blouses. I feel like a cow. If men carried babies, one child per family would be all she wrote."

Sticking to my gender preference, I remind Anna, "She? It could be a 'he' you know."

Anna is quick to respond. "He or she... it can be an orangutan for all I care. I just want it born. I can hardly waddle to dinner."

Realizing Anna will not be consoled by anything I say, I sit on the bed next to her, take her in my arms and just hold her. This seems to work better than words for my very pregnant wife.

Perhaps this baby is going to take a while because Anna seems to have plenty of energy. We walk to dinner even though I offer to bring food to her in our cottage. Now, after dinner, she's cleaning the house and packing for the trip to Kansas. Where she gets the energy is beyond me. I'm tired out just watching her.

We go to bed early and I barely get to sleep when Anna puts a death grip on my arm and says, "JASON! are you awake?"

"If I wasn't, I am now." I reply.   "Can I get you something?"

"YES," Anna says.  "Go get Jackie and Lisa. I'm having this baby."

"I thought you said Marge was going to be midwife?"

"Marge said Lisa's has more experience. JUST GO!!!"

Well, the Viking is back.  I nearly kill myself trying to get my pants on in the dark.  Stumbling out the door, I say to myself,

*"You'd have to pick a moonless night too.   Whatever happened to that full moon thing?"*

Jackie and George are in the Perry Mansion rooms and I manage to get word to them first.  Lisa and Bob are in one of the larger cottages with their three children and it's only after nearly reaching their door that I am drawn to the attention of my bare feet and this being snake country.  Worse is remembering Lucas telling us that snakes are very active at night.  I'm really not interested in having my wife become a single mom but snakes or no snakes, I'm on a mission.

[Knock, Knock, Knock!]  "Bob! Lisa!  It's me, Jason. Anna sent me to get you, she says it's time.  She's having the baby!"

You know how sound travels over long distances at night?  Well, I guess I could have called Lisa and Jackie from our porch because with the lamp starting to glow in Bob and Lisa's cottage, nearly every place in the ghost town begins to wake up. I don't doubt a few ghosts are out of their graves and standing watch over this event. Our porch is crowded with people before I can even get back. If any snakes are out tonight, they better be careful or they'll get squashed under foot.

"JASON, GET IN HERE!  I NEED YOU!"  Nothing pierces the night like a woman calling her husband in mid contraction.

I'm not sure what Lisa and Jackie are doing but my attention is fully on Anna. Trying to help her relax, I'm holding her hand as she squeezes the life out of my arm. We are having this baby.

As Lisa says, "push", I tell Anna, "OK little Viking, it's show time. PUSH."

Anna's expression is eyes closed, teeth clenched, and her lips open so that I can see all her teeth. Her face is red and she's pushing with all she has.

I'm wondering where the baby is. Anna pushed, I saw her do it. So where is the baby? I'm not understanding this.

Marge comes in to assist Lisa and Jackie. Lisa tells Anna to breath but she has been except for when she was pushing. Now Lisa says to push again, I wish they'd make up their minds.

Anna nearly breaks my arm with both hands squeezing and she goes all red faced again. This time she must have done it right, or Lisa did it right, because here comes our baby, crying and beautiful.

"Anna, we have a beautiful baby girl! Great job! She even has your red hair. Another Viking in the family!"

Having no traditional family bible with a genealogy page, we enter her birth information on the inside front cover of Anna's bible.

*Anna Marie Iverson Connors,*

*married to Jason James Connors,*

*Born this day, February 26 2021,*

*Mandy Marie Connors,*

*7lb, 2 oz., 19 inches long.*

The planned move to Hazel Creed is delayed for a week to give both Anna and Mandy time to recover. Marge and Lisa think she should take more time but Anna is up and walking a few hours after Mandy's birth and Mandy is nursing well for a new famished Viking. What an appetite.

It was good thinking that Randy and Chris set up the radio for Hazel Creek. We've been in nearly nightly communications and they understand our short delay. It is giving us time to get to know each other from a distance before our two very different groups attempt to merge.

'Different' fails to describe the chasm between our avoiding adversity at camp and Hazel Creek battling monsters daily. Keith Reed is a nice kid but hearing his account of the weeks past default and then as it got worse when the power failed, is chilling. What gets my attention most is how he tells it without the emotion you would expect. He tells it like from a history book. Chris says it's typical of combat veterans. He says,

"After a while, nothing surprises you. Your emotions callous over and you turn hard. Hopefully, in time, you can come part way back to humanity."

I hope we're making the right move. Time will tell.

# About the Series:

If you enjoyed Days of Ragnarök: End of the Gods, please drop me a line at: **contact@the11hr.com**

You can also give a book review at: http://www.goodreads.com/

An account is free and it allows you a part of a community of readers and book reviewers.

I am currently working on the next in the Ragnarök series "Two Worlds Meet." Ask for it at your bookstore.

Made in United States
North Haven, CT
17 December 2021